PRAISE FOR *CAMPAIGN RUBY*
AND *RUBY BLUES*

'After I had laughed three or four times in one sitting,
I started to keep count. A few dozen pages later,
I had lost count. *Ruby Blues* is funny, warm-hearted
and clever.' *Sydney Morning Herald*

'A page-turner.' *Sunday Herald Sun*

'Laugh-out-loud moments abound; the scrapes, foibles
and follies are hilarious, and the bitchiness is biting.
Someone, please, grab the film rights.' *Good Reading*

'Don't underestimate this delicious comedy
of political manners.' *Adelaide Review*

'From the first page...you know you are in for a
fabulous time. It's a roller-coaster, high-heeled
adventure...Extremely enjoyable.' *Woman's Day*

'Genuinely snort-worthy.' *Weekend Australian*

'A light-hearted, skillfully written political romp...the
Gen Y comedy of manners par excellence.' *Age*

'Very funny.' *West Australian*

'A fun, heart-warming read.' Cosmopolitan

T0363446

ALSO BY JESSICA RUDD
Campaign Ruby

Jessica Rudd, 28, had three career changes in as many years—law, PR, politics—but she is now going steady with her life as a writer. She is based in Beijing.

Jessica Rudd

Ruby Blues

TEXT PUBLISHING MELBOURNE AUSTRALIA

textpublishing.com.au

The Text Publishing Company
Swann House
22 William Street
Melbourne Victoria 3000
Australia

First published in 2011 by The Text Publishing Company
This edition published in 2012

Cover design by WH Chong
Text design by Susan Miller
Typeset by J&M Typesetting
Printed in Australia by Griffin Press, an Accredited ISO AS/
NZS 14001:2004 Environmental Management System printer

National Library of Australia Cataloguing-in-Publication entry

Author: Rudd, Jessica.
Title: Ruby blues / Jessica Rudd.
ISBN: 9781922079046 (pbk.)
ISBN: 9781921921070 (ebook)
Subjects: Man-woman relationships—Fiction.
Interpersonal relations—Fiction.
Australia—Politics and government—Fiction.
Dewey Number: A823.4

For every woman, and one man—mine.

Stupid head

I yawned in his face.

It was the ugliest yawn in my repertoire, the kind that made my eyes squint, nostrils flare and chin multiply.

But Luke still wanted me.

How my anti-tooth-grinding mouthguard wasn't a shattering turn-off was unfathomable.

Tell him you're exhausted, Ruby, pleaded my head. *This is the first night you've been in bed before 2 a.m. in weeks.*

His hands crept beneath the covers and under my carefully selected, greying, oversized *Financial Services Association* T-shirt—the most unbecoming of all my nightwear. Take that, Luke's libido!

'I love this shirt.' He pushed it up and kissed between each rib. 'It's the one you wore when you locked yourself out of your hotel room on the campaign, remember?'

Sucked in, head, said my body. *Oh*, it writhed, *I love*

it when he does that! Just go with it, Ruby. Fuck, for fuck's sake. Release some of that tension—

And then watch it rebuild in the tactics meeting tomorrow, my head protested. *Have you even set your alarm?*

I can't remember. Yes. No. Yes. I think I did. Unless that was yesterday—

Your first conference call is at five.

Yes, but—

Not to mention breakfast with the US advance team. We're leaving on Saturday.

Plenty of time. Tomorrow's Wednesday.

Tomorrow's Thursday. Did you book the committee room for the meeting?

Shit. Why did I even agree to organise that?

And have you charged your BlackBerry?

I think so—

It's too late now, mocked my body. *Shirt's off. Woo hoo!*

Fear not, head. He's about to discover my Amazonian armpits.

I put my elbows in wing position, revealing tufts as plentiful as pom-poms. He pulled back.

Success.

Well played, said my head.

Luke headed south.

My body rejoiced.

He's a trooper, said my head. *I'll give him that.*

Maybe this wasn't so bad after all. My body's right, I reasoned. Many sexless weeks had passed and I was stiffer than a body builder's six-pack.

I took a deep breath, felt my muscles loosen, my head

slow. My heart quickened, my skin sizzled and my eyes closed.

I sat bolt upright. My mouth was tinder dry; my cheek sticky with drool. I checked my phone and sipped some chilled water from the bedside glass. Ten to five. That would do.

I snuggled down, rustling the linen enough to disturb Luke's slumber. His skin was warm beneath the blankets, cool above, hinting at the freezing Canberra morning awaiting us outside.

My hot breath defrosted his right earlobe.

'What?' grunted Luke. He was in a foetal coil so tight it would've taken a melon scoop to spoon him.

'I just had the weirdest dream that we were'—I trailed my fingers from the dip between his collarbones to the base of his sternum—'you know.'

Luke stretched and flipped to face me. His impossibly long lashes blinked as his eyes adjusted to the partial light.

'Was I doing this?' He wriggled down to nibble at my sides.

'As a matter of fact, you were.' I kissed his fingertips.

'And then'—lower still—'this?'

'Yes,' I gasped. 'Exactly that.'

'And then what happened?' He stopped.

'Remind me,' I said, channelling my inner temptress.

'You snored.' He about-faced. 'All night.' The downy duvet covered his face.

Stupid head.

Dorothy-on-cock

A large, yellow envelope hit my in-tray with a thump. I put aside my nectarine, tore the seal and shook out its contents. A slim, black folder slid onto my keyboard. Paper-clipped to the inside cover was the usual With Compliments slip, dated yesterday.

R,

As discussed, enclosed are our December holiday options. I have catalogued them in order of best weather conditions for that time of year. I am partial to Rio, but amenable to alternatives.

We must decide on both *destination* and *time* abroad no later than *close of business Friday* so the travel agent can arrange flights. Accommodation options can be determined as late as Monday.

More than anyone I appreciate the stresses, time constraints and pressure that come with your job, but we've been together for two years and haven't been away since that weekend in the Yarra Valley. Please make time for us.

Love, L

Luke Harley, CEO, Liberty Australia Foundation

My head sighed. *How does he manage to make even the most romantic of gestures feel like the final notice for an overdue parking ticket?*

I flicked through the transparent plastic sleeves, all marked with colour-coded flags, and found a page headed 'Wairapara Wine Region' with photographs of a quaint country cottage. Average December/January temperature: 20–29 degrees. Average December/January weather: dry, long summer nights. Pros: Wherekauhau Lodge & Day Spa, pinot noir on tap, quiet, limited BlackBerry coverage, WiFi, three-hour flight from home. Cons: Three-hour flight from home, limited BlackBerry coverage, WiFi.'

Buzz, went my BlackBerry. I answered it.

'Christ almighty, your aunt is sucking the life out of me.'

'That better not be sexual commentary, Debs—I'm eating.' I stared at the half-gnawed nectarine in my hand.

'No such fuck. Ever since I got knocked up it's been all foot massages and shoulder rubs and bloody herbal tisanes and you're-so-beautiful bullshit. I'm disgusting, Ruby. I'm breaking out like a chocoholic cheerleader. And she's keeping a fucking photo journal of my circumference. Can you imagine the cruelty? Other fat people aren't subjected to this kind of ridicule by their loved ones. I can't sleep because I can't roll. And I can't *poop*.'

'Did you just say "poop"?' I ditched the stone fruit in the nearest empty wastepaper basket. A press sec scowled at me and used a pair of pencils as chopsticks to put it back in mine, which was overflowing with paper and muesli bar wrappers.

'She's reading a book called *Parental Readiness*. Some sick fuck reckons you can't bring a baby into a home of cursers, so now I'm only allowed one swearword: poop. I shit you not. Every shit, fuck, and even dick is a fifty-dollar donation to the swear jar. Poop doesn't even *begin* to describe what I'm going through. Fifty fucking bucks, Ruby.'

'So this would be an expensive phone call, then?' I swapped my overflowing bin with the one at the empty intern's desk. The press sec shook his head at me.

'It's highway robbery, that's what it is. We've got Junior's school fees out of it already. She's driving me to drink. And here's the irony: *I can't drink*, because it might harm the baby. *Everything* might harm the baby. Cheese, sashimi, medium-rare meat, uncooked fucking tautological salads. I can't even open the lid on my eye cream without her confiscating it and googling the ingredients.'

'Just put it in your handbag. Apply when you get to work.'

She took me off speaker. 'You think I haven't thought of that, sunshine?' Her shouts became hoarse whispers. 'Stan is *worse*. He and Daph are in on this together. He's her spy. He's about as subtle as a Mardi Gras float, mind you. He gathers intelligence and emails her. I ask for a latte and he brings me a soy chai. Do I look like a lactose-intolerant sub-continental yoga instructor to you?'

'Well—'

'I've tried explaining it to him. He's such a sook.'

'What did you say?'

'"Thank you for wanking into a cup—that was real nice of you—but big ducking feal. I'm carrying the cargo." He's my PA, for crying out loud, not the father of my child. Says so in the contract. I drafted it. He and Massimo—'

'Massimo?'

'—his Italian stallion boyfriend—are dropping in every weekend with water-birth DVDs and homeopathic stretch-mark ointments, and cooing about nursery-safe wallpaper with Daph over fully caffeinated coffee. Buttercup gingham or lemon-meringue stripe? I mean, are we having a baby or a southern belle?'

'Luke's worse.' I leaned back on my creaky swivel chair. 'I just got an alphabetised catalogue of holiday options in the post.'

'Good grief,' she said. 'That's dire.'

I sighed. 'Get this: a week ago I made the effort to go to that fundraiser he was hosting at the Opera House and my flight was delayed. Not my fault. I arrived at Act One, Scene Two, but the door-Nazi wouldn't let me in until Act Two.

'Anyway, I had to push past a few people to get to my seat and when I sat down I dropped my phone. It was dark so I couldn't find it. And then it rang. Again, not my fault. So I had to get under the seat to find it but the lady next to me accidentally kicked it into the next row so I had to crawl past Luke. It was Max ringing, so I had to answer it—he was in The Hague. I did it very quietly, but it was the middle of O *mio babbino caro*.'

'Did he crack the poops?'

'I wish. At intermission I said I loved the duet. He said it was pedestrian. The next morning I made him a cup of tea; he said he wanted coffee. Anyway, I should get some brownie points when I go to Melbourne at 4 a.m. tomorrow to speak at Dan's show-and-tell.'

There was silence on the other end of the line.

'Debs?'

'Yep, hang on a tick.'

Flush.

'Did you just use the loo while I was talking to you?'

'I'm thirty-one weeks up-duffed, Ruby. Had to wee. Anyway, you were on mute.'

'How very proper.'

The bat phone on my desk lit up, then blinked off. Phew, false alarm.

'I'd better go, Debs.'

I'd dubbed it the bat phone; it was really just an old-school intercom that Chief had put in when Max won office so that I was within cooee of her.

I recalled the day they installed it. The receptionist kept answering the phone, 'Leader of the Opposition's Office—er, I mean, Prime Minister's Office,' and we all struggled to call Max PM instead of LOO. Boxes cluttered the hallways of PMO; art slumped unhung on the floors. Theo, our Hawaiian-shirt-wearing policy wonk, had a screaming match with OH&S over the placement of his miniature golf course. I knocked my African violet off the desk, creating the now-permanent, suspect brown stain beneath my chair. Foreign heads of state sent congratulatory gifts—a petrified-wood paper-weight from the Chinese and a case of Louis Roederer from the French. Workmen chiselled the nameplate from the Chief of Staff's office door and put a new one up for Diana Freya in its place. That was the day Luke stopped being my boss and the day Di became Chief. Two years had passed since then. My accent was now somewhere between English Breakfast and Bushells and I still missed Theo—I hoped he was happy building boats in the Bahamas.

The bat phone lit up again. Bollocks. Mute.

'Roo, it's me,' Chief said.

Every time I heard her voice, I imagined a life-sized hologram of her hovering above my desk, her face shrouded in frustration, faded-black shirtdress fastened with a safety pin at the bust.

'Roo, are you there?'

Unmute. 'Yes, Chief?'

'How are you going with the Question Time brief?'

Mute. 'Shitfuckshitfuck.' Unmute. 'I'm on it.' Mute.

Bugger. Max's pack. I put Luke's folder aside and focused. Tried to focus.

'Miss Stanhope?'

I looked up. A pair of celadon-green glitter-lined eyes appeared over the top of my five-foot partition.

'Hello?'

'Is this a good time?'

'I can only see your forehead,' I said, bewitched by black hair so neat it could have sprouted from the kicking end of a mint condition My Little Pony and by the precise symmetry in the polka-dot hairclips that pinned it back.

'Um...the thing is...Diana Freya called...'

'Who *are* you?'

She cleared her throat and stepped out from behind the partition. Decked out in an indigo seersucker shirt under a purple tweed vest and matching pencil skirt, a round-faced, wide-eyed pixie extended a quivering hand. 'Bettina Chu,' she said. '*Totally* awesome to meet you.'

I shook it, dumbfounded.

'I'm your new intern. It's *literally* the most *gimungous* honour to work for you, Miss Stanhope.'

'Call me Roo.'

'OMG, I'm Chu and you're Roo! How cool is that?'

'Oh em gee?'

'It means, like, oh my gosh or oh my God'—she kissed the gold cross around her neck—'depending on your religion. I'm Catholic, so it's strictly gosh for me.'

'I know what OMG means, I've just never heard it spoken as an acronym. What do you mean *work* for me?'

'Well, Diana Freya—'

'We call her Chief.'

'Chief?' She clapped her hands. 'That's, like, *so* Dub-Dub.'

'Dub-dub?'

'WW.'

I shook my head, bewildered.

'*West Wing*, silly!' She giggled. 'OMG, are you CJ? When I'm your age I want to be CJ and marry Josh and give Toby a hug—he's such a sad sack. Actually, you look a bit like Donna. Do you have a Josh?'

'Something like that. You were saying something about Chief.'

She smiled through the glossiest of lips. 'Chief said I would be reporting to you, CJ—Roo. I *adore* your earrings, by the way. Tiffany?'

'Thanks.' I grabbed my earlobes to check.

'From Josh, I bet. He's a keeper. How long have you guys been going out?'

Going out?

'Two years, but—'

'Sick! What's his name?'

'Luke.'

'That's one of my top ten.'

'Huh?'

'My top-ten desirable boyfriend names. *Tell* me you have one.'

My head shook.

'OMG, how do you decide? Mine are Henry, Luke, Alessandro—that one has good mouth-feel, doesn't it? Sebastian, Jeremy—'

'Are you here on work experience, Bettina?'

'No way, José. I'm part of APIP.'

'The what now?'

'Australian Parliamentary Internship Program. It's an annual program. I'll give you my curriculum vitae—always keep a copy on me just in case I meet Oprah.' She opened an eggplant patent purse and pulled out a piece of paper so pristine it was as if it had just come off the printer tray.

I skimmed it. Bettina Chu. Twenty-two. Fluent in Italian, Mandarin, conversational Korean and Spanish. Masters in Public Policy, ANU. Honours in Law, University of Queensland. Head Girl, Brisbane Girls Grammar School. Founder of an NGO. Young Queenslander of the Year. Youth Representative, Constitutional Convention. Interests: marathons, scrapbooking, nuclear non-proliferation, stationery, and dumpling/raviolo-making.

'What's raviolo?'

'The singular of ravioli—Dad's Chinese, Mum's Italian. I'm trying to learn as much cooking from Nai Nai and Nonna before they pass. OMG, does that sound awful?' She flapped French-manicured hands in front of her mouth. 'It *does*!'

'Listen, Bettina, I'm in the middle of putting together the PM's pack for Question Time.'

Her eyebrows asked a question.

'It's a list of everything he might be asked by the Opposition and also by our side. We call these Dorothies—what are you doing?'

'I'm taking notes,' she said, scribbling into a notebook, her i's dotted with spirals. 'Are they called Dorothies because answering them is as easy as clicking your ruby slippers together? Or is it a reference to friends of Dorothy, because you're on the same team?'

'Neither.'

'Can I see a copy of the pack?'

'When it's finished. I really need to concentrate.'

'Promise I won't say a word. I'll just sit here. I'm super keen.'

Super.

She perched on the corner of my desk.

'Bettina?'

'Mmm?' She read my expression. 'Too close?'

'Just a bit. How about you set up your desk and I'll show you the brief later.'

'Okey-dokey.'

Thirty minutes and a paper cut later, I was outside Max's office armed with two sleek black folders of cross-referenced, double-checked speaking points—one for Max, the other for Chief.

Di stuck her head out the door. Her short, neat hair framed tough, tired eyes. A frayed, once-white lanyard cluttered with passes hung low around her neck and her trademark cherry-red heels were scuffed like cricket balls.

'I've got the packs for you, Chief.'

She thumbed through the pages. 'We've added to the SME notes on page seven. I've emailed you. Do you mind amending Max's copy? I'll change mine.'

'Sure,' I said. 'Listen, about Bettina—'

'Later, Roo.' She shut the door.

I printed out the amendment, pulled the seventh page out of the brief and replaced it.

'Run and make yourself a copy of this,' I said to Bettina. 'I have to give it to the PM in two minutes.'

Her eyes enlarged to anime proportions. 'I won't let you down!' She seized the folder from me, ran to the copy room and returned with a whole minute to spare.

'Um, Roo, is this going to the *actual* Prime Minister?'

'Yes.'

'OMG.'

'What?'

'I've touched something that the Prime Minister will touch.' She pulled out a dictaphone and pressed record. 'Day one. Noon. Got first Question Time pack. PM will actually touch it. Very Dub Dub. Will devour, no doubt, over snack-sized Skittles—'

'What are you doing?'

She hit pause. 'I'm creating a time capsule.'

Don't ask.

'A time capsule?'

Ruby!

'Yes. This is a unique experience and I feel duty-bound to capture its essence and bury it so that, in the future, when iPhones are imPlants and only women can vote, someone like me will dig it up and discover this: the diary of an APIP.'

Can we slap her yet?

Folder in hand, I knocked on the eight-foot red-myrtle doors and entered.

Behind them sat a pensive Max Masters. Glasses in one hand, pen in the other. He had chewed his thumbnail to the quick. It was red raw.

Grey light spilled through the windows and onto his white shirt, which was as creased as a deconstructed paper plane. There were deep circles under his eyes, now a permanent feature and darkening with each slide in the polls. A spot of salad dressing near the knot of his tie bled across the ribbed silk. I opened his cupboard and pulled out a fresh one, tearing off its dry-cleaning tag.

'Your brief, PM.' I put it on the desk with the new tie.

'Thanks, Roo. What's this?'

'You need to change ties.'

He looked down at it. 'I liked this one.'

'We'll get it cleaned.'

'No point. It's balsamic.' He flipped his collar up to loosen the knot.

'Anything in particular I should be aware of?' He nodded at the folder.

'They're going to go for the jugular on the small business policy. We've got some pretty tight language in the brief as well as talking points on the previous government's policy black hole on SMEs. We also have a few Dorothies in there about our good relationship with the US—one for you, one for the Trade Minister.'

It was the last sitting day before our US tour.

Max inspected his tie. 'Bugger.' He'd tied it too short. He started again.

'Did you see what the focus groups are saying?'

'No,' I fibbed.

'Apparently I'm incompetent, uninspiring and disappointing. And overweight.'

'Every first-term government goes through this. Come on, PM. We've had a few hiccups. Things will pick up.'

'That's what you said last week.'

A knock at the door saved me. I pushed back through the doors and answered my buzzing BlackBerry. Private number.

'Hello, my name is Gloria and I'm calling from Denning Chambers in London. Might I put you through to Ms Francesca Stanhope?'

Sigh. 'Now's not particularly convenient—she's listening, isn't she?'

'Yes, I am you great twat. Thank you, Gloria. Hang up now.'

'I *was* going to call you back.' I walked towards my desk.

'You were not. See, this is why you could never play hide-and-seek when we were children. You would hide and I'd find you—always behind the curtain in Daddy's study—then when it was my turn I'd hide for so long I'd nearly wet myself. I'd sneak into the bathroom and you'd already be there, pulling faces in the mirror.'

'That happened once. Twice at the most.'

'Ruby, the point is, I am your sister and I reserve the right to seek you, because I know you'll never seek me.'

'I'm sorry. It's been very busy. The government's on the nose, the PM's approval ratings are down again, one of our major election commitments has fallen over entirely—'

'I don't give two hoots about the government. I'm worried about my sister, the one who probably hasn't even noticed the last Harry Potter film has been released.'

'The one who, when last we spoke, referred to Great Aunt Mildred in the present tense, when they put her in the ground eighteen months ago.'

'I meant Gertrude!'

'The one who is doing everything she can to avoid her birthday on Tuesday.'

'What a neat rhetorical device. I take it you're enjoying the bar?'

'Answer the question.'

'There was no question.'

'Are you or are you not planning to use a trip to the United States to skip your birthday?'

'I will be crossing the international dateline at the time, rendering me twenty-nine forever more.'

'You'll be thirty this time next week.'

The number made me gasp for air like a deep-sea diver. 'Give it a rest, Fran.'

'Speaking of rest, Luke tells me you're planning a holiday for the end of the year.'

'Does he also tell you he uses ringbinders and With Compliments slips to correspond with me?'

'Don't be melodramatic. It was a plastic folder and he's just trying to be nice.'

'There's nothing *nice* about a deadline,' I said, taking the black folder from my in-tray.

'I'm sorry,' said Fran. 'Did he cheat on you, divorce you, marry his junior counsel and make you fight for custody of your seven-year-old daughter?'

'Touché.' I remembered the look on my sister's face two years earlier when I'd picked her up at Melbourne Airport after her husband told her he was rogering junior counsel.

'Is London in the folder, Ruby? I can't handle Christmas alone with Mummy and Daddy again. They keep trying to set me up with their colleagues' sons, all of whom have nose hair, wear vests, drive Volvos and say, "Yes. Quite".'

'Let's see.' I opened the folder in the middle, 'I'll look under L for London, shall I?' I read from the top of the page. 'Dorothy on—cock.'

You idiot.

'Is that in Essex?'

'I'll call you back.'

I hung up and ran to the telly in the press office. My trachea closed as I watched the Prime Minister of Australia, my boss, walk in to the House of Representatives, take his Gumby-green seat at the dispatch box and put a black folder on the table in front of him.

Instead of the folder containing his Dorothy Dixers and likely questions from the Opposition, I had given him Luke's holiday catalogue.

'Fuckasaurus.'

I skidded through the corridors of power, passing a clock. Two minutes to two. My thumb fumbled, dialling the Chief. Straight to voicemail. She was in parliament, sitting in the advisors' box. On national television.

I knocked over a lanky man with a bundle of Hansard proofs while texting.

GiVE PM ur briefs

Stupid auto-text. Another clock. Two. Oh, cock. They'd be doing the commencement prayer by now.

'Almighty Father,' I prayed. 'Thank you for rescheduling the rapture. I know I'm lapsed, but please, have mercy. Let me get to the doors before the Leader of the

Opposition's question about Christmas Island turns into a detailed dissertation on where to find the best baklava in Beirut.'

I punched my fists into the leather-padded door of the House of Representatives. A uniformed attendant opened it slightly, revealing a glimpse of the brightly lit green chamber and public galleries full of school children above. 'Shhh! They're doing the prayer!'

'Please,' I panted, shoving the folder through the door. 'Give this to the Prime Minister.'

'After the prayer!'

'...hallowed be thy name...'

I dropped to my knees. 'No, now! It must be now! Official business. Pretty please—'

'Stop begging. It's unprofessional.'

'...our daily bread...'

'I'm not begging. I can't get up because I ran here. Have you seen the shoes I'm wearing?'

'Louboutin?'

'Yes! Good eye. What size are you?'

'...forgive us our trespasses...'

'Nine.'

'Bet you'd squeeze into an eight with those narrow beauties.'

'You're bribing me?'

'...lead us not into temptation...'

'Would we call it a bribe? Gift would be more fitting.'

'You are. You're trying to bribe me.'

'No, I'm ordering you: give this to the PM.'

'Ordering me?' She narrowed her eyes. 'On whose authority?'

'The Prime Minister's.'

'He's not my boss.'

'...the kingdom, the power and the glory...'

'The Queen's, then. I'm English.'

'Good for you, love, but she's *certainly* not my boss. I'd do anything for the Duke of Cambridge, though. Or Kate.'

'Now I'm begging you. I shall tiptoe on my tippiest of tippy-toes—'

'...Amen.'

She smiled. 'How can I help you?'

'Questions without notice?' grumbled the Speaker. 'The Leader of the Opposition.'

'Hear, hear.'

It was too late. I bowed, entered the chamber and took a seat on the bench beside Chief, ready to watch my fate unfold.

Adelina Pepper reached up to the microphone opposite Max, her signature Hermès scarf knotted at her collarbone. 'Would the Prime Minister please enlighten the House as to how he proposes to clean up his latest quagmire to lighten the load borne by the hardworking small businesses of this country as a result of his government's rushed implementation of the SMEdiation program?'

Max got to his feet.

Chief nudged me when I groaned. 'Shoosh!'

'I thank the Leader of the Opposition for her question. As I've said in this house and other forums on many occasions, this government is not perfect. It comprises human beings, Mr Speaker; and human beings, whatever their intentions, are prone to error.

'We're not perfect,' he shouted over the scoffing Opposition, 'but we're a damn sight better than our predecessors.

Getting the budget back into surplus was step one—'

'Thanks to Cecil Berth!' Adelina interjected.

'Yes, thanks to the hard work of an excellent treasurer.'

'Hear, hear,' mumbled the backbench.

'So now that the budget is back in surplus we on this side of the house are focused—focused on cleaning up the mess *that* side of the house left for us. But we don't shy away from that task, however herculean. No, Mr Speaker, we embrace it. We will continue to clean up their mess until the regulatory environment for SMEs is spick and span. That's our focus. That's our priority.'

More guffaws. Eyes rolled across the press gallery. A nearby backbencher let out a panicked 'Oh God', gripping her seat like an extra on the set of *Air Crash Investigations*.

'What are you doing here, Roo?' whispered Chief through clenched teeth.

'This is my fault,' I heaved. My heart was beating so hard you could pasodoble to it. 'Max has the wrong brief.'

'No, he doesn't. I gave him mine.' She handed me a slim black folder. Inside was a rainbow of colour-coded flags. 'He's messing this up all on his own.'

My trachea reopened.

There was a Post-it note on the cover:

Roo,

Funniest leave application ever. Granted.

PM

Girls' Club

Gossip hushed and rushed like adrenaline through the usual corridor chit-chat. Staffers glanced over their shoulders between phrases. Press secretaries smiled. At 4 p.m. glossy copies of the *Australian Monthly Profile* had hit pigeonholes gallery wide and on its cover, Chief.

I had gone to the shoot with her. They'd styled her in a Bianca Spender black silk blazer. Strong shoulders plunged into a precision-cut V, which fastened at her navel with a single covered button. Brushed gold and lapis beads lapped her slender neck. Her short hair was blow-dried with body, her make-up was simple, elegant; coal kohl winged each eye. The look was Di at her best: warm and human, but not a human you'd want to fuck with.

But that wasn't the shot they'd used. I looked down at the black and white image in my hands. Chief stared back at me, her brow bone and the bridge of her nose dotted with concealer like tribal war paint. Tissues tucked into the collar of her make-up gown threw harsh light onto her stressed face. She was in a director's chair on the phone to Max, her shoulders hunched and legs crossed, shoes off.

The click of the camera had startled her, I remembered. Her neck craned towards the noise.

'Just checking the light,' he'd said, taking another, and that was the cover shot under the title: *Di bitch? Perceptions of the country's most influential woman.*

The article was worse. Keywords ranged from 'inadequate' to 'inexpert'. A host of unattributable anecdotes from bureaucrats, staff, politicians and industry heads fattened the pages, dense with criticism. The most scathing stab came from a 'senior party figure' who said, 'I didn't rate Luke Harley, but he could have gone part-time and done a better job than Diana Freya.' It was a hatchet job and there was nothing we could do about it but pretend we didn't care.

Bettina skipped along the corridor beside me, oblivious to the surround-sound muttering about our boss. Her bouncy shadow faded in the disappearing light.

'I know you told me not to do any prep work, but I thought you might like to see this.' She pulled a pink candy-striped folder from her bag.

'You know you can just use the stationery provided.'

'Ha! Funny.' She assessed my expression with a tilted head. 'Um, no offence, but it is the boringest stationery cupboard I've ever seen. I literally cried. I cried on my first day at Parliament House because what smelled so promising from the outside was as drab as All Bran on the inside. Such a shame, too, because obviously the highest office in the land should have the best stationery.'

'Obviously.'

'So I'm just going to use my own if that's coolio.'

'Fine. So what is this?' I opened the striped folder.

'A backgrounder on each of the people who have said they're attending the meeting. I've asterisked some of the ones I'd like to meet, in case you have time to introduce me.'

'They all have asterisks.'

'That's because I'd like to meet all of them.'

'Bettina,' I said, my head rumbling with the beginnings of an excellent idea, 'how would you like to minute this meeting? I mean, it'd be an excellent opportunity for you to get to know the women present and you're clearly very—'

'STFU!'

'Excuse me?'

'Shut the bleep up, silly.' She smacked my arm then squeezed it.

'Ow!' We walked into the committee room.

'Sorry, it's just'—she lowered her voice—'That's Connie Fife. I love her shoes. Doesn't she look hot in olive?'

'Yes.'

'And that's Anastasia Ng. She looks smaller in person. And Melissa Hatton! Has she had her hair cut?'

'Yes.'

'And that's the new *Politico's* panellist and OMFG that's Adelina Pepper! Not that I even like her; but still, she's the Leader of the Opposition!'

'Bettina.'

'What?'

'My bleeping arm.'

'Sorry. It's just that these hands are about to record the words uttered by those wonderful women. I'm the luckiest girl in the world.'

'I'll let you get in the zone.'

My eyes turned to Chief. She had refilled her wine glass since we'd entered the room. I grabbed a glass, filled it with miserable merlot and went to sit beside her. She was pretending not to play Brick on her BlackBerry. I knew because of the concentration in her eyes, one of which was closed because she didn't have time to see the optometrist about adjusting her prescription contacts.

'Hi.'

'Just sending an email,' she lied, her speech already slurring.

'Right.' Painful pause. 'Want some cheese and biscuits?'

'No.'

'Or just cheese?'

'No.'

'Or just...biscuits?'

'No.'

'The biscuits look nice. I know you like those Jatzes.'

'The plural of Jatz is Jatz.' Another swig. 'And no.'

'Ladies, ladies, I call this meeting to order.' Senator Flight struck her gavel on the table. 'Ladies!'

Nattering died down until all that could be heard was the glug of wine bottles and delighted squeals from the senator's twins, who were busy building blocks in the corner.

Bettina sat beside the senator, pen poised, ready to serve her country.

'Before we commence—'

Bettina wrote that down and looked up.

'I'd like to acknowledge the traditional owners of the land on which we convene, the Ngunnawal people. Now, given the mixed nature of this group—journalists, politicians and staffers—you will all appreciate that the Chatham House rule applies. I'd also like to thank Bettina Chu, who is here on the Australian Parliamentary Internship Program working in the Prime Minister's Office, for volunteering to take the minutes.'

Bettina stood in her place and smoothed a non-existent crease from her purple pencil skirt.

I shook my head. *Oh God*, it said. *Don't do it.*

'Thank you, Senator Flight OAM. OMG—'

'Pssst,' whispered Melissa Hatton MP, who was sitting behind me. 'What's an OMG?'

'An Order of My Gosh.'

'When Miss Ruby Stanhope—she's Roo, I'm Chu, how cute is that?—when Roo asked me to take the minutes at this meeting, on this, my first day in parliament and my first meeting in parliament, it only took me about a millisecond to say yes.'

'Are we being punked?' whispered the Opposition leader over my shoulder.

I had to think about it. 'No.'

'It is the hugest thing to happen to me since I took out the national title for most money raised through Jump Rope for Heart. Distinguished women, I will not let you down. You will all receive the minutes of this meeting in your inboxes by 9 a.m. tomorrow morning. That's my promise to you.' She sat down.

I contemplated filling my ears with Jatzes.

'Um, yes. Thank you, Bettina. It's lovely to have such enthusiasm in this building. That's the housekeeping done. I'd like to welcome you all to this, the inaugural meeting of the—well, that's the first item on the agenda. What are we going to call ourselves?'

Melissa's hand shot up.

'The Member for Donaldson?'

Melissa uncrossed her stockinged legs, revealing a dotted back-seam. 'How about the Parliamentary Women's Association?' she asked. 'It's simple. It says what it is. It withstands the test of time.'

Bettina scribbled furiously, the glittered pom-pom on the end of her pen bobbing like a buoy at the Sydney to Hobart.

'The Parliamentary Women's Association. A fine name. Anyone else?'

Press gallery doyenne Anastasia Ng pointed her long index finger in the air as she did at the end of every press conference. 'I get a Country Women's Association vibe from that. How about Women In Parliament?'

'WIP,' said Senator Flight. 'There's a nice double entendre in that.'

'I don't see what's wrong with the CWA,' said Chief. 'At least they don't label each other bitches.'

Murmurs erupted from a pride of Opposition press secs.

'How about,' I improvised, 'the Women's Fellowship?'

'Christ, it's a sex, not a religion.'

Chuckling trumped gossip.

'Order!'

The senator's two-year-olds flinched and faced her.

'Sorry darlings, Mummy just didn't expect such boisterousness from a bunch of women.'

'If I may, Senator?' said Adelina Pepper.

'Yes,' said Senator Flight. 'The Leader of the Opposition.'

Adelina Pepper adjusted the knotted silk scarf at her neck and stood to address the room. In height she was barely five feet but she towered over us in stature. 'We're here to respond to the boys' club. If we can't join 'em let's beat 'em.'

That got a laugh.

'I'm serious. Senator Flight, you're here with your children, which is wonderful. But how many male MPs do you see with nannies in their offices, unless they are'—she censored herself for the twins—'themselves being taken care of. It's the same for staffers and journos. We all work long hours in this building. We need to get better at networking, at helping each other out rather than being at each other's throats. The boys' club is good at that. So let's call this the Girls' Club.'

There was a contemplative pause.

'Do we have a mover?' asked the senator.

'I move that we adopt the Leader of the Opposition's recommendation that this organisation be called the Girls' Club,' said Education Minister Connie Fife, brushing Jatz crumbs from her skirt suit.

I seconded it with a nod.

'Right, all those in favour of the motion say aye.'

'Aye.'

'To the contrary, no.'

'No.'

Everyone turned their attention to Jacqueline Sloane—Jack—Chief of Staff to Treasurer Cecil Berth. She twiddled her bullet-shaped cufflinks. Her uniform said it all: sharp, dark suits and avant-garde white shirts, her face bare but for a pair of cat-eyed, brushed-silver frames, her hair a sleek grey bob. Her father's dog tags sat at the hollow of her throat. She lived politics, breathed cigars and ate her opponents for breakfast.

'I'd never have expected it,' said Connie with an eye roll.

'I'm sure we'd all like to hear why, Jack,' said Senator Flight.

'Because we're adults, not children. Girls' Club? Bloody hell, when are you lot going to start taking yourselves seriously? We'll be ridiculed.'

'Lighten up, Jack,' said Connie. 'It's a play on words.'

'I started my career at Old Parliament House in 1968. Back then, the only women in politics outside the typing pool were wives and girlfriends. It was hardcore. We had to fight for the basics. This was before the Sex Discrimination Act. We weren't allowed in bars, we had our bums patted at the photocopier and got paid less because we weren't breadwinners. "Fix us a cuppa, will you, love?" they'd say. I'd tell them to get their girl to do it. So I vote no. I'm not a girl—I'm a woman—and I'm sure as hell not going to be part of a Girls' Club.'

'I was there too, Jack,' said Connie. 'You weren't the only pioneer. Times have changed.'

'The times didn't change; *we* changed them, or at least *I* did.'

'What's *that* supposed to mean?'

'It means I worked my arse off to earn the respect of my colleagues and opponents and I'm not about to lose it on a cheap gimmick.'

'All right,' said the senator. 'Let's vote again. All those in favour, you know what to do.'

'Aye.'

'To the contrary, no.'

'No.'

'No,' I heard myself say.

Chief glanced at me.

'Motion carried.'

Jack got up. 'Phone call.' She winked thanks at me. 'Excuse me.'

'Thanks for dropping by,' said Connie, but Jack had already shut the door.

'Goodness,' said Senator Flight. 'We're not used to that kind of drama in the upper house. Next on the agenda: why are we here? Anyone?'

'I think we're here because women don't have time to network unless it's organised,' said Melissa. 'Women have a million things on their minds.'

'And men don't?' asked Anastasia.

'Of course they do,' said Melissa, 'but they're capable of shutting everything else out and becoming totally single-minded. I can't have a conversation with my Chief of Staff when there's a television on in the room, because there are two people talking to him, but my PA can type an email, answer a phone call and read a newspaper at the same time.'

'Sounds like you should promote your PA,' said Adelina.

'Every man's the same,' said Josephine Braddon, a rookie journo at the *National*. 'Don't get me wrong; I'd love to be like that. Multi-tasking's as much a curse as it is a skill. My thoughts are always crowded.'

'*Your* thoughts are crowded?' muttered Chief, more over her breath than under it. People stared. The whispering started up again.

Do something, Ruby.

'Tell me about it,' I heard myself say. 'My boyfriend was trying to, well, y'know, head south for the winter on me last night and it was the first night I'd gone to bed early this week—'

'I'm sorry,' Josephine interjected. 'Did you just say "head south for the winter"?'

Good question, said my head.

'Is that a British thing?'

'Erm—'

'He *does* that? How long have you two been together?'

'Is this Luke?'

Pants.

'Luke as in Luke Harley?'

'Didn't you two get together on the campaign?'

'Luke Harley gives head?'

'Erm—'

Sweet potato. Backpedal. Immediately.

'The point is, without wishing to become too personal, we were engaging in an act of intimacy—'

'Engaging in an act of intimacy?' said Josephine.

'Can I just point out,' said Melissa, 'that you journos always do this. We speak our minds in plain, accessible English and we're chastised for crudeness, then we tone it down and we're accused of doublespeak.'

'Diddums,' said Adelina, tweaking her scarf. 'Carry on, dear.'

'Right. Anyway, we were, as it has been established, horizontal—'

'You didn't say you were horizontal.'

'This changes everything.'

Senator Flight banged her gavel. 'Shoosh, chooks. Come on, Ruby. You have the floor.'

'I fell asleep.'

'You fell asleep?'

'Yes, I fell asleep. I was extremely tired and in bed and my mind was thinking about alarm clocks and whether

I had enough pages in my passport to go on the US tour on Saturday and I guess I just switched off.'

'Bet he took that well,' said Connie.

'No,' I said, 'not particularly.'

Overshare.

'My husband was telling me a fascinating story the other day about his fishing expedition,' said Adelina. 'I was thinking about whether I had time to have my eyebrows waxed before doing the *Breakfast* show the next day and apparently he told me he caught a twelve-tonne salmon and I said, "Well done," and he got all stroppy.

'Then I apologised for failing to celebrate what was clearly a brilliant catch and he said of *course* he didn't catch a twelve-tonne salmon or I would have read about it in the papers. I mean, how the fuck should I know how heavy a salmon should be?'

'Being a woman in this building, or anywhere for that matter, is like being on one of those medieval torture devices,' said Senator Flight. 'You know the stretching machines in the movies?

Di looked up.

'You want to share your life with someone,' the senator went on. 'But if you do you're a shitty partner and if you don't you're a loner. You want to be a mum but if you have children you're negligent and if you don't you're barren.

'You like pretty clothes but if you wear them you're a vain bimbo and if you don't you're ugly and mannish. You want to be kind and warm but if you are you're weak and if you're not you're a bitch. In parliament, you want to stand up for women but if you do you're a feminazi and if you don't you might as well be a bloke.'

Solemn nods filled the room, Di's the most emphatic.

'That's why I think we're here,' she said. 'Because we're all victims of the same stretching machine. We're being torn, whether we're MPs or senators, party leaders or backbenchers, cartoonists or press secs. We mightn't agree with each other's politics but we need to help each other out because we're the only ones who understand what that's like.' She leaned down to remove a pen lid from one son's nostril. 'See?'

As we left the meeting, Bettina looked like she'd Jumped Rope for Heart all over again. She was sweating and blushing. A hairclip sat askew on the crown of her head.

'Are you okay?'

'No. I am not okay. I am excellent. I don't think I missed a single word, except maybe for the whispers. Do you think the participants would enjoy a transcript alongside their minutes, in case they want to go back over anything?'

'Just the minutes will be fine, Bettina.'

'And do you think hard copies as well as soft copies? I thought I'd work on a special letterhead, now that we've agreed on a name for the club.'

'Um—'

She slapped her forehead. 'Der! What was I thinking? Of course we'll have to vote on a design. I'll circulate logo prototypes in the morning to be decided on at the next meeting. So much to do, so little time! I'm going to hightail it back to my desk.'

She left a trail of fairy dust in her wake.

It was time for me to regroup. I consulted the washable To Do list on my left hand. Three months ago Chief had thrown my official To Do list—a delicate construction of A4 sheets, bookmarks, receipts, boarding passes and serviettes—into the shredder. 'Get. That. Away. From. Me.' she'd said. I hadn't committed another one to paper since.

1. Fix watch

Fuck.

Wouldn't hurt to put fuck on the list, said my body.

2. Petrol

When will petrol stations do home delivery? Why pizza and not petrol? If they delivered petrol I'd probably go out for pizza more often.

3. Exercise

Ha!

Ruby, it's been weeks. Everything aches and we're beginning to look portly.

4. Fill pill script

Not pressing. Failure to complete item three is a natural contraceptive.

5. ner

Ner? The biro had faded. Stupid hand cream. Maybe it was an acronym. NER. National Energy Regulation? No, that was done. A suffix, perhaps. What ended in ner? Cloner? That would be handy, I thought. Miner? Blast, I must write that mining industry speech for the PM.

'Roo.'

'Chief.' I tried not to look at Chief's purple-stained lips.

'Come back to the office with me, okay?'

I checked my watch. 4.27 a.m. Shit. I underlined Item 1 in red. 'What time is it?'

'Eightish. Could I just borrow you for a minute? It's important.'

Our stilettos pecked discordantly against the parquetry floor before sinking into the plush carpet of PMO.

'What was with you backing Jack?'

'Nothing,' I said. 'I just get where she's coming from.'

'I can't stand her.'

'I know. I must be the only woman in Canberra who can.'

Blu Tack fixed one of the last two Fs in Chief of Staff to her office door. Inside, she stepped out of her shoes. 'Shut the door,' she said.

Wind in the courtyard outside whipped spindly branches against the windows. She drew the blinds and poured a whisky with shaky hands, sloshing a little on her blotting pad.

'Want one?'

'No, thanks.' Goose pimples formed on my forearms and shins. 'I know the article's a shocker, but it'll blow over.'

'It's not about the article.' She drew breath. 'Take the phone off the hook.'

My hands trembled as I dug around on her desk, finally unearthing her phone from under a pile of paper.

She sat on the floor. Her lips parted and out came a wild, visceral sob, the kind you might expect to hear from a wounded lioness. There were no tears, just blank, wide eyes, an open mouth and pure anguish.

'It's going to be okay,' I said, reaching out to comfort her.

Neither of us believed me.

When she had caught her breath she crawled under her desk. 'I need to tell you something,' she said, 'and I need to know I can trust you.'

'Sure,' I said, sitting opposite her on the carpet.

'I mean it, Roo. This kind of information is a burden. If you can't, I will understand.'

'You can trust me.'

She swigged whisky. 'Years ago, when I first started working in parliament...Max and I...'

I didn't mean to recoil.

She looked into her crystal tumbler as if she might find answers there. 'He was a backbencher. We were in Opposition. I was junior press sec working for another MP. He and Shelly were having problems...'

My eyes closed to give my head the space to process this information without additional stimulus.

'It was before they got married. That sounds terrible. I'm not making excuses. It was wrong. I knew he was engaged but I was pissed and lonely and he was pissed and lonely and—I know what you must think of me.'

'These things happen,' I heard myself say. 'Why are you telling me this?'

'Late last night I received this.'

She reached up to her desk for a battered Filofax, unzipped it and handed me a white envelope. Inside was a single piece of paper with small black type in the centre of the page:

I know.

'That could mean anything,' I said.

'Turn it over.'

And there's proof.

'So?' I asked. 'Seriously, it could be about a parking ticket you didn't pay twenty-five years ago or about that time we forgot to declare Max's interest in that house at Bateman's Bay or it could be about nothing at all—just a nutter with a vendetta.'

'It's not the first one. Every time I get one I feel sick.'

'How many have you received?'

She thrust a pile of envelopes into my hand. There were a dozen or so.

There was a knock at the door. Chief shook her head. 'Get rid of them.'

'Um, Roo, are you in there?'

'Not now, Bettina.'

'It's kind of urgent.'

'Bettina, go away. Seriously.'

'But—'

'Seriously.' I turned back to Di. 'Sorry about that. Look, you need to tell the federal police. You're Chief of Staff to the Prime Minister, Di. If someone is threatening you, they are threatening the PM and his office. That's serious.'

'Are you crazy? Then I'd have to tell them why I find this frightening. They report to the Attorney-General. It'll get out. We can't cope with that politically. We're already vulnerable. We've lost three ministers in six months: two to corruption, one to incompetence. The focus groups seem to be saying they'd prefer to spend a summer in Mordor than vote for the PM again. A sex scandal would destroy us. You know that.'

'Did you tell Max?'

She nodded. 'I offered my resignation.'

'You did *what*?'

'He rejected it. He said it was a cop-out and that if I was going to resign over it, so should he. But I thought it was the only responsible thing to do.'

'How is he?'

'Not good.' She bit a fingernail. 'I have a sinking feeling about this, Roo. The kind that makes me want to drive out to Yass, dig a hole and get in.'

'Remember that time on the campaign when you were so freaked out I made you breathe into a sick bag?'

The corner of her lip lifted into a half smile. 'That's why I'm telling *you*.'

'Right.' I stood up and opened the blinds. 'You've had your meltdown; now get up, put down the whisky and go home. We'll sort this out.' I extended a hand to pull her off the floor.

She swallowed the rest of her whisky before she took my hand.

'Get some sleep.'

'Thanks, Roo.' She put her coat over her shoulders. 'See you tomorrow.'

Bettina was clicking her pen lid at the desk next to mine.

'What was that about?' I asked her.

'I'm sorry, but I thought you should know—'

'If you're going to work here, you need to understand the rules. When the Chief closes her door, there's a giant, virtual DO NOT DISTURB sign on it, like in a hotel room. So unless there's a military coup and the navy's used jumper cables to get our submarines going and has them lined up in Lake Burley Griffin ready to take us out, don't knock. Just wait. She'll open it again when she's ready. Clear?'

She nodded, her ponytail bobbing.

'Great, now what was it that you needed to tell me?'

'I could hear voices from my desk, but no one was here, so I looked around to find them.'

Good grief. The poor girl's unwell.

'The voices were coming from your desk. They were two female voices. When I got closer I realised they were coming from that thing.' She pointed.

'What thing?'

'*That* thing.'

My eyes tracked the direction of her pearlescent nail polish. Shitfuckshitfuck. The bat phone.

Bettina gulped. 'When I heard what I heard, I quickly tried to turn it off, but it wouldn't go off, so I was saying, "I can hear you, whoever you are," and "hello," which is when I realised it was you, because of your cute accent, and Chief, because you said "Chief," but you couldn't hear me, so I went to tell you.'

'What did you hear?'

She winced. 'That the PM and Chief—' She thrust her pelvis and made a pumping motion.

I sat down on the edge of my desk. 'Faaaaaaaaark.' I must have bumped the bat phone when I took Chief's phone off the hook.

'I tried to warn you.'

'It was on mute.'

'I even tried to unplug it, but it's—'

'Indestructible. Did anyone else hear?'

'No, just me. I was designing letterhead prototypes when it happened. The only other person who was here was the cleaner, but he had his headphones on.'

I held up my hand.

'Bettina, it's vital that you forget everything you heard.'

'Done,' she said. 'Erased. Wiped. Control Alt Delete. Nada. Empty.'

'Good.'

'It's just...'

I bit my tongue. 'It's just what?'

'It's just, who would want to do something like that to the Chief?'

'Bettina, I thought you just said you'd erased it.'

'But isn't it our duty to investigate it?'

'No, it's your duty to respect the confidentiality agreement you signed when you entered your office. Listen, we'll talk about this tomorrow. Do me a favour. Forget about it. Go home and get some rest.'

'Okay. Sorry Roo.'

'It wasn't your fault. It was mine.'

I looked at my BlackBerry. Eight missed calls. It rang again. Luke.

'Hi, babe,' I said. 'Rubbish day. How are you?'

'Don't "hi babe" me.'

'You sound cross.'

'Cross? No, cross is the feeling you get when your favourite TV show has been rescheduled for the second week in a row. Furious is the feeling you get when your partner is ninety minutes late to dinner with your parents.'

'Ner!'

'Ner?'

'Ner. Din-ner. I had written it on my hand but I—never mind. I'm sorry. Could we possibly do breakfast tomorrow?'

'They leave town tomorrow morning!'

'Right. Of course. I'm on my way. Where is it again?'

'Ruby!'

'I'm sorry, I'm sorry.'

I dashed to the car park and got into the car. The petrol gauge had dipped below E. If a car could contain less than zero fuel it could get me from Parliament House to the Manuka shops—it was all downhill, after all.

I turned the air-con off and the ignition on and rolled in neutral to the boom gate.

'There's a good boy.' I rubbed the dashboard like the rear of a donkey as we rounded the first of an estimated eleven roundabouts in the three-kilometre journey.

An angry cyclist pinged his bell as we coasted along Canberra Avenue. 'It's a sixty zone,' he yelled, speeding past us.

'You've laddered your lycra!' I yelled out the window. 'Ignore him, buddy,' I said to the car, 'you're doing a tremendous job. Only one roundabout to go.'

Suddenly the road flashed blue. A man in leather with orange batons conducted us into a makeshift laneway. Bollocks.

'Good evening, officer,' I said.

'You've been selected for a random breath test to assess your blood alcohol level. Take a deep breath and blow into this for me. Stop when I say so.'

I inhaled and blew.

'Stop. Thanks, you can go now.'

I put my foot on the accelerator.

'You're free to go ma'am.'

'Erm—'

Cars behind us honked.

'Ma'am?'

Luke was even less impressed than the police were when he came to my aid with a jerry can and funnel, his Leaning Tower of Pisa tie so skewed that the tower looked straight.

'I had to leave dinner with my parents, Ruby—a dinner you were supposed to be at two hours ago—in order to go to the petrol station because you forgot to fill up the car.'

'I didn't exactly know. The petrol gauge light thingy didn't beep.'

'The word "petrol" is written in block letters on your hand.'

'I've had a hell of a day.'

'What happened?'

'Chief...' I trailed off. 'Nothing.'

'What?'

'It doesn't matter.'

'Shit a brick, you don't want to tell me because you think I might tell someone.'

'No.'

'You're unbelievable.'

'I'm really very sorry.'

'You're always really very sorry.'

'That's not quite fair,' I said, as we got into separate cars.

'Ruby. Seriously. Don't talk to me about fair right now.' He slammed the door.

Ner was finished by the time we got to the restaurant. Luke's parents danced politely around the big, grey elephant in the room while I ordered a super-sized helping of humble pie for ert.

Mi toolkit es su toolkit

I shimmied free of the tangled sheets, pulled on some pyjama bottoms and crept barefoot out the front door, across the frosty lawn to get the papers and back again.

On cue, JFK and The Widdler panted with leaf-blower force and smacked their tails against the floorboards. I braced myself for certain slobber and stepped inside.

'Shoosh.' I waited for my feet to defrost.

Dogs don't respond to whispers, Ruby.

I bent down to scratch The Widdler's ear and glimpsed myself side-on in the hall mirror.

My frame wasn't as slight as it used to be. I wasn't fat, was I? The drawstring of my pyjamas seemed shorter. I had convinced myself that was the fault of the tumble dryer but, on reflection, perhaps we didn't own one.

I pulled up my top and drummed four fingers on my pale stomach. It rippled. When I inhaled there was one roll, when I relaxed there were two.

On the upside, my chest was fuller—I had gone from the curvature of a knife to that of a teaspoon.

The taxi's horn startled me. I waved through the window and raced into the bathroom for my toothbrush to the sound of the dogs' barking.

My head lectured me. *Do your make-up in the car. And your hair: you look like Edvard Munch's muse. Of course, you've selected the wrong bra. Joy of joys: another fun-filled day of awkward strap-adjustment ahead. What inspired you to choose this dress, you crumpet?*

My fingers fumbled with the tiny, covered buttons.

'Allow me, milady.' Luke yawned and stretched.

'Thanks. Sorry to wake you.'

I pulled my hair from the nape of my neck and watched Luke's concentration in the mirror. He was beautiful in the morning, his hair skewed to one side, his skin shiny and warm to the touch, his face content and not a terrible tie in sight.

'Am I fat?' I asked.

'No.' He didn't flinch. 'Why? Am I?'

'No.'

'Good talk,' he said. 'See you tonight at half-past eight.'

'I don't know if I can.' I kissed him, zipped up my boots and picked up my bags.

'You promised. And you owe me after last night's debacle.'

'I'll try,' I said, trotting out the front door and down the stairs.

'And I need your holiday preferences. Make sure you give Dan that permission slip—it's in your wallet.'

'Bye!' I waved out the window of the taxi. 'Driver, can you take me to the RAAF base—'

43

'I already told him.'

I turned so fast I hurt my neck. Beside me sat Bettina, fresh as a Tic Tac. 'What are you doing here?'

'Chief said I should come today.'

'We're just down and back to Melbourne for an RSL breakfast. Are you sure you want to?'

'Am I sure I want to get on the Prime Minister's private jet? Is Jesus Catholic?'

'No.'

She kissed her crucifix. 'You have toothpaste on your cheek. I have a make-up wipe if you want one.'

'No, thanks. I have one in my toolkit.'

'OMG, I have a toolkit too!'

'My dear,' I chuckled, 'you haven't seen a toolkit until you've seen this, er—'

I rummaged through my handbag, past the squashed receipts full of chewed gum, the name-tag from that conference, boarding passes, several lipsticks, hotel keys, umbrella case, half-eaten muesli bar, old passport and the swipe card I'd reported stolen. 'Somewhere in here is my—voila!'

Broken-zipped, holey and lipgloss-smeared it might have been, but that simple case was still my pride and joy. 'Bettina, meet my toolkit—the key to my success, the essence to my being.'

I removed the hair band holding it together and shook its contents into my lap. Out fell a mangled toothbrush, scrunched-up tissues, a lidless whiteboard marker, a rusty purple razor and a lone chicken fillet. I poked around inside and held it up to the light. Two tampons. Super.

I saw my disappointment in her pink-mirrored aviators.

'Don't worry,' she said. 'You can use mine.'

The gold teeth of her handbag's zipper parted with German precision. Inside, the Dalmatian silk lining shimmered untarnished in the morning light. There were pockets for everything in there. Her BlackBerry, her screen-protected iPad, a concertinaed file for paper, lipgloss on a retractable leash, and Velcro harnesses for her crystal-studded memory stick, pencil case and matching wallet.

But I'd seen nothing yet. When she unfastened the magnetic-sealed python clutch from its designated spot, I expected fireworks, nay, an operatic chorus. It popped open to reveal an arrangement of instruments resembling the inner-workings of a Swiss watch.

'Help yourself,' she said, handing me a mirror. 'Mi toolkit es su toolkit.'

'Thank you.'

While I dabbed at the corner of my mouth with rose-scented wipes, Bettina ran through the morning's media coverage.

'I've condensed the coverage into a hyper-linked email but also provided a hardcopy. When you get a chance, please let me know which of these formats you prefer. I'm a bit of a greenie. Shall I give you a verbal brief too?'

'Please.' Un-clumpy mascara glided over my lashes with one of five disposable brushes.

'Shall I start with the poll?'

'I read it last night before bed. They're fifty-four to our forty-six.' It hurt to say it aloud. 'What's the analysis?'

'The *National* says we're dead in the water, the *Queens-lander* says the government is more on the nose than a mid-summer sewage leak in Venice.'

'Bit harsh.'

'The *Herald*—'

'That's better, surely.'

'—says these first-term blues are likely to become only-term blues if the government doesn't immediately lift its game. And the *West Weekly* said they had a back-up feature on standby in case by the time they went to print the government had been rolled by the people's revolt.'

'Right, I'll read that later. Anything else?'

'Cecil Berth's speech last night...'

There's a selection of perfumes in here, all labelled with relevant moods. This one's called Peppy. If that's a mood, it's not in my catalogue. Oh my pants! Is that a battery-operated straightening iron? Everything in here sparkles. Even her setting powder seems to contain gold dust. Or is that crushed pearl? I say! Pink tweezers, Ruby.

'...he's a "national treasure" on account of his vision and leadership.'

I blotted my lips. 'Max will be happy with that.'

'I totally heart Cecil Berth.'

'Why?'

'Because he's tall and a Rhodes scholar and he's the only government minister to use German import, triple-A-grade recycled, recyclable, photo-finish paper with a GSM of 120.'

Tragic.

'No, I meant why are you talking about Berth?'

'Because of his speech last night and the *Queenslander* calling him a national treasure.'

'Sorry, wasn't concentrating. Must've been an excellent speech.'

'Visionary. By the way, they're doing a profile of Connie Fife for the *Queenslander* magazine this weekend. I'll talk you through the rest of it on the plane. You have a conference call now.'

'Yes, thanks.' I scrolled through my battery-poor Black-Berry for the dial-in details.

'Here,' said Bettina. 'I've dialled in for you—let me charge your phone while you talk. And FYI, the letter-head prototypes and minutes from last night are at the back of your brief.'

As we stepped onto the VIP, Bettina caressed the raw-silk cladding as if it was her dream wedding-gown.

'Oh Roo,' she said, fanning her face, 'if we're shot down by extremists, I will die happy. Excuse me.' One of the attendants turned around. 'Could I have my picture taken with you?'

I moved to the empty seat beside Jack.

'G'day, sweet pea,' Jack said, cradling her Mont Blanc pen between two fingers like a Davidoff. She ashed it. 'Hope you guys don't mind me hitching a ride.'

'Not at all,' I said as an attendant handed me an orange juice.

Behind her back, the men called Jack 'Mother' because she was the least maternal person in the capital. I didn't—it was counterproductive to the cause. Rumours about her sexuality did the rounds like a public servant on the Lake Burley Griffin bike track.

She did nothing to stop them—she revelled in the mystique, used it to her advantage. The fact was, Jack enjoyed screwing men almost as much as she enjoyed screwing them over. They liked it too.

'Thanks for your support at the Sheilas' Club the other night.'

'I hope you're coming back.'

'I don't have much in common with the rest of you, anyway. No bubs. No hubs.'

'We could use someone with your experience.'

'Not a chance.' She grinned. 'Especially while Fife's on it.'

'What *is* it between you two?'

'Went to uni together. Loathed each other. That's a story for a longer flight.'

'What are you in Melbourne for?' I asked.

'Another fucking surplus celebration roundtable. Cecil's already there.'

'I read his speech from last night,' I lied. 'It's good. Great coverage.'

'Ta. Hopefully it'll put us in good stead for next week. What's the PM doing in Melbourne?'

'Just the RSL breakfast this morning and an electorate commitment—back for the new Japanese Prime Minister this afternoon,' I said. 'I'm going to speak at Luke's son's school's show-and-tell.'

'Three apostrophes.' Her glasses perched on the end of her nose. 'Sounds serious.'

I smiled. 'It is.'

'You're young, muffin. Don't settle down. Have some fun.'

'Thanks for the tip.'

'Anytime. The poll's a bit of a bitch,' she said.

'I'm in two minds about it. It's good for people to know we've got a fight on our hands before we go to the polls.'

She shook her head. 'This is the eighth government I've worked for. They all make the same mistakes. Over-promise in Opposition, under-deliver in office—not for want of trying, it's just much tougher than anyone expects it to be. Two years into the three-year term means we're in election-date-speculation territory. Look.'

She flipped a newspaper over and fingered an article.

'They're saying the PM will delay calling it until he has some wins on the board, and I hope he does. The surplus goes some way towards that, but we have to lift our game if we want to avoid becoming a one-term wonder. We wouldn't be the first, pet, that's for sure.'

I nodded.

'Whose daughter's that?' Jack threw her head back, pointing her chin at Bettina, who was posing with the copilot.

'She's my new intern.'

'I know. You didn't answer my question.'

'I'd say she's Mr and Mrs Chu's daughter.'

'I figured someone had asked you to take her on. Fuck me. You'd think when you get to the highest bloody office in the land they might give you some decent talent to play with.'

The truth was, I didn't know what to make of Bettina yet. Intelligent? Yes. Clueless? Yes. Thorough? Yes. Annoying? Absolutely. She was a glittering enigma.

So I decided to give her a test. 'Psst, Bettina. What do you know about Twitter?' I led us into the corridor.

She took a deep breath. 'I have six thousand seven hundred and forty followers at last count and a followed-to-follower ratio of two to one. My account has been active for four years. I follow every Australian federal and state politician and have selected a handful of international leaders to watch. Generally speaking, I think most politicians, political parties and NGOs tweet poorly.

'Tweeps want a more active role in democracy and

as the medium expands it's becoming more representative of public opinion—not just the chattering classes. My honours thesis was on the evolution of social media etiquette and the way that intersects with defamation law and—'

'Stop. How would you like to take over the PM's Twitter account?'

Bettina's eyes widened to the size of twenty-cent pieces. 'I would totally die.'

I smiled. 'Please don't. Take a taxi to our Melbourne office when we land. The techies will give you the passwords and fill you in on our security measures. Draw up a communications strategy and we'll chat about it at the end of the day.'

'Roo,'—she squeezed my hand until my fingertips numbed—'it means so much that you have faith in me.'

'Good.'

'And Roo, I put a bit of thought into...' She stopped, then winked so obviously that I had time to discern the three shades of eye shadow on her lid.

'Bettina,' I whispered, 'we went over this.'

'But I've come up with a list of possible—'

'Come with me, please.' I marched her into the bathroom at the back of the plane, opened the door and pushed her in.

'Wowsers, why didn't you tell me how shiny I was?' She produced a piece of blotting paper from her pocket. 'I need a new mattifier.'

'Bettina, I need to make sure we have an understanding. You are not to mention what you heard. Ever. Like, ev-er.'

'But I only mentioned it to you and you already know so it's not like I'm telling anyone new. I drafted this quick list of people who might want to hurt the Prime Minister.'

She put it in writing?

'You put it in writing?'

'Yes, but I encrypted it.'

'Using what?'

'A password.' She leaned in and whispered in my ear. 'Rainbow Bright. The I's are exclamation marks.'

'You can't write about this or talk about it or time capsule it or even think about it.'

'Okay, but just look at this.'

I looked down at the document, a family tree-like chart of political relationships headed PEOPLE LIKELY TO HAVE IT IN FOR THE PRIME MINISTER: A DICHOTOMY OF BLACKMAIL SUSPECTS.

'Dear God, you printed it?'

'Yes, I thought that'd be better than email. Unless, do you have a Hotmail account?'

I took the piece of paper and tore it in six and put it in the stainless-steel toilet bowl.

'I wouldn't do that if I were you. You're not supposed to—'

I pressed the blue button. Flush. 'Gone. Out into the atmosphere. Never to haunt us again.'

'Not exactly.'

'Yes, exactly. It made the whooshing noise.'

'The whooshing noise doesn't mean it's in the air, silly. That would mean you could be, like, truffle-hunting in the fields of Lyon and be hit by a flying poo from BA37. A tiny spray of water and the vacuum mechanism make it flush.'

'Well, where does it go?'

'LOL. The age-old question: where does my poo go?

It goes into the septic tank underneath the toilet.'

'Well, it's not like anyone's going to go through that.'

'Unless there's a blockage. In small jets like these, special toilet paper is required so they don't clog what is a very sensitive system.'

'So?'

'So, you're not supposed to put anything in there that doesn't satisfy the disposable-paper requirements. See the cute little spray of water in the bowl?'

'Yes.'

'It's like a baby sprinkler. It's trying to move the blockage.'

I flushed it again.

'And now the bowl is filling up because it has nowhere to go.'

'How do you know all of this?'

'Dad's a pilot. Mum's a flight attendant.'

A guttural noise filled the tiny cubicle. Then there was a loud clunk. The bowl filled. A tiny puddle pooled at our feet.

'Licorice ball sorts! Quick, Bettina, get some toilet paper!'

'I'm wearing suede ballet flats!' She pushed past me and jumped onto the toilet seat.

There was a knock at the door. 'Excuse me, ladies, is something the matter?'

'No, everything's fine,' I yelled. 'Just a small mishap—'

'Gross!'

'Do you happen to have any more paper towels?'

'Ladies, let me in!'

The puddle grew and formed something of a pond. We burst through the door into the aisle.

'What have you done?' asked the flight attendant, whose nostrils had flared to equine proportions.

'I just flushed something.'

'What did you flush?' He rolled blankets into makeshift sandbags.

'A, erm—document.'

'We have a shredder on the plane!'

'You do?'

'Wow!' said Bettina. 'Is it the C-100? I have that one at home.'

Gutter politics

It was Zimmer-frames galore, and a maze of false-toothed smiles and horn-rimmed glasses at Max's RSL event in the ballroom of the Grand Hyatt. I nicked off to the toilet to change my soggy stockings and came back to the last two paragraphs of Max's speech. 'Now,' I mouthed to Flack the Cop, who nodded to his team.

Applause.

Flack steered us down a path through the mild-mannered sea of blue-rinse. Max stopped occasionally, shaking hands, posing for photographs.

I caught a glimpse of dark frizzy hair as a woman pushed past me, towards Max.

Flack and his flunkies had seen her. They closed in. 'This way, Prime Minister,' Flack said, navigating through a group of medal-wearing veterans surrounded by the bright lights of a single camera crew.

'One sec, Flack,' said Max, who was having his ear

chewed about the ethnic background of 'taxi drivers these days'.

'You see, Mr Masters, they just don't know where they're going and I've had enough of it.'

Max smiled. 'You know, Shirley, I did a quick stint as a cab driver when I was at uni. I was lucky enough to have passengers who pointed me in the right direction—'

'PM,' said Flack, listening to his earpiece. The halo of frizz was getting closer.

Max read the severity of Flack's expression. 'It looks like we're off, Shirley, but it was lovely to meet you.'

Suddenly Shirley was shoved aside.

'You're a fraud.'

Max turned around to face his accuser.

She was nervous, her mass of hair trembling with her body.

Flack stepped in.

'No, it's all right, Flack,' said Max. 'Max Masters,' he said, extending a gentle hand.

'I know who you are!' she bristled. 'I lost everything. Everything. My job. My husband. My house. The interest rates, the tax—and you don't even have the decency to answer a letter. So don't come in here preaching compassion. You dis*gust* me.' And with that, she spat on him. And not just a bit of spittle: a giant wad, which landed on his neck and tie.

'Everything! Everything!' she screamed as the cops frogmarched her towards the exit at the side of the stage.

One of the diggers stepped forward to Max with a striped handkerchief. He took it, then Flack shepherded a white-faced Max away. 'We should get you into a room to get cleaned up,' said Flack.

'No, I want to get out of here,' I heard Max whisper through gritted teeth and a forced smile. He held the handkerchief at his neck.

Cameras flashed and a journo forced a microphone in his face. 'Prime Minister, will you be pressing charges for assault?'

'Happy to answer your questions shortly,' I said, 'but give the man a minute, will you?'

I followed them through light rain to C1. I got into the back beside Flack the Cop. Snappers and the camera crew pressed their lenses against the windows; Flack spoke into his cuff. Soon the bonnet flag was flapping in the breeze.

'Is it still on my face?'

'No, PM,' I said. 'Here.' I reached into my bag and handed him a KFC towelette.

The rain slid down the windscreen.

'Did it get in your eyes or your mouth?' asked Flack, reaching for the first-aid kit. 'We should get you medical attention.'

'No.' He wiped his face. More colour seemed to come off with it. 'How could anyone hate me that much?'

'She's barking,' I said. 'She hates herself.'

The windscreen wipers screeched against the glass.

'No, she hates me. This isn't working.' He looked down at his hands. 'I can't seem to turn it around.'

'It will get better.'

'Did you see that cartoon of me this morning?'

'The Grim Reaper one?'

'There was a cartoon of me as the Grim Reaper?'

'Um.' *Think, think, think.* 'It could have been Yoda.'

Max leaned forwards. 'Mitch, can you put the windows down?'

56

'Can't, PM. The windows are bulletproof. They don't go down.'

'I need air.'

Mitch cranked the AC. 'Just breathe, PM. We'll be there in a minute.'

'I think I'm going to be sick. Pull over, Mitch.'

Mitch indicated and slowed. The wipers notched up a speed with the intensity of the downpour. It got loud. I looked out the window. We were on Flinders Street, almost at the clocks.

'Mitch, wait a sec,' I yelled above it. 'We're almost at the office, PM, and it's raining—can we go there instead?'

'No, I need to get out.' He yanked at his tie.

'Or maybe use this?' I gave him my handbag.

'Pull the fucking car over!'

'It's Federation Square!'

Mitch put on the hazard lights. Heavy rain weighed down the flag.

Why is there a red carpet?

'Mitch,' I said, calm as I could, 'keep driving.'

'No, Mitch, stay here. I'm getting out.'

Flack leaped out of the car to open the PM's door.

I got out to investigate, covering my head with a newspaper. I squinted through the deluge to get a clearer picture.

Police?

Max got out and doubled over the gutter at the foot of the red carpet. Flack's team surrounded him, their coats open and an umbrella up to give him shelter and privacy.

The rain eased. That's when I noticed. About thirty metres away, a mob of teenage girls with running mascara had gathered in a cordoned-off zone. BE MY FIRST, read a sodden cardboard placard. I LOVE YOU MORE THAN SHE DOES, read another.

Not a good sign.

Photographers behind temporary metal fences spanned the carpet, their lenses poised, zooming inquisitively towards us.

Uniformed police rushed over. 'You can't park here.'

'Charlie Flack, Federal Police.' Flack held out his hand. 'Mate, we'll be out of your hair in just a minute. What's with the teeny-boppers?'

'They're here for Saxon Vibe.'

'What's that?'

'You don't have daughters, do you?'

'Nah, mate,' said Flack.

A woman with an in-built, flesh-toned microphone and clipboard pushed the cops aside and marched towards me in drenched, pony-skin wedges. 'Gestapa Brown,' she said. 'Who are you?'

Gestapa?

'Ruby.'

'There are no Rubies on my clipboard!' She stomped so hard she got splash-back from the carpet. 'Go away! Fuck the world, is that the—?'

'No.'

'Yes it is! It says C1.'

'Personalised number plates.'

'And the flag?'

'I'm a patriot.'

'Stop it! That's the Prime Minister.'

I turned around. Between a gap in the cops' coats I saw Max sitting on the curb, deep-breathing and deathly pale.

'Checking the tyre pressure,' I said.

'*Checking* the *tyre* pressure?'

That's quite enough spit for today, thank you.

'Yes, checking the tyres. We heard a bump. The PM was in the navy, so he knows, you know, mechanical stuff. We'll just be a minute.'

She blinked. Her eyelids trembled, then opened. 'The world's highest-grossing pop star is about to set foot on this carpet. He will do so in'—she looked at her watch, raising her voice—'sixty-eight seconds. Then, *those* photographers will snap and film and those girls will scream. The Prime Minister is not part of the image we're projecting here.'

'AAAAAAAAAAAAAAAAAAAAAAAAAAAAAAH! HE'S HERE! SAXON!'

'No, he's not!' Gestapa shouted. 'False alarm! Stay behind the barriers!'

It was no use. Cheap heels clacked against the wet pavement. Blood-curdling cries bounced off every surface and plastic ponchos rustled.

The force of their affection broke the barricades. Then, the stampede.

'AAAAAAAAH!'

Flack's team surrounded Max. It was no use; iPhones were out, ready to record.

'I WANT TO HAVE YOUR BABIES—Oh my God. Is he—?'

'Feral!'

'Who's *that* guy?'

'Is that—?'

'He's fully barfing!'

'Oh my God.'

'Ewwwwww!'

A black stretch Hummer pulled up behind our white Holden. The door opened. Out came two men so large they made the Hummer look like Mary Poppins' carpetbag. They stood on either side of the car door, arms crossed, shades on.

Then a white sneaker hit the pavement. Jeans fastened mid-thigh struggled to contain ballooning boxer shorts. A black T-shirt with S@XON spelled backwards across it sprouted an adolescent head of product-laden hair. He forked two fingers into a peace sign.

'AAAAAAAAAAAAH!' went the girls.

'BLERRRRGH,' went Max.

His security looked at ours, ours at his. Confused camera crews panned between the two newsworthiest stories of the day—pin-up, upchuck, pin-up, upchuck.

'Saxon, I'm Gestapa. Di*vine* to meet you. I'm going to take you down the red—'

'Who's the old-timer in the gutter?' Sneakers squelched towards us. 'I'm just going to say hi.'

Gestapa frowned. 'Nobody. This way, Saxon.'

He ignored her.

A bamboozled Max pulled himself to his feet, his eyes still red and watery. The cops stood back. I rushed over and handed him a tissue. 'PM, we need to get in the car now.'

'AAAAAAAAAAAAAAAAAAAAAAAH!'

'I can't just *leave*, Roo,' he said, close-mouthed. 'Look at them all. They're beside themselves.'

'PM,' I tried.

'I LOVE YOU!' squealed a twelve-year-old.

Max waved. 'Isn't that nice.'

'You okay there, man?' said Saxon.

'A bit under the weather,' said Max, reeking of hurl. 'What's your name?'

Having never been asked the question, he tilted his head to one side to check Max wasn't joking. Nope. 'Saxon,' said the heartthrob.

I cleared my throat and stepped forward. 'PM, do you mind if I talk to you for a minute?'

'Is it urgent, Roo?'

'Um, sort of—'

'LET ME HAVE YOUR BABIES!'

Max blushed. 'They get a bit overexcited, from time to time. Occupational hazard.'

'I hear you, dude.'

I stood back. I couldn't watch.

'Where are you from, Saxon?'

Gestapa sloshed over. 'Saxon, we should probably—'

Saxon held up a hand. 'Peace out.'

She backed off.

'My spirit animal hails from the Galapagos,' said Saxon, 'but I grew up in California.'

'I've never been to the Galapagos but my wife and I honeymooned in the Napa,' said Max. 'Do you go to school there?'

'I'm homeschooled. My guru travels with me. I spend a lot of time on the road. You know how it is.'

'Sure do. Parents in the army?'

'Saxon's a singer,' I said, pointedly. 'He sings—'

'I was in the choir when I was your age. How old are you?'

'Sixteen.'

'My voice broke when I was fourteen. That's when they banished me to the altos. Which part do you sing?'

'I'm a solo act, but I've done a few collaborations, you know, with EZPZ and Talisha, mostly for charity,' said Saxon, waving at his fans, who shrieked with glee at the gesture. 'I'm here on tour.'

'What a fantastic opportunity for you. Welcome to Australia.'

'I love it here. The chicks are rad and your sashimi is better than anything in Osaka.'

'Such a well-travelled young man. You're lucky to have parents who take you everywhere. When I was your age, the farthest I'd been was Cairns.' A photographer broke free of the barriers, pushed past Gestapa, and surged onto the scene. 'Saxon! PM!' he called.

Max smiled. 'Is this your Dad?'

'No.'

'Don't worry, mate. My daughter, Abigail, disowns me all the time.' Max laughed. 'Happy to have a photo if you want one, Saxon.'

'Sure,' said Saxon. 'You're not my usual demographic, but whatever, man. If dudes are your thing, that's cool.'

Max frowned, perplexed.

Saxon clicked his fingers.

Gestapa hurried forward with a pen and photograph of Saxon.

'I should probably go and see some of the others. The cops don't like it when I keep them waiting.' He signed his headshot. 'Namaste, sir.'

'Why didn't you say so?' Max seized the pen. He signed an autograph, shook the bemused boy's hand, waved to the crowd and got in the car.

'Feeling a bit better, PM?' I asked, handing him some gum.

'Yeah, sorry about that guys. I panicked a bit.' He popped two pieces of PK. 'Nice young man, that,' he said, as we drove to his next appointment. 'Bit arrogant, though.'

His family phone rang. 'Hi, sweetie.' His smiled turned upside down. 'Who?...No, I'm not trying to destroy your reputation...yes, he said his name was Sax—oh, well how was I supposed to know that? I've got slightly larger things on my...no, Abba, the entire world doesn't know who he is—I certainly didn't. Calm down...Abba? Abigail?'

Laugh, kookaburra

'Advance Oz Tray Affair.' The recorder-accompanied national anthem at Kirner Primary squawked to a halt.

Broad-brimmed royal-blue hats returned to the heads from whence they came. There were hundreds of them, sitting cross-legged on the covered bitumen. Parents and teachers sat in plastic chairs under the shade cloth on the sidelines, surveying the perimeters like generals inspecting their troops before battle.

'Good morning, boys and girls,' said the principal, whose slacks came up to her bosom, or whose bosom came down to her slacks—I couldn't work it out.

'Goooood mooooooorning, Missssussss Maaaaaaaaartin.'

My chair was plastic too. In the full glare of the bright noon sun it felt like a hot car bonnet beneath my bum. One of its four legs was shorter than the others, so every time I shook, which was a lot, it rocked. Sweat trickled down my spine, saturating the waistband of my knickers.

I longed to remove my coat but my fingers couldn't work the fiddly buttons.

'A few quick announcements first. Miss Jones will be teaching 6D while Mrs Burke is away.'

Falsetto murmurs broke out.

'Excuse me, fingers on lips, children.'

The cavalry followed the order.

'Much better. Where was I? Yes. There will be a notice going home in your school bags this afternoon regarding contraband seedling donations to our kitchen-garden project and we're still waiting for some parents to get back to us with their lamington-drive funds, so let's remind our mums and dads about this when we get home today.'

Some parents looked smug, others shifted in their seats.

Bollocks, it's Bella.

Her long, golden hair fell softly on tanned shoulders. She wore jeans, a white T-shirt and a pair of oversized sunglasses but looked as glamorous as a film star spotted stepping out of Starbucks in a gossip magazine.

'Before we introduce our very special guest, we're going to hear a round robin from the Kirner Kernels.'

The conductor signalled for her choir to huddle closer.

Bella waved a few fingers at me and flashed a perfect smile.

I tried to reciprocate, nerves springing, lips twitching.

Why did you agree to do this?

Because Dan said he wanted me to talk to twenty-five year 5s not the entire school assembly. Oration shouldn't be a problem for a seasoned prime ministerial advisor, I thought. They were children, after all. But it was a problem, a bladder-fillingly terrifying one, especially now that my rival was in the audience with her camera at the ready.

I'm sure Bella didn't see herself that way. She and Luke enjoyed the kind of friendship most current girlfriends dream their partner might have with their ex-wife. Luke spent Mondays and Tuesdays in Melbourne while Bella was on night-duty at the hospital, and Dan came to Canberra every second weekend. I didn't mind that Luke stayed at her house, not one bit. Okay, one bit; but still, he was in the spare room.

And when, by total coincidence, I was in Melbourne as well I'd stay there and it was completely normal, aside from the his and hers towels in the bathroom. 'Wedding presents,' she said. I bought her new towels for Christmas.

Why did she have to be so lovely? Most people have flaws. Bella was bella inside and out. She had a berry garden. Her hips swayed when she did the dishes. She served tea in a pre-warmed pot and shared articulate thoughts on the latest Sofia Coppola film, the kind I'd have to draft and put on palm cards if I was to deliver them. Her playlists were always current. Not top-100 current, just new and interesting and unusual. Even when she snort-laughed by accident it was charming, like a very sweet spring piglet. If I recorded her snort-laugh and put it on the internet it would become a bestselling ringtone.

Luke should never have let her go. What a first-class fool. He would still be happily married to Bella if his job hadn't led to their divorce, he and I getting together and him quitting his post with Max, the buffoon.

Whenever he said her name or Dan's, I pictured the three of them playing beach cricket or flying a kite or picking berries for breakfast. He must wonder why on earth he was with unlovely, ugly-in-a-T-shirt me when he could have lived happily ever after with that goddess and their son.

I didn't have berries. I didn't even have parsley, just a wealth of dog poo, struggling turf and a hose with canine-inflicted puncture wounds. I didn't have time to read novels. And who's Sofia Coppola? My lips are thin and meagre unless I eat chilli—by which time they've swollen along with my tongue, and then Luke just laughs at me because of my tempowawy wisp.

'Laugh, kookaburra, laugh, kookaburra, gay your life must be.'

The troops applauded.

'Wasn't that wonderful? Thank you to the Kernels and their conductor, Miss Polly.'

'Now, I'd like to invite Dan Harley from 5F to come up. Dan is going to introduce his dad's—um—friend who has come all the way from Canberra to speak to us today. I'll let Dan tell you why.'

Dan, who was a carbon copy of Luke, except smaller with freckles and hair that parted on the other side, approached the microphone and stood on an upturned wooden crate. He poked his tongue out at me.

I returned the favour. Our customary greeting surprised the principal.

He unscrunched a piece of paper. 'Good mooorning Principal Maaartin, teachers, parents and fellow students. My name is Dan Harley and I've been arksed to introduce my dad's girlfriend, Ruby Stanhope. Roo is from England but now she works for the Prime Minister.' He scratched his knee. 'I arksed Roo to speak to my class, 5F, because today we're having show-and-tell and our theme this week is government. But when I told my teacher about Roo, he rung up Principal Maaartin and she said she reckoned Roo should speak to everyone at assembly.

'Today, Roo is gonna tell us about her job. So, without much further ado, put your hands together for Roo.'

There were claps and cheers for Dan as I approached the microphone.

Pants.

I cleared my throat. The mike screeched. 'Thank you Principal Martin and Dan for that lovely introduction. He's a hard act to follow.'

More screeching.

'I thought I'd start by making a few short remarks before handing it over to Q&A, but feel free to intervene with any poignant questions as and when they arise.'

This is a primary school, Ruby, not an accounting-standards seminar.

'Right. Yes. So, I used to be an investment banker. Investment bankers make money grow and travel around the world at speed to make people richer.'

A pigtailed girl in the front row put up her hand.

'Yes?'

'Does the money go in a rocket?'

'Erm, no. No rockets. But in 2009 a rocket would have been a safer option than the subprime vehicles most of my colleagues were investing in.'

Her brow furrowed.

'One day, I got an email from some horrible, troll-like people called human resource managers.'

A boy with glasses waved his arm at me.

'Yes?'

'My dad's one of them.'

'Oh. Right. Well, not all HR managers are trolls. In fact, Australia has some rather nice and un-troll-like HR managers, like your dad. So, the email said I had lost my job. I packed up my things, went home, opened a case of wine and drank—in moderation, of course. Just a thimbleful.'

The shade-cloth inflated with a collective parental sigh.

'It happened to be quite powerful wine and it made me do funny things, like book plane tickets to Australia. That's why wine is bad and should be avoided at all costs.'

The same boy put his hand up.

I nodded.

'My nanna's a winemaker in the Yarra Valley.'

'Excellent,' I said. 'On second thoughts, perhaps we should leave questions until the end.'

Principal Martin appeared anxious.

I powered on. 'So I ended up in Australia at my aunt's house with nothing to do. Then I met Dan's dad, Luke, who said I might like to come in for a job interview. The day I met with him was the day my boss's predecessor stabbed her predecessor in the back—'

Gasps.

'Not literally in the back, she just took his job and called an election and I joined the election campaign for the other guy.'

I relaxed a little. 'It was the most marvellous experience of my life. If any of you get the chance to work on a campaign, you should seize it with both hands. I travelled the country, met incredible people and my boss ended up becoming prime minister. We won the election. The people voted for us. We got government and I became the strategic communications advisor. I will always remember that night. It was my proudest hour. So, that's about it really. Any questions?'

There was an uncomfortable silence. Parents whispered to each other. Bella had put the camera down.

'Yes, you, up the back.' I spotted a hand in the crowd. 'Stand up and speak with a big voice so everyone can hear you.'

'I can't, I'm in a wheelchair.'

Dive, dive, dive.

'Sorry about that. Not sorry about *that*, sorry I didn't notice—I mean, erm, what was your question?'

'What is a strategic communication?'

'A strategic communication is a communication which is, you know, strategic.'

'What does that mean?'

'Oh. Erm, the thing is, I think it's just a title they made up because nobody knows what I do. I sort of do everything—a bit of this and that. A little from Column A, a little from Column B. Does anyone else have a question?'

'Was government the prize for winning the election?'

'Yes, sort of.'

'Why did you want to win it?'

'Because—that's a ripper of a question. You should come and work at the press gallery. How old are you?'

'Six.'

'Bravo. Was government the prize? Sort of. We wanted to win government because we wanted to make a difference for the country. We wanted to change policies to help people. Of course, it's one thing to want to make a difference and quite another to actually make one. A lot of the time we just swing from disaster to disaster and hope to God we'll have a day of reprieve in which we can think a bit and do some real difference-making. Like in football. Does anyone play football here?'

About a hundred hands shot up.

'Excellent! Yes, being in government is like playing a game of football. When the other side is scoring goal after goal and your goalkeeper is exhausted and a bit downtrodden because, frankly, he's not *that* good at his job, that means everyone on your team is focused on defence—even the striker—so nobody has the time or the energy to score goals and then the secondary striker retires hurt. And then the fans turn on you and start booing and hissing—that's what it's like. We just want to get to half-time so we can have some oranges.'

Well done. That shut them up.

'Any other questions?'

A tentative hand. 'Yes?'

'What's a goalkeeper? And what's a striker?'

'They're football positions—soccer, you'd call it.'

'That's not football.'

Heathens.

'Anyone else? How about you in the blue hat?'

Everyone's in a blue hat.

'What differences have you made and how many people have you helped?'

'Another superb question. We had a plan and presented it to voters before the election. Then we won government and tried to make the plan work. We implemented some of it, but much of it was harder than we thought it would be. Things were changing all the time and there wasn't as much money as we'd have liked. Also, the people who didn't vote for us didn't like the plan at all and tried to stop us making it work, so that made it tricky. How about you, in the middle?'

'My dad says if you vote for a politician, you get a politician. Is that true?'

'Yes, but if you vote for a politician who used to be a rock star, you get a politician and a rock star. Two for the price of one. Anyone else?'

A tall girl with braces and a neat, blue hair ribbon stood up and adjusted a shiny, gold badge. 'My name is Jemma and when I grow up I want to be the prime minister, I think. I'm school captain. My plan was to make tuck-shop free on Fridays but I can't make the plan work because it costs too much money.

'Yesterday, one of my friends said she should have voted for Cory. I tried to make up a new plan, but it's not as good as my old plan, even though the new one works. Is being prime minister like being school captain?'

Screech.

'I don't want to lie to you, Jemma. The PM is laughed at, lied about and today he was spat on. We all put on a brave face, but it's hard.'

I saw a patch of bright pink at the back of the blue.

Why is Bettina here? And why is she pacing?

'I—I don't know what else to say. Jemma, you've chosen a hard road. Godspeed.'

Principal Martin took the mike from my hands. 'Well, what do we say to Miss Stanhope, Kirner kids?'

'Thaaaaaank yooooooooou, Roooooooooooooooooooooo.'

I hurried towards Bettina, who was busy drowning herself in the water fountain.

'Ruby.' Bella grabbed my wrist. I was always oxygen deficient when talking to Bella. Breathtaking beauty has that effect. 'That was honest,' she said, her smile radiating warmth. 'Are you okay?'

'Not really. I didn't prepare properly.'

'You were fine. Anyway, it's my fault. I thought Dan had told you about the assembly thing. I should've checked. He really looks up to you, Roo.'

'That's a worry.'

'Luke told me about dinner with the parents.'

'He did?'

She laughed and rubbed my arm. 'Look, they both think the world of you.'

How does she know that? She still talks to her in-laws? She's perfection on legs!

'Excellent. Listen, I have to run. Suicidal intern. Tell Dan I'm sorry I fucked it up. Except without the expletive.'

'Will do,' she said. 'And can you tell Luke he left his favourite tie at my place?'

'Tutankhamun stripes?'

'No, the seventies Le Creuset orange one.'

'That's not his favourite!'

'Thank God,' she said. 'Want me to bury it?'

In the berry patch.

'Yes, please.'

'Get some sleep, lovely. You look shattered. And happy birthday for next week.'

Shattered? Bit harsh.

'Bettina,' I said, rushing towards the water fountain, 'is everything okay?'

'No, everything is totally not okay. Do you know what TweetDeck is?'

I shook my head, leading her past the kitchen garden to the school gates.

'It's an application allowing users to run multiple social-networking accounts from a single portal. It's very useful. For example, you could have several Twitter accounts and Facebook pages going at once, or LinkedIn or—'

'I get it.'

'So, I set up TweetDeck on my BlackBerry, with Max's Facebook and Twitter account alongside mine, so I could get a feel for how it's run at the moment and how I might like to develop it—'

She couldn't have.

'—and then I tweeted from Max...I'll just show you.'

@MaxMastersPM: Hanging out for my mani/pedi this Sunday. #pamperporn

My heart rattled my rib cage in search of a way out. 'Recall it!'

'You can't recall tweets. You can delete them.'

'Delete it, then!'

'I tried to delete it but by the time I noticed what I'd done, it had been re-tweeted about seven hundred times and I thought it might look worse because he has about a zillion followers and the re-tweeters probably have twice as many between them'—she breathed—'so that's two zillion so I got in a cab and came straight here.'

'When was this?'

'Twenty-one minutes and thirty seconds ago. I'm totally going to be sick.'

'No, you are not. I've had my fill of sick today. Get us back to the electorate office. If you must, you can vomit in the taxi.'

She ran into the middle of the pedestrian crossing, waving her arms like Olivia Newton-John in *Physical*.

I switched on my phone. Missed calls: thirty-four. Chief, Chief, Chief, Chief, Chief—I called Chief.

'Roo, someone's hacked Max's Twitter account.'

'Not exactly,' I said. 'I asked Bettina to look after Max's Twitter and she accidentally—'

'You did what? She's a fucking intern.'

'I know, listen, it's my fault.'

'I know it's your fault! Fix it. He's in the middle of a speech at the opening of his electorate office. There's already footage of him parking tigers on YouTube. There are at least eight journos there—TV, print and radio—and he's about to be blindsided.' She hung up on me.

The cabby turned up his radio. 'Listen to this. It's bloody hilarious.'

'If you've just joined us here on 3PV Mornings, we've been taking calls on prime ministerial nail colour. You heard right. The Twittersphere is abuzz after the Prime Minister used the micro-blogging site to reveal his manicure and pedicure plans for the weekend, describing them as "pamper porn".'

Bettina wound her window down an inch and dry-retched.

'As we broadcast, Max Masters is speaking at the opening of his new Melbourne electorate office after an eventful morning, going from being spat on at an event in the CBD to being sick at a Federation Square press conference for teen idol Saxon Vibe. Onlookers described the brief encounter between the pop star and the PM, during which neither knew whom the other was, as awkward. Joyce from Jimboomba, are you there?'

'Dear future, this is the end of my political career. It has been a brilliant twenty-eight hours—'

'Bettina! Now is not the time to capsule! Driver, I'm going to have to ask you to speed up.'

'Yes, hullo, Harold. I listen to you every morning.'

Creepy.

'Thanks, Joyce. Tell me, what do you think of Max Masters' manscaping ritual?'

'Well, Harold, I think it's lovely when a gentleman takes care of himself, especially a busy one. If I were him, I'd either go for something patriotic, like a green and gold, or classic, perhaps a French manicure. Or red, white and blue for his US visit?'

'Joyce, good suggestions but I'm going to have to leave you there. We're crossing now to Max Masters' electorate office where the Prime Minister is winding up his speech...'

We pulled up on the curb. Balloon-lined rows of chairs filled the car park. A makeshift stage had been set up outside the office door. The media advisor waved me over.

I elbowed my way through the huge sniggering media presence and walked up the side aisle to the front row as surreptitiously as I could. An elderly lady scowled at me. I smiled like a Colgate commercial.

'This is my community,' said Max. 'It's where my heart is. It's where I met my wife and where my daughter grew up. It's where I belong.'

He paused when he saw me, perplexed.

I tried to think of a non-verbal way to convey the message. It was harder than I thought. On the spot, I came up with downward-pointing spirit fingers.

He blushed, looked down at his fly, back at me and continued. 'So, it is with great joy that I declare this office open!'

He picked up a pair of scissors and cut the ribbon, neither of which were great props in the circumstances.

Snappers swarmed, all zooming in on his fingers.

A journalist jostled to the front of the pack. 'Prime Minister! Prime Minister! Will you be pressing charges against the woman who assaulted you this morning?'

'Do you always get your nails done before the Midwinter Ball?'

'Gels or acrylics, Prime Minister?'

'Saxon Vibe has just tweeted. He said, "My Aussie fans taught me 'fully sick' is a good thing down under, so your prime minister must be pretty popular."'

I stood in front of him. 'Ladies and gentlemen, the Prime Minister looks forward to taking your questions in just a moment.'

Max smiled, waved and followed me through the office door.

I handed him a bottle of water.

He looked at my face. 'Oh God, please don't tell me we've lost another troop.'

'No,' I said. 'I gave control of your Twitter account to an intern who tweeted this morning, thinking it was hers. It's her second day. I didn't want you to be blindsided out there. I'm so sorry, PM.'

'Oh,' he said. 'Not about the poll, I hope.'

'No, it's—' I showed him on my BlackBerry.

His jaw dropped. His eyes creased. He clutched his belly and laughed like a kookaburra. 'Lighten up, Roo,' he said, wiping a tear from his smile lines.

He took his phone out of his pocket.

'Erm, PM, what are you doing?'

'You'll see.' He opened the door and stepped out onto

centre stage. 'Before I take any questions,' he said, 'you might want to hit the refresh button.'

The hungry hoard fumbled with their phones while I looked down at mine.

@MaxMastersPM: Sorry about before. A new staffer's second day on the job. I think she nailed it. PM

Sacrificial lamb

My Louboutins clip-clopped as I dashed across the marbled foyer at Parliament House that night with plastic-covered couture slung over my arm.

They used to have a perfect clop-clop until I sprinted in them at Admiralty House, tripped over a soccer ball and flew headfirst into the Spanish Ambassador. Her Excellency broke a thumbnail, I sustained minor facial bruising and the stiletto heel of my left Louboutin lost its tip. Now they go clip-clop, clip-clop, like a neglected donkey.

I had been meaning to take them to the shoe repairman but there wasn't time. That I'd managed to pick up my dry-cleaning was a miracle.

'I thought you were dead,' the drycleaner said when I handed him the crumpled ticket from January. He went to the back of the store. 'There are summer dresses in here—it's three degrees outside. I was ready to put them in the charity bin.'

I didn't have the heart to tell him I'd been unfaithful. Promiscuous, in fact. I didn't know which of his competitors we used now that Luke had taken over dry-cleaning responsibilities, as he had everything else in our lives. He insisted on it after waking up one day with an empty wardrobe. 'Babe,' he'd said, peering into a cupboard containing hangers, a wetsuit, stonewash jeans, a tux, two cummerbunds and a wall of novelty ties. 'Do you know where my clothes are?'

I suggested we might have been robbed by a man with terrible taste, which would have been convincing if he hadn't discovered the bulging garbage bag full of laundry in the boot of my car.

The wall clock said 8.50 p.m. when I swiped myself out through security. Crap. Luke would be cross.

The security guy winked. 'You're leaving early tonight. Hot date?'

'Something like that. Can you hold these for me?' I zapped him with static electricity as he relieved me of the slippery stack of dry-cleaning.

'Call Capital Cabs,' I said into my voice-activated Black-Berry.

'Welcome to Capital Cabs. Would you like to book a taxi?'
'Yes.'

'If so, say yes, if—'
'Yes.'

'I'm sorry, I'm having trouble understanding—'
'I said yes.'

'Please wait for me to run through the options. If you would like to book a taxi, please say yes. If you have a lost property enquiry, please say lost property.'
'Yes.'

'Transferring you to our lost property desk now.'

'No, I said yes.'

'I'm sorry, did you say yes?'

'Yes.'

'Okay, transferring you now.'

Thank fuck.

'Welcome to Capital Cabs. Our lost and found desk is now closed. Please call back during business hours, Monday to Friday excluding public holidays. Thank you.'

'The daft cow hung up on me.'

Security Guy found this funny. 'Here, use my land-line—they recognise the number here.'

'Thanks.' I dialled.

'Welcome to Capital Cabs—'

My BlackBerry rang. It was Luke. I held it to the other ear.

'Where are you?' he sighed.

'Running out the door.'

'You were running out the door forty-five minutes ago.'

'I'm sorry, I'm having trouble understanding you. Did you say yes?'

'Yes!'

'Don't snap at me,' said Luke, 'I'm just trying to figure out whether to cling-wrap your dinner.'

'I'm not snapping at you, I'm snapping at Capital Cabs. I'm on two phones at once. It's a superhuman ability.'

'I'm sorry, did you say bookings for people with disabilities?'

'No!'

'Just press nine until someone answers, Ruby. It always works.'

'You mean I'll get to speak to a human being?'

'I'm sorry, I'm having trouble underst—'

I punched nine repeatedly with an angry knuckle. 'Welcome to Capital Cabs, how can I help you?'

'It worked! Bye.'

They both hung up.

I threw my handbag to the ground like it was the racquet of a frustrated Wimbledon champ.

'You haven't changed a bit,' said a honey-laden voice behind me.

I swivelled, but I already knew whose it was. Those action-figure arms, those dimpled cheeks, that ridiculous new length and curl in his dark brown hair. Were they highlights?

'Oscar.' I blocked an attempted kiss with a firm handshake. 'What brings you here?'

He flashed me a kilowatt smile. 'A bit of this and that, you know.'

'Last I heard you were in training for the foxtrot, something you ought to be rather good at.'

'I'm flattered, Roo. I thought you'd be too busy at PMO to take an interest in my career trajectory.'

'About a million Australians watch *Celebrity Dancefloor* every week. That doesn't mean they all take an interest in you or your career trajectory.'

He laughed. 'You crack me up, gorgeous. How are you, anyway?'

'Terrific, thank you.'

'Good to hear. Are you and Luke Harley still—'

'Verily so.'

He smiled. 'So, your boss is on my show next weekend.'

'I know,' I said. 'What are the ratings like for *Sunday Roast* at the moment?'

'Usually about eight hundred thousand, but we're expecting more for your guy. But probably best not confuse that with an interest in him or his career trajectory though.'

Insert witty comeback here.

A taxi pulled up outside. I yearned for it.

'Is that your cab?' asked Oscar.

'Yes,' I lied.

Security Guy handed me my dry-cleaning. 'Looks like they got the message after all.'

Oscar opened the heavy bronze-framed door with two fingers, as if it was a bamboo-beaded curtain at the local convenience store. 'After you,' he said, looping a scarf around his neck. 'Do your coat up—it's freezing out here.'

Scoundrel, said my head. *How dare he think he can tell you what to do.*

He's right, said my body. *Button up.*

Harden up, body.

'Name?' asked the cabby through the passenger-side window.

'It may have been booked under our receptionist's name,' I shivered, 'you know how it is.'

'Is your receptionist's name Oscar Franklin?'

'Take it, Roo,' said Oscar, smiling.

'I couldn't possibly.'

Yes, you could. Your teeth are chattering.

'I insist.' He opened the car door for me. 'I'll order another one—I have the CapCabs app on my phone.'

Apt.

'Thanks.' I got in.

'Not at all,' he said over the doorframe. 'It was good seeing you again, Roo—you look great.'

'You too. I mean—'

He grinned. 'Look, there's a cocktail party on next Friday night—a bit of a celebration. I'll text you the details. Say hi to Luke for me.' He shut the door.

'What a gentleman,' said the cabby. 'Isn't he on TV? My wife loves him.'

I texted Chief.

Just bumped into Pretty Boy. WTF? R

She replied.

I meant to tell you. Let's chat about it tomorrow before you fly. D

Fly? New York. New York tomorrow. Cripes.

Ten minutes later I was home. The grass had stiffened with frost underfoot. Smoke wafted above the chimney and the warmth of candlelight softened the windows. The sensor light came on as I walked up the steps.

'Sit,' I urged in my gruffest tone as The Widdler's clumsy claws tore a gash in the dry-cleaning bag. 'Sit!' JFK sniffed my skirt and licked through the holey tights encasing my left ankle. 'Please, sit?' At least theirs was an affectionate welcome. Luke was at his piano.

I didn't even know he could play until our first Christmas party at The Lodge. We were outside in the beautiful early summer evening, standing barefoot beside the vast rose garden. I was wearing a blue hydrangea-print halter dress for the occasion. Luke said I looked like a siren in it.

'A blue siren,' said Chief, as she pricked sausages at the barbeque, in her black parachute-silk maxi-dress with tiny straps.

Jack smoked Cubans, with her feet dangling in the

pool and the Treasurer played Monopoly with Max and Shelly's daughter, Abigail. Our hosts danced like love-struck teenagers until the sky blushed pink.

After one too many champagnes I ran back up the hill to the house in search of a bathroom and found my Luke sitting at the piano, bashing out an unrecognisable melody with his right hand, a glass of red in his left.

I observed quietly from behind the couch like David Attenborough behind a sub-Saharan bush. Luke hummed and muttered profanities with every wrong key, his long fingers desperate to remember where they were meant to be. He clicked his tongue against the back of his teeth in place of a metronome. Before long, he rediscovered rhythm.

He set his glass down, cracked his knuckles and closed his eyes. Ten fingers hovered above the monochrome keys and out poured Luke's soul. *Somewhere Over the Rainbow* had never meant more to me than falsetto munchkins until Luke played it. Hopeful and mournful all at once, there was a longing in his playing, in the unspoken lyrics. It was the sexiest I had ever seen him.

That Christmas Eve there was a knock at our door. Luke answered it in his boxers.

'You Luke Harley?' asked the removal-truck driver.

'Yes.'

'Sign here, please.'

'For what?'

'Your piano.'

The dusty black baby grand I had purchased from a Yarralumla lady was wheeled into our living room beside the under-decorated tree. I saw Luke's eyes twinkle then glisten, just for a second. He spent the next week becoming reacquainted with his eighteen-year-old self, paying his way through law school as a lounge pianist at the Windsor.

Now, Luke played the blues. I hung the dry-cleaning on the hat stand, unzipped my boots and pulled my dress over my head and my tights down to my ankles, wrapping myself in a towelling robe.

'Luke?' My nose led me up the hall to the kitchen where a hot bowl sat cling-wrapped on the stove. 'Is this lamb ragout?'

He switched songs. *Suppertime.*

It *was* lamb ragout. My favourite, the gamey sauce enriched with orange rind, bay and rosemary-coated crinkled pappardelle. 'I'm starving. Have you eaten? It smells amazing.'

No response. He was going to make me sing for it.

The dogs followed me across the cold tiles into the warmth of the living room and slumped in front of the dwindling fire. I added a log and puffed the bellows. Tea candles on the dining table had melted into transparent pools in their tin casing. A bottle of my best pinot noir sat on the runner with two glasses, one greasy with fingerprints, atop an open issue of the *New Yorker.*

I straddled the piano stool. Luke's tie—a kind of bubbled, greying beige, like mouldy Victoria sponge under a microscope—was undone and draped around his broad shoulders. I slid it off him, and put it around my neck to practise my half-Windsor. 'Sorry I'm so late.'

He kept playing—*Georgia On My Mind* now—in a sort of melancholic trance. I ran my fingers through his hair and down the back of his shirt. 'Who is Georgia and do I need to worry about her?'

He smiled. 'That depends.'

'On what?' I kissed his neck.

'On whether you're going to be late for everything for the rest of our lives. Georgia is very tardy.'

'Tarty?'

'No, tar*dy*.'

'Yeah, well, Georgia doesn't work at PMO. Anyway, cut me some slack. I'm home at a quarter past nine on a weeknight. And I'm going to New York tomorrow and you won't see me before my birthday.'

'What birthday?'

'Very funny.'

'Oh, that's awkward,' he said, deadpan. 'I forgot.'

'You did not, you big tease.'

'Give me five minutes and I'll duck down to the servo for a bunch of yesterday's carnations and a block of Dairy Milk.'

'You can make it up to me later,' I said with a cheesy wink.

He segued into a basic rendition of *Sexual Healing*. JFK crooned with the music.

'Dan called me,' he said. 'He said his school captain offered her resignation saying she wants to spend more time with her family, all of this after one of her constituents went on an angry rampage because everyone was calling his dad a troll.'

'Oh. Sorry about that. I'd had a bad morning.'

'So I saw. What made you pull over outside Federation Square?'

'Please don't tell me how to do my job,' I said. 'You know how it is. He wanted air.'

'You should've just put the windows down and driven him to the office.'

And you should stop seeing fungus as an appropriate wardrobe palette.

'You can't put the windows down in C1 because it's bulletproof.'

'I know.'

No, he doesn't.

'Anyway, all I'm saying is, sorry I'm late. Haruko is in town.'

'What's in town?'

'The Japanese prime minister.'

He stopped playing. 'I know who Haruko is, Ruby.'

'Okay, well, you asked.'

'Because you mispronounced it.'

'I always put the em*pha*sis on the wrong syl*la*ble with Japanese words. Anyway, so Har*u*ko's addressing the parliament tomorr—'

'You don't believe me, do you? You think I don't know who the new Japanese prime minister is.'

'Huh?'

Here we go again.

'You think I don't follow basic current affairs. I run one of the most successful and influential think tanks in the country. Of course I know who the fucking Japanese prime minister is. He was sworn in after a close-fought—'

'She.'

'What?'

'Prime Minister Haruko is a woman.'

He stood up and poured himself another glass of wine. 'That's what I said.'

'I must have misheard you. So then we had to meet with the US ambassador—'

'You seem to forget that I *hired* you, Ruby. And frankly,

if I had known you'd become this fucking arrogant I'd have just asked you out for a drink so there wasn't all this bullshit competition between us.'

Fury bubbled. Or was that hunger? 'I'm going to heat up my dinner.'

'What, Ruby? You think people with no understanding of Australia let alone its politics are often hired to work on major election campaigns?'

I turned on my heel. 'Now you're being hurtful.'

'Truth has that effect on people.'

'I worked my pants off on the campaign.'

'You sure did!'

I knew he wanted to eat his words as soon as he'd let them out, but that didn't forgive them.

Stomp into the kitchen and reheat that bowl of deliciousness.

It's quite difficult to be angry with someone when you're eating your favourite meal, especially when they've cooked it. We sat in silence for a few minutes—me on the couch, him on the piano stool, eating pappardelle with muted slurps—until finally he said, 'I don't like who I am with you—who I've become. I leave work at eight with an empty in-tray. I come home and cook gourmet meals for you, which you *never* eat.'

'This is lovely,' I said between slurps.

'You get into bed last and out of it first. I do all the house stuff: cleaning, washing, ironing, gardening—everything. I'm organising Debs' baby shower and extending our travel agent's deadline. Could you not find five minutes, Ruby, to tell me where you want to go on holiday?'

'I got the dry-cleaning today,' I said. 'It's on the hat stand, in case you're interested.'

'That's impossible. I got the dry-cleaning yesterday!' He marched into the hallway and returned, waving a tiny piece of paper.

'What's that?'

'This? This is a receipt claiming that these clothes were dropped off by R. Stanhope on the eighth of January.'

'So?'

'So, it's June!'

'The second quarter.'

'No wonder I couldn't find my tux for the opera. It's been at Ahmet's since New Year. I had to hire one!'

'It looked great on you.'

'It had a sewn-in cummerbund!'

'I work hard. You're jealous. I get it.'

'I'm not jealous.'

'Yes, you are. Nobody fired you from PMO, Luke. You left. Everyone begged you to stay. It was pretty selfish, leaving Max just as he was elected, but we all supported your decision.

'I didn't ask you to email me twenty-five times a day or catalogue my holiday options. I didn't ask you to slave over a hot stove or plan a baby shower for my aunt's missus. I just want you to be happy.' I felt the prickle of tears behind my eyes but willed them away with a greedy breath. 'Did I tell you I broke the toilet on the plane? There's been spit, vomit and toilet water, all in one day. The trifecta. I just can't cope with another fight and I still have to pack for New York.'

His elbow struck B-flat as he stared into the fire. 'I left work for Dan—he needs his dad. And for me. God knows I needed a break after working twenty-hour days for ten years. I hate that I sound like the whiny, nagging woman who divorced me for doing the job my girlfriend does. It's pathetic.'

'I'll tell you what's pathetic.' I approached the piano and put down the ragout. 'You expected Bella and Dan to live their lives on standby for you, and the second you get a taste of it you flip. How many dinners with Bella's parents were you late to when you worked for Max? Did you mow the lawns then? Did you go to her work functions? Or Dan's concerts? This is sexist tosh of the highest order.'

A single droplet escaped my eye. It bounced off his synthetic tie onto the velvet-upholstered piano stool, creating a dark spot. I sat on it, beside him.

He sighed. 'Fucking hell, Ruby, why don't you just marry me?'

Huh?

'Huh?'

He pulled a black suede box from his pocket, flipped it open and slammed it on F-sharp. A fat, round, multi-faceted, platinum-set ruby flanked by a pair of diamonds sparkled in the candlelight.

I looked up at him. 'What?'

'I want you to marry me.'

'No.' I took off his tie and got up.

He drew back, wounded. 'Did you just say no?'

'Yes, I said no.'

'No. Well, that's nice.' He shut the box.

'What did you expect me to say to, "Fucking hell, why don't you just marry me"?'

'Yes?'

'We were in the middle of a row. You can't just propose to someone because you're losing an argument!'

'I wasn't losing the argument.'

'You were!'

'Was not!'

'You were so!' My gesticulation sent my bowl crashing to the floor via my little toe. 'Ow fucking ow!' Now in five big pieces the white china looked like the Sydney Opera House on a harbour of ragout. The dogs rushed in to lick it up. 'No, Widdles! Stop it! No!'

They didn't listen to me.

'Sit,' said Luke, heading for the kitchen.

They backed off.

He brought my toe an icepack.

'We're good together, Ruby, but we need to get away from here, from the fights. For once in my life I have time to invest in my relationship, and the one person that matters most to me doesn't. I'm asking you to make that time for us.'

He reopened the box and got on his knees beside me.

'Let's travel the world, share newspapers in bed, take turns cooking breakfast, host barbecues for friends—settle down together. Just you and me. I have enough to sustain us, to—to get you away from all of this.'

'I don't need rescuing.'

'You do. From this—your—the job.'

'My job. You want me to *resign*?'

He nodded. 'Just take a year off.' I don't think he even thought about how it sounded. There was disbelief in his eyes and a quiver to his mouth.

'I am no damsel in distress. Not even a damsel in— whatever the opposite of distress is. This is what I want to do. I chose this work and I love it. There is nothing loving about a conditional proposal.'

Luke swallowed hard and shut the box. He stumbled as he stood.

'I have to pack for New York. I'm leaving for the office at five.'

'You're going to New York?'

'You knew that,' I said.

'But you're *still* going to New York?'

'Of course I am.'

'Well, that is a definitive no, isn't it?'

'No. Yes. I don't know, but I can't just not go to New York. I work for the—'

'Prime Minister,' he said. 'I know. I hope you'll be very happy together.'

I heard the front door open.

JFK and The Widdler thought it was time for a walk.

Luke thought it was time to walk out.

Cloak and dagger

JFK howled with my 4.30 a.m. alarm.

'You are not a rooster,' I reminded him.

It didn't matter. I hadn't slept.

Moonlight shone through the gap between the curtain and rod, spotlighting the unrumpled quilt on Luke's side of our bed.

Shrouded in a crocheted blanket on the window seat, I tried to make sense of it all over a steaming mug of Earl Grey. He had a ring. When did he buy it? I wondered. What if he had asked my father's permission? I said no, didn't I?

Yes.

I turned down a marriage proposal. From Luke, no less. I love Luke. Why didn't I want to marry him?

Because he wants you to divorce your job.

Oh.

I doused my face with icy water to numb my stinging

eyes when my BlackBerry buzzed with a private number. 'Luke?'

'It's me,' said Chief. 'Get in here and talk to Cecil. This is not good.' She hung up.

Toothbrush in mouth, I threw a few things into my suitcase and switched on the radio.

'...has been rocked by the extraordinary release of a document revealing the government's plan to pull funding for its controversial Serve the Nation policy...'

Fuck me. I threw my hair into a loose ponytail and dotted concealer around my eyes.

'Serve the Nation, a key election platform for the Masters' government, incentivised school leavers to take a community service gap year in order to halve their university fees...'

I stood in front of the mirror with two hangers. Black shift dress or grey wrap dress? Shift. I stepped in, but my arm wasn't long enough to reach the zipper. 'Can you—?' I stopped myself. Phantom him.

It's a wrap.

'...memorandum between the Prime Minister's Office and Treasury discusses the planned cut and canvasses anticipated public backlash, proposing different ways in which to spin the news. Treasurer Cecil Berth, who will be acting Prime Minister following Max Masters' departure for the United States this morning, is due to convene a press conference at half past nine. It's four-forty on a foggy morning here in Canberra. Two degrees with an expected high of...'

Taxi? Booked. Radio? Off. Dogs? Fed. Keys? In hand. Passport? In bag. Tights? On legs. Little toe? Sore. Door? Locked. Life? Fucked.

I bumped my suitcase down the steps and wheeled it to the waiting car. 'Can you pop the boot please, mate?'

My heart stopped. It wasn't a cab. A dark figure rushed towards me and stepped into the sensor light.

'Argh!'

'OMG, Roo, I *totes* didn't mean to scare you.'

'You were sitting in the dark outside my house!'

'It's dark because it's early. Did you go swimming this morning?'

'No.'

'Your eyes are red. You look like my mum does when she watches Hallmark movies. I have drops in my toolkit. I'll put some in for you later. PS, does this beret clash with my coat? I mean, I was in two minds about it, but pink and yellow can kind of work if you accessorise—'

'Bettina, what are you doing here?'

She opened the boot to her purple Monaro. 'Waiting to drive you to work, silly.'

'How about a text, like, "Hey Roo, I was in the neighbourhood. Do you want a lift to the office?"'

'I probably should have texted you but I thought you'd be mad at me for yesterday. I wanted to apologise. Seriously, my bad.'

My pulse steadied. 'Don't sweat it, Bettina. Um, the boot's full.' I stared at the four-piece, quilted peach luggage set.

'Sorry, that's all my stuff for America.'

I opened the back door to put my bag in. A menagerie of soft toys was sewn onto the shoulders of Hello Kitty seat covers. On the dashboard was a fluorescent-pink lace tissue box. 'When are you going to America?'

'Um, hello! Today. Wow, you really didn't get much

sleep last night, did you? Are you sure you don't want to talk about it?'

Hang on, does that mean she's—

'You mean you're coming on the trip?'

She nodded and turned the key in the ignition. Kylie Minogue blasted through the sub-woofers. My thighs wobbled with the vibration. We tore away from the curb. The pink fluffy dice hit the windscreen.

She turned the stereo down to nightclub level and whizzed around a roundabout. 'Chief said she'd like me to be there to support you because one of the advancers has appendicitis. This is going to be *amaze*balls!'

Amazeballs.

I turned off the music. 'We'll be back on Wednesday. You can't bring all that luggage. We need to be able to get off the plane and run.'

'What if the President invites me to a state dinner? I can't just say no and I won't have time to shop, I guess, even though Saks Fifth Avenue is having its annual sale and it would be madness to just walk past it—was that a stop sign?'

I don't want to die in a purple Monaro with Hello Kitty seat covers.

'Downsize. One suitcase.'

'Okay.' We jerked around the corner. The V8 revved. 'Um, Roo?'

'Yes.'

'Before I give you your brief, I just wanted to raise something with you.'

'Yes?'

'It's about, you know.'

'No, I don't know.'

'The thing we're not supposed to talk about.'

Beat her with the dice.

'Bettina, I do not have the patience to go through this again. I've had a *terrible* night and I just want to get to work, have the meeting and get on the plane. Okay?'

'Okay, understood.' My fingers let go of the seat as we squeaked into a narrow bay.

I wheeled my suitcase past the smattering of identical cars in the ministerial car park.

Luggage-laden, Bettina hurried after me. 'This morning's coverage is pretty bad, you know, with the spit and the spew and the star and the—'

'Let's not relive it.'

'The front pages are all about how rattled he was to be spat on. No, der. How'd they like it if some feral lady spat on them? The photos aren't pretty. No chunks, though, which was a positive. The *Queenslander* has that profile on Connie Fife. OMG, you should see the photos! They put this stunning colour on her lips, like a dark burgundy, and she's in this incredible peplum jacket—'

'Anything else?'

'The *Melbournian* says the PM's bringing a doctor on the US trip. Is that for real?'

'Fuck me. Every prime minister since Barton has travelled with a doctor. That's just what you do.'

We got in the lift. 'I've taken the liberty of assembling the coverage on the Serve the Nation leak.' She handed me a ring-bound bundle. 'Do you have a highlighter colour preference? I like orange and pink, but if you have a preference—' She unzipped a pencil case, resting it on her vanity case.

'Is that an *eraser*?' I stared at a tiny faux strawberry.

'Yes. It's divine. Bought it in Japan. It's tutti-frutti. Feel free to smell it.'

We beeped through security.

'Back again, Bettina?'

'Morning, Frank—erm—love the tie pin! Where was I? I've put relevant press clippings in chronological order and highlighted any inconsistencies in the stories in orange.' She lowered her voice. 'He's a total hottie.'

'Frank?'

'No! Although I'm sure he had moments in his day. I meant Oscar Franklin.'

I snapped to attention.

'He broke the story,' Bettina said.

Of course.

'You need coffee. And muffins. I baked. Hope you like sour cherry and almond.' Her purse popped open to reveal a pink-lidded Tupperware container. 'Voila! Okay, unless there's anything else you need, I'd better do my re-pack.'

She trundled down the hallway, vanity case slung over her shoulder.

'There is one last thing,' I said mid-mouthful.

God almighty, this is a good muffin.

She turned.

'Why did Frank say, "Back again, Bettina"?'

'Huh?'

'You heard me.'

'Okay.' She scurried back towards me, checking over her shoulders. 'This is what I wanted to talk to you about. I staked the place out last night. Just me, my thermos of hot chocolate and about a year's worth of *Cosmo* magazines.'

'You staked which place out?'

'PMO.'

'Bettina!'

'We have to keep an eye on the place.'

'Frank keeps an eye on the place. As do the Australian Federal Police.'

'Well, how are the threats getting in?'

'By post.'

'No, the stamps aren't postmarked with corresponding dates.'

'What?'

'The stamps. They have postmarks on them, but they were sent two years ago—'

I held up my hand and boxed my muffin. 'How do you know this?'

She looked down. Today's eyeshadow looked neutral from one angle, but when the light hit it it was the psychedelic rainbow sheen of an oil spill.

No way.

'*Please* don't tell me you went into the Chief of Staff's office and rifled through her papers.'

'I only glanced at the envelopes. I didn't open them.'

'Look into my eyes.'

'They're very red. Do you want me to get the drops?'

'Shut up. What you did last night was a direct violation of the direction given to you by a senior member of staff. As your supervisor, I am formally warning you that if you mention this again I will have no option but to report you. *Capisce?*'

She nodded. 'Actually, it's pronounced "ca-pee-shay" not "ca-peesh". Gangsters misappropriated it in the forties from the Italian mafia, but in Italian it's—'

I stormed into the kitchen in search of breakfast, poured myself a bowl of cornflakes and opened the fridge. No milk. Brill. Eating from the packet like crisps, I went to scavenge better food from the Treasurer's waiting room and opened Bettina's brief.

The leaked story was the debut post on a new blog called *Franklinly*. Bettina had cut and pasted the 'about' section; it read:

> Franklinly is *Sunday Roast* host and *Celebrity Dancefloor* contestant Oscar Franklin's first foray into the blogosphere.
>
> The new blog, an Eleven Network first, will provide readers with daily insight into the often out-of-reach world of politics.
>
> Oscar will head the Canberra bureau of the soon-to-be-launched cable news channel 24/11.

I turned the page. The leaked memo had passed by email through the hands of at least three ministers and thirty-five advisors from four offices and two departments, excluding administrative staff. It might have been left in a printer tray, at a café or on a plane; or it might have been deliberate.

'Cecil will see you now,' said Jack. She looked me up and down. 'You look worse than our lot.'

'Thanks.'

'What's up?'

'I don't want to talk about it.'

'I'm guessing you haven't been crying over leaked memos.'

'I don't want to talk about it.' My eyes welled.

'That looks terminal. Iris,' she yelled. 'Get Roo a double-shot latte. And a pastry.'

I calmed myself and followed her in.

Cecil Berth was a fierce but fine treasurer. We spoke the same language, both of us former bankers, both of us comfortable with cutthroat efficiency.

His office was tense: all untucked shirts, sleepy eyes, half-empty coffees and messy hair. It smelled like a university study hall at midnight during exam week.

Advisors fussed over briefs, press secretaries barked into BlackBerries and Cecil sat among it all, clicking his pen like a broker watching the Lehman's collapse.

'Treasurer,' I said.

He looked up at me from his desk, his blue eyes bloodshot and striped shirt sweat-marked.

'I'm here to brief you on how we intend to handle this with the gallery.'

He grunted and wolfed down a piece of Vegemite toast.

I continued. 'First thing's first: it's not true. We're not cutting Serve the Nation. It needs fine-tuning, sure, but we're not giving up on helping students help their communities.'

'Blah, blah. I know all the pap. Cut to the leak. What do you know?'

'When we get to New York, the PM will say he takes the breach very seriously and that his office is investigating the matter—'

'Tell Max I want the language to be about both of our offices collaborating to get to the bottom of it. We can't have it looking like his office is looking into mine. I'm acting PM. Clear?'

'Crystal,' I said, grateful for the warm coffee now in my hands, 'but we don't want this to grow bigger than it already is. The resources of two offices leading an investigation into a single leak will stink of panic.'

He contemplated this. 'Are you guys any closer to figuring out where it came from?'

Staffers stared.

'Clear the room,' said Cecil, reading my expression.

The office emptied with the wave of Jack's pointed cuff. She shut the double-doors and returned to her desk.

'The document passed through about forty in-boxes on our count. We're no closer to narrowing it down.'

Cecil pounded his fist against his other hand. 'I don't have to tell you how serious this is. We're lucky we rejected the funding cut weeks ago but I'd be lying if I said the leak wasn't a major concern.'

'We're on the same page, Treasurer. If it was an accident, we've got internal control issues. If it was malicious—'

'If it was malicious, we're up the creek. Morale's already low thanks to the polls. Question Time was horrendous this week. Not a single win. We had the spitting incident followed by spewgate yesterday, which was bloody careless. I'm doing everything I can, but it comes down to Max. He needs to lift spirits.'

'We'll pull out of it, I'm sure, Treasurer. In the meantime, your tone needs to say you're taking this seriously but it's not the end of the world. Put it in perspective.'

He sipped a cup of tea. 'This may be out of line, Roo.'

'Yes?'

'You know that Oscar bloke, don't you?'

Breathe, Ruby.

'Yes.'

'Anything you can do to get a sense of where it came from would be appreciated.' He pushed back on his chair. 'Thanks for the pep talk, Roo.'

'Come with me,' said Jack. I followed her into a freezing courtyard. She lit one up and sucked it down. 'He shouldn't have asked you to do that, I'm sorry.'

'It's fine,' I said, my teeth chattering.

'Don't say that. Set an absolute bottom line for yourself. You shouldn't have to dredge up whatever personal history you have with someone for something like this.'

'Whatever. I don't care. I'm exhausted, as I'm sure you are. I'm just going to get on that plane and go to sleep. See you next week.'

My phone buzzed. Private. Luke?

'Ruby Stanhope,' I said, shooting inside to let my feet thaw.

'No, this is Clementine Gardner-Stanhope. I am *looking* for a Ruby Stanhope, though. She's my aunt.'

'Clem, it's me.'

'Hello, Aunty Wooby.'

'Hi, Clem.' Disappointment addled my insides.

'Mummy said I should call you for your birthday now because you're going to see the President to avoid it, just like everything else in your personal life.'

I chased away the lump in my throat. 'Mummy's a cow.'

'Birthdays are the best days, along with Christmas, Easter and snow days, wouldn't you agree?'

'They wear off over time.'

'My seventh birthday was the best yet. I woke up. Mummy gave me a skipping rope, every Harry Potter book ever printed—Mummy won't let me change my name to Hermione—and a mobile phone. Then I ate four pieces of French toast and went to Daddy's to get more presents. He took me out for McDonald's. Then I came home and opened my parcels from you and Luke and Aunt Daphne and Debs and Grandma, and then Samantha Fingleton came for a sleep-over. She's eleven turning twelve.'

'You have a mobile?' I walked towards PMO.

'*Everyone* has a mobile. I'm calling you on mine now. I tried to call your home but Luke said you weren't there so that's why I'm calling you on your blueberry number. Mine isn't a blueberry.'

Luke?

'Clem—'

'I wanted an Apple, but Mummy said no way because it's too expensive. Samantha Fingleton has an Apple. Mummy said just because someone else at school has one doesn't mean I need one, but then I said just because all the other people in court wear ugly old-lady wigs doesn't mean she has to wear one too.

'Clementine—'

'Anyway, my mobile is blue too and shiny and it flips. It's a gnocchi. It's only for emergencies, like the axe on the school bus or Mummy's special bottle of Grey Goose water. I am only allowed to use my mobile if there's a fire or Voldemort or probably an aunt's birthday—'

'You spoke with Luke?'

'Yes, and JFK, but he was just barking because he doesn't like suitcases. Luke said he doesn't like sprinklers either. Or postmen.'

'Why were there suitcases, Clem?'

'Where?'

'At my house.'

'Because Luke is going to Dan's house which is nice because the lady next door is going to look after JFK and Widdles.'

The wrap dress constricted. Cornflakes ran amok in my

stomach. I imagined them using last night's pappardelle as surfboards to comb the waves of my lower intestine. There was a lump in my throat the size of a ping-pong ball. I coughed to clear it, but it wouldn't budge.

With Dan means with Bella. Berries.

'I like Dan. He has a PS3 like Samantha Fingleton. She doesn't have a cubby house though, but Dan does. I'm not allowed to get a PS3 but Daddy said if I keep it a secret I can play on his Xbox, but I don't like Xbox because the X is green and I really, really hate green, pacifically neon green and car key green. Car keys aren't even green so it's a silly name. Do you have green car keys in Australia?'

'No.'

'I didn't think so. Car key green isn't green. It's more brown. I call it breen, like the spinach at Daddy's house or horse droppings at Buckling Ham Palace. So anyway, I didn't need to keep the secret because I didn't even want to play Daddy's Xbox, so I told Mummy and she said Daddy is in the Chewer.'

'In the what?'

'The Chewer.'

'Where's that?'

'It's where grown-ups go when they want to misbehave like children. Okay, I have to flip my phone now because Helga says it's time for bed. If you see him, say hello to the President for me and tell her I like her dog.'

When I hung up there was a new message on my phone.

Going 2 Melb. Need 2 think. When u get back, pls fwd my mail to B's, pay Telstra and return DVDs. Dogs have vax appt at 11 on Wednesday. Not optional. Rest of list on fridge. L

I deciphered the shorthand. Bills. Blockbuster. Bella's.

Bettina was waiting at the door for me with two suitcases and two handbags. There was no turning back.

The humungous apple

Our wheels squeaked and bounced as they hit the hot tarmac at the air force base in New York.

I rubbed my eyes and turned around to find Bettina time capsuling. Again.

'Thanks to the international dateline I get two day threes. This is day three, episode two. OMG, I can't believe we're actually here, in the *humungous* apple. So far, everything looks American. The guy waving the paddles on the runway has a jaw like GI Joe's with shiny, neat teeth. OMG! There's a red carpet and cameras and a limo—'

'Bettina, stop waving!'

'Sorry.' She paused her dictaphone. 'OMG Roo, how cute were the Hawaiians with their leys when we refuelled? Real frangipanis. I've never had a ley.'

That explains it.

She hit the record button. 'Poor Roo didn't sleep at all. Lucky I brought extra lilac shimmer powder. Mind you, everyone's probably just digitally remastered at birth in the future. Believe me, in the past, it took creativity to get rid of dark circles. You might all have CO_2 poisoning, but at least you look fab, so that's something.'

BlackBerry on. Twenty-seven text messages. Eight of those from my sister. One hundred and eighty-three emails, one from Oscar about the cocktail party. Thirty-five missed calls, most of which were either Fran or Daphne. Lukeless. Hang on. Fran. Daphne. The baby!

I dialled. 'Aunt Daphne, I'm so sorry—I've been on a plane. Is Debs okay?'

'Debs? Debs is fine, aside from the occasional kick in the guts from our unborn child.'

'Is it my parents? Clem?' I felt sick at the thought of it.

'Ruby, stop, darling. It's you I'm worried about,'

'Me?'

'I spoke to Luke.'

That jolted me. 'You spoke to Luke?'

'He rang to ask if I could come to Canberra on the weekend to look after the pups. I asked why and he told me you two had—'

'How good of him. How's he enjoying the berry garden?'

'What?'

'Never mind. I'm fine. It's for the best.'

'You're so much like your mother, Ruby. You are not fine. You need to talk about this.'

'I have a full day ahead of me in New York. I don't have time to wallow.'

'This is your relationship—your future. Jobs will come and go, prime ministers will come and go—'

'And so will boyfriends.'

'Sweetheart, listen to me. Don't bury yourself in work right now. Take a bit of time off.'

'Time *off*?' I lowered my voice and took my phone into the toilet, folding the bifurcating door behind me. 'Have you seen the polls lately? I know you mean well, Aunt Daphne, but I didn't ask for advice.'

'I know, darling, but you need—'

'Let me tell you what I need. I need to get back to work. Debs needs a glass of wine and a dermatologically effective eye mask. And you need to calm down, back off and quit catastrophising! You're driving us all nuts.' I was looking in the mirror as the words flew out of my mouth like a swarm of bees through an open window.

Outside the door there was the soft thud of someone passing.

'Aunt Daphne, I—'

'I was trying to help, Ruby. Have a nice trip.' She hung up.

Look at you.

Eyes red-rimmed and forehead creased, the woman in the mirror surprised me. No make-up, hair unkempt, lips dry and shift dress threadbare, she was unfamiliar. People are allowed to grow, I thought. They strengthen and grow wiser. And the people who love them shouldn't hold them back.

I tore the loose thread from my hem, threw my bedraggled hair into a bun and stepped out to face the day.

'There you are,' said Bettina. 'I've prepared the briefing pack for you, but I took the liberty of adding a little Lady Liberty to it. I found this hole-punch online in the shape of the Statue of Liberty—look at the little torch. How cute is that? And red, white and blue highlighters—what?

I thought you'd like it.'

I opened it. US flags separated each segment.

'Everything's in there, as you asked. The UN address. Shelly's Met speech. Today's press—local and back home—and backgrounders for each of the people they're meeting.'

'Great.'

'I've got something else for you.' She opened her purse. 'You're going to love me even more for this.'

The only way is up.

'My dad *swears* by this stuff for jet lag.' She handed me two pills and a bottle of water. 'You're only supposed to take one, but I think you deserve two.'

I squeezed her hand—'You're a life-saver'—and knocked them back with a swig of water.

'The PM's ready when you are,' said the RAAF flight attendant. 'I put an extra sugar in your cuppa. It's on the table in their cabin.'

I knocked and entered. Shelly wore a white, belted sundress and coral cardigan with a turquoise necklace and tan sandals. She looked a million bucks, but less green. Her cheekbones were bronzed, dark hair slicked back and eyes kohl-lined to perfection.

Max, in a navy suit, white shirt and sky-blue tie, made notes in the margins of his brief.

'You two look fabulous.'

'You don't think the suit's too tight? asked Max, tugging at his waistband.

'No,' I yawned.

Shelly smiled. 'You okay, Roo?'

'Peppy as Miss America.'

So. Damned. Tired.

'Now, in a minute you'll get a quick intro to the secret service guy before doing a few smiley, wavy shots on the steps and then onto the red carpet. Our ambassador to the UN will introduce you to the mayor of New York and his wife, then you'll get into the limo and be driven with them to Jenny's residence.'

'What's Jenny's husband's name again? Ned?'

My phone rang. Fran. I killed it. 'Excuse me?'

'Jenny's husband. What's his name?'

'Oh, sorry. It's—' Yawn. 'Yes, Ned. I think. And their sons…'

'Adam and Stuart.'

'Their sons will join you for afternoon tea. Then you, Shelly, will get your hair and make-up done—I'll meet you beforehand—and then open the indigenous art exhibition at the Met and you, PM, will go to your first meeting with Jenny about the situation in—'

Blank.

I clicked my fingers.

'Jordan,' said the PM.

'Who's that?'

'The situation in Jordan.'

'Jordan, of course.'

Shelly rubbed her teeth with a finger to check for stray lipstick. She smiled at me.

'All clear,' I said, reading her question. 'Is that a new colour?'

'Coral's back.' She straightened Max's tie.

'I haven't seen her in years,' said Max.

'Huh?'

'Coral.'

'Terrible joke, darling.'

Eyelids heavy. Must. Close.

There was a knock on the cabin door. 'That'll be what's his name with what's her name. Come in.'

'Flack with Jenny?'

'Yep.'

Shelly and Max stood to greet the curvaceous ambassador, her long, dark hair pinned into a fulsome chignon, revealing exquisite, antique cameo earrings.

'And you must be Roo!'

My lips sealed to conceal a yawn, making my nostrils flare. 'Lovely to meet you Jenbassador.'

'I've heard all about you. Really looking forward to working with you. How was your flight, Prime Minister? Get any sleep?'

Who said sleep?

Another yawn.

'Yes, thanks to the Brookings speech I'm supposed to deliver in less than forty-eight hours. Powerful stuff.'

Flack stepped in and cleared his throat. 'PM, Shelly, I'd like to introduce you to my US counterpar—'

'Welcome to the United States of America, Prime Minister,' said a man so wide he'd snap a hula-hoop. He pushed Flack aside with the flick of a wrist. 'Agent Monger of the United States Secret Service.'

Flack rolled his eyes.

I rubbed mine.

'Good to meet you,' said Max, shaking Monger's hand, which was the size of a basketballer's foot.

'My team is responsible for your and the first lady's protection here on US soil. We have a special subdivision assigned to the first lady. Three agents will accompany you on the ground at all times.'

'Shelly,' said Shelly. 'We don't have first ladies. And you mean when I'm with Max?'

'Negative, ma'am. I mean at all times.'

'Nobody knows who I am here. I don't have security back home.'

Flack puffed out his chest.

'With respect, ma'am,' said Monger, at ease, 'what my counterparts do or don't do on their territory is none of my business, but the United States government takes the protection of all visiting heads of government and their families very seriously. There have been thousands of visits and not a single loss—not even to a hotdog with E. coli—and that's not about to change on my watch.'

The Ambassador stifled a smile. Max gave Shelly's hand a gentle squeeze.

'Sir, at 1600 hours I will lead you and the first lady downstairs onto the tarmac where you'll be greeted by New York mayor Crawford Soccer who is accompanied by his wife, Chastity Cox. Any questions?'

'Agent Monger,' said Max.

'Yessir.'

'It's four.'

'Four, sir?'

'I think the Prime Minister is saying it's 1600 hours,' said Flack, concealing a smile.

Monger checked his watch and spoke into the microphone beneath a gleaming gold eagle cufflink with blue sapphire eyes. 'Go, go, go.'

Yes. Go, go, go to sleep.

Not helping, head.

At the top of the steps, Max and Shelly stood. They smiled, waved and descended. Cameras flashed.

The tarmac felt like a hot griddle underfoot as I followed the Ambassador.

My phone rang. 'Get out of shot,' said Chief. 'I'm watching it live.'

'Sorry.' I peeled off my cardigan and veered away from the eager snappers towards our minibus. 'I wish you were here.'

'You look terrible,' said Chief in my ear. 'Sleep much?'

'No,' I said through a yawn. 'Bettina gave me some pills to wake me up but they're not working yet. What time is it there?'

'Six in the morning. Listen. I got another one.'

'Another one?' The bus doors whooshed open. I sat in the front seat and checked my periphery. Policy advisors shouted into their phones, speechwriters flogged decrepit laptops with flustered fingers and the bus driver whistled along to Roy Orbison's *Crying*. It was safe to talk. 'What does it say?'

'It's the same as the last one.'

'When did it arrive?'

'The post guy put it in my in-tray this morning. That makes it four in two weeks.'

'Did you, erm'—I lowered my voice—'get a chance to check the postmark?'

Bettina boarded the bus.

'Why?'

'No reason.'

Toast crunched in my ear. 'That is the skinniest woman I've ever seen.'

'Which woman?'

'The mayor's wife.'

I looked out the window to where Max and Shelly

were chatting to the mayor. 'TV adds bumf. You should see her in real life. She's thinner than a credit card.'

Chief cranked the volume on her TV. '...air force base in New York where Prime Minister Max Masters and his wife, Shelly, have landed and disembarked. On screen now is Chastity Cox, standing next to her husband, Crawford Soccer.'

'Imagine if they hyphenated,' said Chief.

'Here they come, Liza. Down the red carpet. Shelly Masters is wearing a Fleur Wood dress with accessories from Dinosaur Designs and shoes by Mimco. She is waving one last time before getting into the stretch limousine— ooh, that looked a bit tricky, didn't it, Liza?'

I couldn't see past the wall of security.

'It sure did, Dave. Not the most elegant of entries. Mind you, I wouldn't want to get into a giant, bulletproof limo live on national television—and here comes Max Masters, ready to join his wife. He waves and climbs into the—is that?'

Chief groaned. 'Fuck a duck.'

'What?' I strained and pressed my face against the glass.

'He hasn't.'

'What?'

'He's split his—no! Tighty-whities! Do something!'

'...the Prime Minister appears to be experiencing a wardrobe malfunction. In case you ever wanted to know, he is not a boxers man.'

Chief hung up.

I smacked my head against the window, partly to stay awake, partly because I was now going to spend the week cleaning up after yet another embarrassing gaffe.

'Roo?'

'Not now, Bettina. The PM's just split his pants live on national television and those pills you gave me aren't going to cut it. I can barely keep my eyes open.'

'That's what I wanted to talk to you about. Please don't be mad.'

My head stopped. 'What?'

'Okay, so I rang my dad to tell him we didn't even land at JFK because we landed at a naval base. And he was like, "I've never been there." And I was telling him about Hawaii and my first ley—'

'Get to the point.'

'Okay. I think you're going to be mad but I think I need to tell you anyway. He said to pop one of the pills tonight to get a good sleep and I'll be right as rain tomorrow, and I was like, "No silly, then I'll be up all night," and he was like, "Betts, one of those things would knock out a rhino on Red Bull."'

The perky one must die.

I looked around for weapons.

Later. Too tired to murder now.

'Oh noes, you're mad, aren't you?'

Koto, I've got a feeling we're not in Canberra anymore

'Triple-shot, venti macchiato with a straw for, um, Me? Is there a Me here?'

'I'm Me. At least I think I am.' I scanned the shop. 'Is there another Me here?'

Two teenagers swirled their index fingers at their temples, the international sign for derangement.

I sucked on the straw. The drug defibrillated my flatlining brain.

I saw the light, said my head. *So shiny.*

Welcome back. I've given you caffeine, now you must focus. You got me into and through Oxford, so you can get me to Eighty-Sixth and Madison. It's a grid.

It's all coming back to me. Why is there sun at night-time?

Focus! Eighty-Sixth and Madison!

I stepped out of Starbucks. The street was hotter than the coffee. Heat penetrated my leather soles, cooking me like a microwave from the inside out. Underwire stabbed my ribcage and the elastic on my tights gave up, lowering them to mid-buttock. My shift dress looked shiftier than usual, its lining dipping an inch lower than the hem. The tag said it was made of cotton. It felt like mohair.

I cursed the concierge again.

'It's three blocks,' he'd said. 'It'll be faster to walk.'

'Do you have a map?'

'Sure, but you won't need one. Just go out of the hotel, turn left, walk three blocks and you're there.'

I'd tipped him too. Arsehole. I mean asshole.

A woman passed me in snakeskin slingbacks with contrasting iPad case under her arm. 'They're listing in Shanghai,' she said into the latest model BlackBerry, its hands-free feeding into her Louis Vuitton handbag. 'You betcha I'm bullish on China.' Her make-up was magazine pristine, not a blotch of anything untoward on her Ralph Lauren shirtdress, which was so tailored she looked like she'd been born in it. Eyes up, chin forward, step, step, step.

I can do that. Eyes up, chin forward, step—

Honk. Swerve. Honk, honk. 'Hey, lady, watch where you're going!'

The man at the hotdog stand stared.

Under the shade of a Central Park elm, a lady sat on the footpath with a sign. THE END IS NEAR, it said.

Thank God. I took a seat beside her. Now, if I could just find Eighty-Sixth and Madison. I held my map upside down to figure it out.

Don't ask me. What about Mr Moccasins with the newspaper?

'Excuse me, sir, can you—'

He shoved a buck in my hand and walked away.

'I don't want your money!'

He sped up.

A horse clip-clopped behind me.

'Your Excellency,' I said to the police officer on it. 'Can you please point me in the direction of Eighty-Madison and Sixth? No, Madison-Sixtieth and Eighth? No, the other one.'

'Are you okay, ma'am?'

'Your horse is looking at me funny.'

'Is there someone I can call for you?'

'I just need to get to Shelly.'

'Is Shelly looking after you?'

'No, I'm looking after Shelly.'

'Okay. And where is Shelly?'

'Eighty-Sixth and Madison. Yes! That's it!'

'See that sign across the road—ma'am, don't lean on my horse.'

'Sorry, I'm a bit tired.'

'I can see that. That white building across the road is the corner of Eighty-Sixth and Madison.'

'I love you! And this is the most comfortable horse I've ever met. Ney, the glossiest and most comfortable horse I've ever met.'

'Uh-huh. Ma'am, I'm going to escort you over there, okay?'

'Can I hold your hand?'

'No.'

'What about your horse's?'

'No.'

'If Bettina was here she'd put this in her time capsule,' I said as we crossed. 'Chaperoned by a horse. No! A chaper-pony. Geddit? Except you're more of a chaper-horse, aren't you?'

He snorted.

As we reached the footpath, Shelly stepped out of her limo. Buff women in aviators surrounded her. Everyone stared. At the horse, I guessed.

'Thank you, officers,' I said, patting them both. 'Found you!' I said to Shelly and propped myself up on a hotdog stand.

'Roo, darling,' she said as the clip-clopping faded. 'Are you ill?'

'I'm abso-fine-olutely. How you are?'

'Come with me,' she said. 'I'm going to get my hair and make-up done for this gig and you are going to have a massage.'

'I need to speech you on your brief.'

'I'll get a speeching from someone else. Put the coffee down.'

'No, thank you.'

'Give it to me, Ruby.' She took it from me.

'Snatchers get snitched!'

She threw it into the rubbish bin. 'We have two hours in New York's finest salon. You and I are going to enjoy it together.'

'You can't make me.'

'Would you rather I tell Max the NYPD escorted you across a road?'

'You wouldn't!'

'I'm dialling.'

'Okay, you big meanie.'

∞

Heritage-green awnings jutted out over the sandstone steps that led to the front doors of Fugiku. They opened inwards—we entered—and slammed shut behind the secret service, who flinched and surveyed the room with the kind of suspicion usually reserved for *CSI*.

It was dark, cool and silent but for the mellow sound of traditional Japanese music. Slowly, a spotlight revealed a man in black robes plucking at a pear-shaped lute.

Sleep.

'Madame Masters, Mademoiselle Stanhope,' said a French woman in a kimono, 'I am Cecile. Welcome to Onsen Fugiku. This way, please.'

She shuffled on wooden clogs into a sitting area with rice-paper walls. In the centre of the room was a bronze gong. She hit it with a padded stick. The sound reverberated through my body as if my bones were tuning forks.

She knelt before us on the tatami. 'Sit.'

Two women shuffled towards us, each with a tray containing a lemongrass-infused, ice-cold wet towel.

'Can I suck it?'

Shelly shook her head and wiped her hands with it. I followed her disappointing lead.

'Your ablutions await,' said Cecile. 'Please.'

The shufflers helped us to our feet and led us into separate rooms. On my wall was a mural, a hand-painted image of two women bathing in a lake under the cherry blossoms.

'Your clothes,' said my shuffler. 'They come off.' She unzipped my dress and turned around.

'Steady on.'

'And the rest, Miss Stanhope.'

'But I'm hairy.'

'And the rest, Harry.'

Bra, tights, knickers, shoes.

She ignored me and turned on a shower with the press of a button. Steam escaped. It smelled of violets. 'In,' she said, and shuffled away with my clothes.

The mist beckoned me. Inside on slate walls were at least thirty jets, each tasked with washing a different bit of me. I stood still, looking up to the skylight two storeys above me.

After a minute or two, it stopped. I stepped out into the arms of a fluffy towel before sliding into an embroidered silk robe and slippers. 'This way,' said my shuffler.

I followed her to another rice-papered room. In the centre was a large bronze egg slick with water, a seated harpist and a single chair.

'Listen, this is all very lovely, but I must get back to work.'

She smiled. 'Sit.'

'Could I at least have my BlackBerry?'

She nodded and left the room.

A long, lean man came towards me wearing linen pyjamas. 'So, you are Harry, yes? I am Koto.'

'Hello, Moto.' I giggled.

'Koto. Moto. So funny. Like the Motorola phone. Never heard this ones before. But I forgive bad humour. You have troubles, yes?'

I nodded. The shuffler returned with a small bowl of fresh strawberries. 'Blackberry not in season,' she said.

'What you want?' asked Koto.

Tears welled in my eyes. 'I'm so tired. I took sleeping pills. I thought they were awake pills. Now I am like this—and Max's pants!'

'There, there; so many pants-men in this town.'

'And Luke. He wants berries. I don't grow berries, Koto. I never pre-warm the pot.'

He cracked his knuckles. 'Pre-warming the pot is man's job. Not yours. You relax, Harry. I make it better.'

Koto pressed his index fingers to my temples and ran his thumbs from my neck to the base of my head. 'Rest.'

I woke up to the low hum of a hair dryer. Two people were massaging my hands while another blow-dried my hair. I was still zonked but much, much better.

I had no idea what had happened in the intervening period; but whatever it was, it felt good. Clean, fresh and light. Koto was rubbing my bare neck. Oh, an up-style, I surmised. How chic.

'And now we finish,' said Koto.

'That was incredible.'

'My pleasure.'

The shuffler returned me to my suite. She presented me with a silk-covered hanger from which hung what looked like my frock and smalls, except they couldn't have been my frock and smalls because they didn't smell of despair.

'How?'

The shuffler smiled and bowed.

I checked my phone. Shit, we had four minutes to get to the Met. I threw my clothes on and followed her to reception.

Shelly looked like a goddess. She wore a waist-cinched, petal-collared orange dress with mute-gold peep-toes and pink sapphire earrings so pretty they looked like raspberry jelly. Her long, dark hair was gleaming and a slash of jet gel eyeliner across her top lids made her look exotic.

'Wow!'

'Roo! Er, I almost didn't recognise you.'

'I know, these people are magicians. One minute I feel like stale potpourri and the next minute, well, voila! Meanwhile, you look incredible!'

'Thanks.' She took my arm as we walked to the limo. 'I—I love it. It's just really very different.'

'The *best* kind of different, Shelly. It's jaw-dropping. Hot, even. Great dress, by the way.' The limo pulled off. 'Onwards and upwards. Now, Bettina will meet us at the Met and lead you in, then I'll head to the UN for the PM's speech. You haven't met Bettina yet. She can be a bit full-on, but means well. All set?'

'Yes,' she said, looking uncomfortable.

'Hey, you're going to do great.' I squeezed her hand. 'And thanks so much for the pampering. I feel like a new woman.'

'I'm glad you like it, Roo.'

We pulled over at the foot of the grand, vast stairs which formed part of the wedding-cake-white façade of the Met.

Bettina, in a scarlet jacket with blue-and-white striped pants and gold star earrings, rushed towards us. The women in black opened the limo door to let her in.

'Mrs Masters,' she squeaked, taking a seat opposite me, 'I am Bettina—OMFG, who *did* that to you?!'

'Bettina! Shelly looks magnificent!'

'Not her. You! It's, it's—'

'Oh, is it my hair? Probably still full of massage oil. Can I borrow a brush?'

'Oh dear,' said Shelly. 'You haven't seen it, have you?'

'Seen what?'

Bettina opened her bag, pulled out a slim emerald compact and flipped it open.

Gone. That was the first word that came to mind when I saw it. Gone was my long, messy, tangly, strawberry-blonde mane.

Instead, my pale, make-up-free, mortified face hung below someone else's beastly, platinum bob. It had a fringe that curled upwards like an Arian handlebar moustache across my forehead. The tips of my ears poked elfishly through the sleek, near-white coif, which hugged the contours of my cheeks. I reached behind me to muss it up only to graze the unfamiliar fuzz of an undercut, a sort of pubescent beard for my neck. My nose looked even longer and pointier than usual.

Barbie called. She wants her merkin back.

I tugged at it. Immovable.

'This is your fault,' I said to Bettina.

'It'll *totally* grow back,' said Bettina. 'Mrs Masters, we really have to go.'

The secret service opened the doors and out we got.

My BlackBerry buzzed. Eight new messages.

Ruby, do you really think you can avoid your own sister? I know where you live—

Delete.

Hi Ruby, I work with the Ambassador. I'm at the UN waiting to sign you in when you get here. Text me when you arrive and I'll meet you at the flags. PM is on his way. Cheers, Sophie.

The limo pulled away. Checking my watch, I stuck my other arm out for a taxi. 4.27 a.m. Shit. I checked my BlackBerry. I had twenty minutes until Max's speech.

A miracle occurred on Eighty-Second Street. A cab stopped.

'I need to get to the UN.' I leaned down to yell through the open window. 'Fast.'

'There's a game on at Madison Square Garden, lady. There is no fast.' He puttered off.

I hailed a pedicab. 'I need to be at the UN by six o'clock.'

'Impossible.'

'I'll give you eighty dollars!'

'Eighty bucks? You've got to be kidding me. It's a hundred degrees out here.'

'Don't be silly.'

'It is, look!' He pointed to a digital barometer atop a distant building.

'You're cheating. Fahrenheit's like a Wonderbra—it makes everything seem more dramatic. Are you going to take me or not?'

'How much do you weigh?'

'Ex*cuse* me?'

'You heard me. How much are you packing?'

'Sixty kilos.' He looked blank. I used my BlackBerry. 'A hundred and thirty-two pounds.'

'You're at least one-fifty-five. A hundred and twenty bucks and you'll be there in fifteen.'

'I'll take the subway.'

'Your funeral—that'll be thirty minutes.'

'Bollocks. Fine. Pedal!'

We tore through the park, cutting grassy corners, our wheels lifting off the ground. Sweat flew from the calves of my chauffeur. Dog-walkers shook their fists at us. Leaves and bugs landed in my ears and mouth.

'Where are you from?' he yelled, as a woman pulled a child out of our way.

'I'm English, but I live in Australia.'

'You're not related to that WikiLeaks guy, are you?'

'Julian Assange? No. Why?' I picked a beetle from my teeth.

'Same hair.'

Good grief. Toolkit. No mirror. Fuck. Make-up.

Eyes first. Oh good. Mascara. I yanked the clumpy wand from its sticky sheath and waited for my driver to reach a pedestrian crossing.

Okay, quickly. One eye. Done. Next—shit! We hit a bump. Ow. I felt it in my eyeball and brow and wiped at it with the palm of my hand.

Eyes stinging, I turned to my lips. What did I have? Purplish red. Excellent. A bit of definition will do the trick. On it goes, easy does it.

'Sir, do you mind warning me when we're about to—'

Speed bump. The lipstick went up my nose.

'What?'

'It doesn't matter.' I shoved my index finger up my nostril to scoop out the goop and waved with my other hand at the mounted officer as we passed her and her glossy steed. Their jaws dropped.

We left the park and skidded onto East 59th.

I reached into my handbag for a tissue. Of course not. Just a lonely, spare pair of knickers. That'd do nicely. I blotted with the crotch and used excess to rouge my cheeks a little.

Now we were on Lexington, the streets were fast descending. Forty-ninth, forty-eighth, forty-sixth, forty-fifth—

'We're here.' He used his bandana to soak up the sweat. 'Definitely one-fifty,' he muttered.

'Well now I'm a hundred and twenty lighter.' I thrust the money into his hand and ran towards the flags, texting Sophie.

I'm here. Roo.

The place was packed with people.

What do you look like? I'm wearing a black suit and have nude shoes on. S

I scanned the crowd. Every second person wore a black suit.

White hair. Shit dress. R

Typo. Bugger.

Shift dress.

A petite woman in a black suit, killer heels and neat braids approached me. Her expression was one of astonishment rather than familiarity.

'Sophie?'

'Roo?'

'Sorry I'm late.'

'Listen, darl, I don't know you from a bar of Dove, so I'm just going to come out with it: you look like an albino insomniac who's been making out with a beetroot in a coal mine.'

'My intern drugged me, a kind man massacred my hair and I did my make-up in a pedicab.'

'Ah.'

'Shall we go in?'

'No,' she said. 'The Prime Minister asked me to give you this note.'

I unfolded the sheet of paper.

Roo,

Anyone who requires a mounted police officer to escort them across the road will be of greater use to me after a kip.

Go to the hotel.

No buts.

PM

Single as a dingle

My stomach creaked like an empty house. In darkness, I felt around for the light switch in my downtown hotel room.

Motorised curtains hummed as they parted. Wrong switch. I squinted to protect my tired eyes from the harsh glare of morning, but it didn't come. Outside there wasn't even a hint of dawn, just the proud glitz of the Chrysler's crowning tiara and the faint twinkle of the Brooklyn Bridge, like Christmas lights strung between distant pillars.

My watch said it was 4.27 a.m. The clock said three. My stomach said lunchtime.

I clambered to my feet, tried to tie my hair up, remembered it was the length of a paintbrush, squeezed into jeans and a black tank top and walked out the door.

The unfamiliar city should have frightened me at that hour. Saturday-night revellers yelled at passing cabs.

A homeless man sat in the shadow of his shopping trolley, nursing himself to sleep with a maudlin lullaby. Two blocks down, swathed in tulle, a staggering hen disgraced her rowdy party with a quick squat on the footpath.

But above the mid-summer stink of sweat, diesel, yellow mustard and percolated coffee, high above the subway's gentle rock, I just walked and walked, trying not to think of all the people I'd usually call if I woke up jet-lagged in another time zone.

I thumbed through my BlackBerry contacts in alphabetical order.

Chief.

'Sure, I've got time for a chat about your miserable life between being ridiculed, blackmailed and leaked against.'

Daphne.

'Hi, Aunt Daphne, sorry for calling you a meddler. Mind if I go on about myself for a while?'

Debs.

'Hey, kiddo, thanks so much for outing me on the eye-cream front. Really appreciate it.'

Fran.

'So now you call your sister?'

Luke.

What would he say?

'I've been an arse-hat, Ruby. I'm on a plane to New York as we speak. They've just arrested me for interfering with the navigational system. They've cuffed me and they're saying if I don't hang up they'll throw me in Guantanamo Bay but I don't care. Say you'll take me back.'

Unlikely.

'Is it urgent? What's that? I can't hear you. I'm in

the middle of very energetic, unconventional sex in my marital bed. We even had to put the His and Hers towels down in case of spillage. I've got a mouthful of fresh berries. And cream. Hang on, she's pulling out the fluffy cuffs and my hands-free is in the kitchen. I'll have to call you back.'

Both scenarios involve cuffs. Disturbing. Next?

'You've reached Luke Harley. Leave me a message.'

Boring. You can do better than that.

'It's over, Ruby. You made yourself clear. Leave me alone.'

Probably.

I put the phone back in my pocket and kept walking.

The door to Kay's Diner tinkled as I opened it. Air-conditioning chilled my clammy skin. I took a plastic booth by the high-set window, the one with a bit of spilled coffee and a preloved copy of today's *Times*.

On page three beneath the fold was a photograph of Max addressing the UN General Assembly ten hours earlier, while I was sleeping:

AUSSIE PM CHANGES TUNE ON CALAMESIAN CRISIS

An eager audience at the United Nations General Assembly gathered yesterday evening to hear Australian Prime Minister Max Masters' much-anticipated address about mounting tensions in the Calamesian Peninsula.

But moments before he took the lectern, the Prime Minister was informed by staff that there had been a prison break in Trufoli and a bomb outside the US Embassy in the country's capital.

Eighteen convicted terrorists are fugitives at large and five Americans were injured in the blast.

Masters fumbled on his feet, finding a half-pregnant position sympathetic to America's activist approach without endorsing it.

'Australia condemns those responsible for the despicable act of violence that occurred in Trufoli today against foreign nationals and Calamesians,' he said. 'We stand ready to find the right way to work towards restoring peace.'

One observer remarked that, 'The Prime Minister managed to tread water in the rapids.'

Shortly afterwards, those rapids became a waterfall when Australian journalist Oscar Franklin published a copy of the Prime Minister's intended speech.

That version shows Masters planned to announce Australia's firm opposition to any international intervention in the troubled region.

'Australia feels strongly that it would be a mistake for the international community to throw its weight around in such a brittle environment. We must find a hands-off way to help engineer peace without placing more lives at risk.'

Masters is due to meet with President Lydia Garrity tomorrow.

I spent five whole minutes on those few paragraphs, reading them over and over. The words refused to sink in. They orbited my head like a baby's mobile, suspended just out of reach.

'What can I get you?'

The waitress flipped her notebook open, pen poised. Gold bangles jangled with her every movement.

'What's good?'

She shifted her weight to the other hip and sighed. 'Do you want me to come back?'

'The cheeseburger,' said a nasal voice in the adjacent

booth from under a well-worn baseball cap. 'And the chocolate shake and, if you can handle it, the key-lime pie.' He lowered the bundle of paper he was reading to reveal grey-green eyes.

I thanked him with a nod. 'What he said.'

She wrote it in a busy scrawl, ripped out the carbon copy and put it on the table.

A quick, embarrassed silence passed before he said, 'You're English.'

'Well spotted.' I twisted towards him.

He looked down again and then back up at me, adjusting his cap off to the side. 'Would you say lavatory, toilet, loo, bathroom or WC?'

'I'm sorry?'

'I'm writing something. My protagonist's a Brit and I need to know what she'd say?'

'Where's she from?'

'She's from London, England.'

'I have two questions for you: one, why do you Americans always say London, England and Paris, France? And don't say it's because sometimes you mean Paris, Texas.'

'And the second question?'

'My second question is what kind of Londoner is she? Where did she go to school? What do her parents do? What does she do for a living?'

'So you actually had five questions.'

'What?'

'You just asked me five questions.'

'Oh.'

'Would you like answers to them?'

'Please.'

'There's room over here,' he said.

I hesitated.

'Or not,' he said. He continued to read then looked up again, catching my stare.

Breakfast with a strange, ignorant man from New York, America when you're lonely and melancholic at half three on a Sunday in Manhattan. Capital idea.

'What are you writing?' I heard myself ask as I rubbed the sleep from my eyes and switched booths.

'That's question number six: a screenplay. We say London, England because we like to err on the side of over-information. My protagonist is black. She was raised in East London, England. Her father drives cabs, her mother's a teacher. She went to Oxford and studied science.'

'Probably toilet,' I said. 'And if you use the word "gov" you will flush your box office success down the loo.'

He wrote in green ink and a steady hand: *Toilet—no gov.*

Close up he was cute. The skin on his arms was tanned beneath tufts of sun-bleached hair. He wore a crumpled, striped shirt, rolled up to the elbows.

The waitress's bangles clattered as she put two shakes on our table.

'What's it about?' I fidgeted with my straw.

'It's about a young man whose girlfriend is abducted by an alien scientist who wants to tag as many human specimens as he can to understand the species. He always throws them back, but he doesn't want to let this one go. He likes her too much. The man tries to find his girlfriend and bring her back, but finds she's happy where she is.'

'Sounds like something my boyfriend might watch. Not my boyfriend. My friend who is male. I am single.'

I tried it on for size. It was uncomfortable. 'Yep. Single as a dingle.' Even more uncomfortable the second time, particularly with the addition of dingle.

I know you don't want to introduce this man to your lady jungle, but the reiteration of your relationship status gives the reverse impression. Just saying.

Our burgers arrived. I sank my teeth into mine, hiding behind it. My mouth filled with the simultaneous pleasure of meaty, cheesy, picklish, sauciness.

He doused his fries in ketchup. 'What's your name?'

'Ruby Stanhope.'

'Hunter Lush.'

'Hunter Lush?' I laughed. 'How does the other Hunter Lush feel about there being two of you in the film business?'

'There's another Hunter Lush? I'll get my people onto that right away.'

I coughed. 'You're Hunter Lush.'

He nodded.

'As in the Hunter Lush who directed *Zion*.'

'You saw it?'

'And *Fuel Dual*.'

'I'm flattered. The ladies don't usually dig my style.'

'My, erm, my Luke friend loves your work. Every time your films come—came—out we are—were—the first in line at the box office.'

'I always used to confused my tenses.'

'Why are you here?'

'Same reason you are, I suppose.' He licked sauce from his thumb. 'I was hungry. You have lettuce on your lip.'

I wiped it off and stocked my mouth with fries so as to stop myself from saying something stupid. Again.

'So, this Luke of yours sounds as though he has superior taste.'

I blushed.

'In film,' he said, smiling.

'Oh. He is not my Luke and I am not his Ruby.'

'So you keep saying—he is Luked, not Luke.'

'Oh. Ah—'

'Hey, for the record, I don't hang out in diners in case cute, weird, jet-lagged Brits stop by. I'm here because the studio's breathing down my neck for this script and I needed a burger.'

'No. Quite. Of course not.'

He wiped his mouth with a checkered serviette. 'Shall we share the key-lime pie?'

'Sure,' I said.

'Just one pie,' he said.

The waitress removed the dome from a cake stand on the counter and sliced.

'What is key-lime pie anyway?' I sucked down the remains of my shake.

His jaw dropped. He stood in his place and cupped his hands around his mouth. 'Forget what I said. We need two.'

'I couldn't possibly,' I said.

The girl rolled her eyes. 'Make up your mind.'

'She's never had key-lime pie.'

'Wow. I really care right now.' She plonked two plates on the table and went back to her iPod.

Two wobbly wedges of goop stood before us, each topped with unashamed lashings of pillowy cream and a hit of citrus zest. Encased in a dark, sturdy crust, the smooth, pale filling was green-tinged like apple flesh.

'I'm not sure I could—'

He handed me a spoon. 'Eat it.'

The mouthful of heaven-sent, bittersweet ecstasy was so cold it hurt my teeth.

Suddenly the world was vivid. Hunter's eyes weren't grey-green, they were peridot. The booth wasn't plastic, it was fairy-floss pink.

'What's in this base?'

'Gram crackers and butter.'

'G-R-A-M crackers?'

'No, G-R-A-H-A-M.'

'Graham? Who would call something this heavenly "Graham"?'

I shovelled more in. I couldn't have cared less about how piggy I looked. I knew this feeling; it was happiness and it had been a long time coming. When I'd finished I ran my fingers along the plate, picking up runaway crumbs and smears of filling.

The waitress took the plate and left me the spoon.

'How was it?' asked Hunter, knowing the answer.

'How could I have lived for thirty years without knowing this?'

He shrugged. 'That's what my mother said when I gave her a joint, except she was seventy.'

'I don't want to live a life of pie-less piety anymore.'

'Pie-less piety?' He scratched his ear.

'I'm going to make a speech, Hunter. It will be a little over the top.'

'Thanks for the warning. Mind if I take notes? I'm always looking for new material.'

I stood in my place, cleared my throat and charged my spoon. 'I shouldn't have to come home every night to a sad sack in bad ties playing the blues and pining for berries and fantasy films—no offence.'

'Good for you—'

'Shoosh. There's more.'

The waitress put the bill on the table.

'Why should I fear flying solo? I'm young. Ish. And attractive, as you pointed out, aside from having Julian Assange's hair. I'm bright and I have a very important job that I love and there's no reason I should be afraid of what comes next. Like your heroine, the alien-abductee, she didn't need some guy to rescue her, did she?'

'I haven't decided—'

'Precisely. And why should she? She was off on an adventure of her own with her Martian mates.'

'But the guy—'

'From now on, Hunter, I shall holiday at a time of my choosing, not when it is convenient for someone else. There will be no binder, no Post-it notes, no deadlines—it will be spontaneous. And if I happen to have a particular craving for berries, I shall buy them from the grocer like everyone else. I will have many towels, all embroidered with the word "Mine". And I will taste every pie the world has to offer.'

I put twenty dollars on the table. 'Hunter, it was a great pleasure to meet you.' I extended my hand.

He shook it.

'You are not nearly as odd as I thought you might be.'

'Thank you.'

'No, thank you for introducing me to key-lime pie. And for the company par excellence. Good day.'

Par excellence? Seriously, sometimes I wonder if we're related.

The sky was navy blue, streaked with glimpses of daylight when I walked outside. Joggers squeaked against the pavement, vast machines swept the streets and the roller-doors of newsstands sprang open. I walked with my head up and a smile on my face.

'Hey!'

I turned towards the voice.

'Gimme that spoon. What are you, loco?'

M to the O

'Can I put a bow in your hair?'

'No.'

'But I think it'd look super cute with your new do. Look, I have this ace cobalt one or this kind of citrine one or sexy red.'

'No.'

Bettina sat on the floor of our twin hotel room in Washington, DC with pink cotton wool between her freshly painted toes, her hair in hot rollers and a stout vanity case full of more bibs and bobs than Dan's Lego set. She sighed and zipped away her haberdashery. 'I wish you'd just embrace brights; you'd look great in them. Sometimes I want to crack open the crayons and colour you in.'

I picked up the hotel phone and dialled nine.

'Housekeeping.'

'Yes, hello. Last night I arranged urgent laundering of a few items through your overnight service and they've not yet arrived. Can you tell me when I can expect them?'

'I'm sorry, ma'am, our system indicates you requested the usual forty-eight-hour turnaround on your laundry.'

'Well I indicate your system is a numpty.'

'A what?'

'Why would I put laundry in to be returned a day after I check out?'

'Ma'am, we've had some personnel changes; it's possible that this is our error.'

'Possible? I guess it's also possible that putting me next to the lift in a twin room with Minnie Mouse was your error.'

'The lift, ma'am?'

'The elevator!'

'Oh, the elevator. I thought you said the lift.'

'I'm going to the White House today for a meeting with your president. As it stands, I am sitting here staring into a suitcase. My choices are: jeans, a mildewy grey blazer, a pyjama shirt, two bras and laddered stockings. What would you suggest I wear?'

'Ma'am?'

I hung up and banged my head against the desk.

'Did something happen with your laundry, Roo?'

I walked into the bathroom, shut the door, screamed, opened the door and said, 'Bettina, may I please borrow something to wear to the White House?'

'OMG. I thought this day would never come. Yes, yes, yes! Okay, I have two conditions for my makeover.'

'Makeover? Let's not get ahead of ourselves.'

'Both conditions are non-negotiable.'

I sighed. 'Hit me.'

It'd be less painful.

'One, Cheryl Crow. Loud. No ensemble assembly is complete without her.'

'Fine.'

'Two, you must wear a bow.'

'Absolutely not.'

'Oh well, I'm sorry I can't help you.'

'Bettina, show a little grace.'

She folded her arms and shook her head. 'The Crow and the bow or no M to the O.'

'M to the—oh. Makeover.' I gritted my teeth. 'Proceed.'

Her rollers wobbled as she leapt across the beds and sunk her iPod into the sound system. 'Hit it!' She wiggled her hips and sang into her deodorant can. 'This ain't no disco, this ain't no country club, either.'

She skipped towards the quilted peach monster in the corner of the room and wheeled it out in time with the beat. Beneath the flap were six segregated compartments filled with dozens of zip-lock plastic bags arranged like a brand new packet of coloured pencils. Each bag grouped like tones. JEWEL COLOURS read one in sparkling emerald. CITRUS GARMENTS read another in sharp lime. It was NASA-standard packing.

'Try this on!' She threw a box-pleat silk skirt at me. It sailed through our hotel room like a hot air balloon, each pleat a different shade of pink.

'Do you have anything, I don't know, a little more... subdued?'

'And this!' She pulled out a banana-yellow pencil dress with cap sleeves.

'But it's glow in the dark.'

'No glow, sadly. Oh and try these pants too—they're the exact colour of your eyes.'

'Budgerigar blue?'

'LOL.'

I put on my bent sunglasses and took the garments into the bathroom.

The skirt was all wrong.

'I look like I'm wearing a garland of musk sticks,' I called out.

'Try the pants.'

I stepped into the side-zipping, wide-legged pants. They knocked the wind out of me as I did them up.

'Um, Bettina? I'm sure these are very fetching on you, but on me they're budgie in more ways than one.'

'What about the pale yellow?'

'Pale?' I stared at the dress. 'This is the kind of yellow all the other yellows gossip about. "Oh, did you see what's her name at number 69, Daffodil? Who does she think she is, frightening the children like that?" "And to think they call *you* a Lemon!"'

'Show me!'

I came out of the bathroom to find Bettina with fresh, bouncy curls.

'Roo, you rock this yellow! It makes your skin sing.'

To be fair, it was a well-constructed frock. Square-necked, defined waist, structured to mid-knee, but, 'No.'

'Why not? Look. Take my make-up mirror into the bathroom and check out your bum; then tell me no. '

I did as I was told, removing my sunglasses to check for signs of cellulite.

The girl has a point, said my head, raising its eyebrows approvingly.

'We have a winner,' I said.

I stepped out of the bathroom into crisscross white

sandals to find Bettina in a gum-leaf-green bubble skirt, into which she'd tucked a gold silk camisole. 'Representing my country,' she said, tucking her hair behind her ears to show me a gold kangaroo in one and a matching emu in the other.

'True blue,' I said. 'We have to go and brief the PM. Come on.'

Ninety minutes later we were in a convoy on the capital's wide streets, all lined with US and Australian flags, headed for Pennsylvania Avenue. Bettina pulled out her dictaphone. 'In case China is the superpower when you're listening to this and you're all "America Schmamerica", don't be, because it was the ant's pants in its day. That's an expression, by the way. Ants didn't actually wear pants in the past. No point—we can't see their private parts from up here. I bet you all have super powers now and ants have started wearing pants just to protect their modesty.

'Yesterday, Shelly went and spoke to a whole bunch of unemployed ladies about picking their lives up after the financial crisis. The *National* thought she was overdressed, but all the ladies said she was lovely, which she is. And then we flew to DC last night and now I'm on my way to the actual White House. OMG, I can see it!'

She hit pause. 'Look, Roo, wanna play truth or dare?'

'No.'

'Okay, I know you don't want to play truth or dare but I want to tell you the truth about something.'

'No thanks.'

'Please? It's been on my mind.'

'No.'

'I need to get it off my chest.'

'La, la, la, la, la, la—'

'I called Mike at the mail room in Parliament House and asked him to keep an eye on the postmarks on all stamped envelopes addressed to Chief. There. I said it. Phew. That feels way, way better.'

'You did what?'

'I thought you weren't listening.'

'Your voice is so high-pitched it operates on another frequency. No amount of la, la, la will block it out. What did you say to the mail guy?'

'Mike. He has a name, Roo.'

'What did you say to Mike?'

'Nothing, I just asked him to do me a favour because I volunteered to contact his daughter's schoolbooks. He was trying hard but it was all bubbly. His wife used to do it before she died—so sad—so now he does it. Anyways, I mixed it up a bit. Some with lace, some Hello Kitty, some Sailor Moon. You know, the classics. I even did one with—'

'And when he asked you why you wanted him to look at the postmarks, you said—'

'That I noticed there had been some delays between postage and receipt and, if so, I'd raise it with Chief. He's going to keep a log of all incoming letters to her, so if the threats are in there, we'll know if they—'

'I'm going to pretend we didn't have this conversation and you're going to pretend you didn't overhear a private conversation between me and the Chief of Staff. End of discussion.'

My phone buzzed.

'But—'

'No conjunctions!'

Her diamante-encrusted phone emitted the sound of Tinkerbell's wand. 'Bummer.'

'What?'

She pointed to a tweet:

@Oldpoll: 2pp: 60/40. Primary: 47/28. PM's approval down three points.

'I know, it's abysmal. We got a heads-up this morning. You should've seen his face when I showed him the figures.'

'He'll turn that frown upside down,' said Bettina. 'When they're forced to make a real decision at the ballot box they'll think about the alternatives and realise they were being way harsh about Max, you'll see.'

'Eighty-two per cent of Americans are happy with their president's performance. That poll came out yesterday. This is not going to be a fun press conference. It'll be two good friends, one popular, one not; one for a Calamesian intervention, one against it. And I'm wearing a canary.'

'You look divine. Speaking of which, don't think I forgot.' She reached into the purple purse and plucked out a thin, gold headband with a yellow and white enamel daisy off to one side.

'Absolutely not.'

'We had a deal!'

'Two words, Bettina: mail guy.'

'His name is Mike.'

President Lydia Garrity and her husband Frank stood a few metres away from us. She was taller than I'd imagined, with the physique of a flagpole, and had a sheen to her skin under that famous mass of cherry-red hair.

Shelly and Max got out of the limo in front of us. They

looked smart—she in navy and white, he in a moss-green tie. They posed, first the two leaders together, then with their partners, before heading inside.

Outside, an advancer nodded.

'Okay, we're going to get out of the car. You're with Shelly, I'm with the PM. Go.' We dismounted the van and, with great care, took the stairs into the White House.

Bettina, Shelly and the first gentleman went for a quick tour while I followed Max and the President with her advisors through to the West Wing.

'We'll meet in my office,' she said with her famous southern lilt. 'It's cosy, but I like it and I had our chef bring in a pitcher of his famous iced tea. Do you like iced tea, Prime Minister?'

'Call me Max,' he said. 'And what's not to like about iced tea?'

A polite laugh, so far it was like a great date.

'Tell me, Madam President—'

'Lydia, please.'

'Lydia. Where do you spend most of your time in this building? What's your favourite place?'

'There's a rose garden just outside. When it's sunny but not too hot like it is out there today, I like to sit out there with my dogs and think. The jonquils remind me of my Gramma's in Lexington.'

I pinched myself to check.

Ow. Yes, you are in the West Wing. Ow! Stop it, yes, you look like a tropical fruit with a great arse.

We passed saluting guards with shiny-buttoned uniforms and enlarged photographs of the President in action, and wandered down narrow halls until we reached a room with striped, curved walls the colour of butter, and gold taffeta curtains framing the lawn outside.

You're competing with the wallpaper.

The Resolute desk was cluttered with gold-framed photographs, mainly of dogs, with irises in the corner. Between stiff couches, a polished coffee table held two tall, frosted jugs and eight glasses.

They put me beside an opalescent vase of freshly cut champagne roses. Sunlight shot through the window at me, just in case I wasn't yellow enough.

'Would you mind, Max, before we get to the fun stuff, if we have a quick talk about your remarks on the Calamesian Peninsular?'

'Not at all.'

She poured the iced tea. 'Your speech was well received. Many people have expressed their gratitude to the Secretary of State for your quick but sensitive condemnation of the attack.'

'I'm glad,' said Max. 'Australia thought it important that we seize the opportunity rather than cancel the speech.'

An aid squinted as he approached me with my glass.

Shit. I shifted to the right, trying to move into the stripe of shade. The chair squeaked loudly like an overused bed.

A serious lady glowered at me.

I cocked my head to one side to fake focus.

Not ninety degrees! You look like you're looking up her skirt.

The President handed Max a glass.

'It was never my intention that the speech I had planned to deliver would become public. It was a leak. These things happen, as you well know.'

Speaking of leaks, I think you're sweating.

I twisted to peek under my right arm. Nope. Phew—shit, fuck, balls, that's cold! I had spilled a bit of iced tea in my lap with a piece of mint to boot.

I used a contemplative sigh to dry it and put my hand over the leaf on my nethers.

The President removed her glasses. 'I guess I could say I was puzzled to read you were planning on providing the United Nations with your views on the need for a soft approach in that region—is that right?'

'I wouldn't describe it as soft,' said Max. 'Before the attack on your embassy in Trufoli, Australia believed the best approach to troubles in that region was one of firm diplomacy...'

I lost concentration as a blowfly descended from the lofty heights of the ceiling, and buzzed into my crotch. I had my own regional issues to deal with. I swatted at it, but it was determined to invade.

'And if the peacekeeping mission fails?' asked the President. 'We have a duty to step in to secure peace.'

I squirmed as the fly nose-dived at my nose. I blew it away. It swooped again and missed.

'The peninsular has never seen true peace the way you and I know it. Calamesians wouldn't know peace if it kissed them on the lips.'

She laughed. 'You're saying where a nation has never known peace, peace is unattainable?'

'Of course not. But for peace to come it will take more than the sudden intervention of a faraway group of well-meaning nations.'

'This has been good,' said the President. 'Now, would your staff like to have a quick photograph before we head to our press conference?'

'I'm sure they would,' said Max. 'Madame President, I'd like you to meet my advisor, Ruby Stanhope.'

That's you!

I jumped to my feet, flicked the soggy herb from my damp triangle, shooed the fly and shook her hand.

'Ruby, what a lovely name,' she said. 'How did you like the tea?'

The East Room heaved with hungry faces testing their dictaphones. Agent Monger and his team spoke into their shirtsleeves, their weapons bulging between muscle and suit. The President's bronzed complexion glowed under studio lights against the tricolour flags. Max's paled in comparison.

Bettina beamed like Muriel on her wedding day from the front row beside Shelly, two seats from the Secretary of State. She pulled out her time capsule.

I raised an eyebrow.

She put it away.

'Prime Minister Max Mass-ters and I are, as the Ossies say, great mates. In fact, our countries are great mates. We have grown up together, fought and died together, helped others together and traded together. Great mates almost always agree, over a Fosters'—laughter—'but sometimes they disagree. It's a mark of strength in any friendship. I am happy to report that the Prime Minister and I are in absolute agreement about the necessity of the United Nations peacekeeping mission, given the recent instability in the Calamesian Peninsular.'

She extended a friendly hand to Max.

He reached to shake it, brushing a sheet of paper from lectern to carpet.

I'd seen it earlier when I'd briefed a dejected Max on the poll: on one side was an email from the Chief, where he'd underlined the bad polling figures; on the other, the familiar slant and curve of his handwritten notes about how he could respond to the poll. I watched it fall to the floor with the slow descent of an autumn leaf and the suspense of a coin toss.

Heads: statistical proof of unpopularity in a private, reassuring email from the Prime Minister's Chief of Staff. Tails: rehearsed one-liners in defence of statistical proof of unpopularity. It was a double-edged sword—either way there'd be paper cuts.

Tails.

'Thank you, President Garrity. Shelly and I are grateful to you and Frank for your tremendous hospitality...'

I couldn't listen.

There, on beige, bristly wool-pile between the two most powerful lecterns of the moment stood a single, folded piece of paper, an origami of Max destruction.

Cameras zoomed and flashed. Max was oblivious.

Pick it up, PM, I willed. Notice you've dropped it, bend down and pick it up.

'We are, as the President has said, one hundred per cent aligned in our support for the UN...'

My heart galloped as my head grappled with the obstacle course between my feet and that fucking piece of paper.

'Excuse me, sir,' I said sotto voce to the staffer beside me. 'I need someone to pick up that piece of paper.'

'Hush,' he said.

Several photographers moved forward, their lenses growing like Pinocchio's nose in a poker game.

'Now, I'd be happy to take your questions...'

Bettina. Bettina was our only hope. I waved to her. She waved back with jazz hands.

I shook my head and texted.

PM dropped piece of paper. Sensitive info re poll. On floor between lecterns. Cameras might zoom and get the image—

She clasped her hands to her mouth.

—Try not to be too obvious. If you can, without disturbing the press conference, go get the paper.

She texted back:

U want me 2 go between PM & POTUS 2 get the piece of paper now? Have u weed urself?

No. Try to be stealthy. Hurry FFS. And silence your bloody phone! Send.

Bettina pulled a Swarovski crystal hairclip from her toolkit and fastened her hair into a neat knot with the flick of a wrist. Next, she bent down and, seconds later, popped up, putting her gold Mary Janes on the seat.

Oh dear.

The rustle of her taffeta bubble skirt against the carpet drew concerned expressions.

I waved my hands to stop her but it was useless.

In the aisle, on manicured hands and stockinged knees, she crawled towards the podium.

Journalists stirred.

Shelly's teeth gritted into the fakest of smiles. The Secretary of State narrowed his eyes; Max's widened. Agent Monger breathed into his cuff. 'Go, go, go!'

'No!' I whispered to the agent beside me, who was

reaching for his taser. 'She's my intern, she's just—'

'Step aside, ma'am—freeze!'

Both leaders and their spouses along with the Secretary of State were whisked away. Reporters ducked and cameramen spun to film the hullaballoo.

'Freeze!'

My phone beeped with a news alert.

AAP: Another day, another gaffe

Ow

A soft murmur followed by a hard shake woke me.

Go away.

My headphones lifted of their own volition.

Aircraft noise inundated my eardrums, punctuated by a high-pitched 'Roo, Roo, wake up!'

Tell her to fuck off.

'Fuck off.'

'Open your eyes!'

Teeth clenched, I yanked at my eye patch, snapping it against sore, over-tired lids. I rubbed them, yawning. 'Bettina, go the fuck to sleep.'

I saw my silhouette in her glossy pupils and looked up past the conical hat.

Scarlet balloons floated above me with a matching banner: HAPPY 30TH BIRTHDAY, ROO. Corkscrew curls of crepe streamers hung from padded panels of cabin walls. A tower of red-velvet cupcakes with my name swirled in cream cheese frosting sat in the middle of my tray table. Red metallic confetti was scattered through the aisle: tiny threes and zeros that looked like OWs if you read them back-to-front and sideways.

Ow indeed.

'How did you know?'

'I diarised everyone's birthdays, silly billy. Anyway, I hope you like red, because I know you're Ruby and Ruby's red, so—'

My cheeks ached from over-smile. 'What time is it?'

'Four in the morning in DC, nine in the morning in London and six at night in Australia, but do you know what these times have in common?'

'No.'

'They all occur on your birthday!' She blew a party horn in my face. 'I set my alarm and everything. Tried to wake up the PM and Shelly but they said they were sleeping and I was like, "Birthday cake won't wait for sleepy heads," but they said they'd wish you happy birthday later.'

I was speechless.

'Cheer up, Charlie.' Her head cocked to the side, making the yellow ribbon in her ponytail flop onto the shoulder of her turquoise velour tracksuit. 'I felt the same last year at my twenty-first, but my BFF was like, "It's just a number, Betts—one more than twenty." And I was like, "true dat". Anyway, check out all your cool prezzies!'

'Presents?'

'Of course!' She opened a big red Santa bag and pulled out the first: something small wrapped in rose-patterned paper.

'Can I open them in the morning?'

'No way, José. This one's from your aunt! She seems nice.'

'You spoke to my aunt?'

'Mmm hmm. And Fran and Luke. Your aunt was the early bird though. I got hers first.'

'Luke?'

'You didn't think your boyfriend would forget you.'

My breath quickened. 'Can I have Luke's present first?'

'Nuh uh,' she clutched the bag to her chest. 'You know the rules. It's lucky dip.'

'Give it to me, you mung bean!'

'No!'

'Bettina!'

'Shhh, everyone's sleeping.'

'Fine.'

I reached into the bag and pulled out gift number one. Daphne and Debs. Shit. Same one. I put it back.

'Don't think I didn't see that, missy!' She snatched the bag and handed me their present.

I tore it open.

'Cards first! Seriously, sometimes I wonder if you're as English as you say you are.'

I opened the card.

Dearest Ruby,

Happy birthday, darling.

For your holidays, wherever and whenever they may take you.

Love,

Aunt Daphne xoxoxoxo & D. Llewellyn

I opened the blue box. Luggage tags. Ruby Stanhope & Luke Harley, 85 Harlot Street. I shut the box.

'How nice is that? Tiffany luggage tags. And to think

she rang to tell me not to give them to you. Geez, you have the nicest family.'

'Next,' I said, reaching into the bag.

I pulled out a red glittery box. Mother fucking—

'Yay, that's mine!'

'Oh. Yay. You shouldn't have.' I opened it. Inside was another box, this one a pearlescent red. I opened it.

Inside box number two was a third, this one silver with red stars. I opened it.

Just one big wooden box, several nails and a hammer would suffice.

The third and final box contained a fold of silver tissue paper, beneath which was a simple, square-shaped, red wash bag.

'Wow, thank you,' I said, holding it up to the light. 'It's very lovely.'

'No, ding-dong. Open it up.'

I unzipped the cover.

Wow.

A flock of miniature plastic bottles with varying nozzles stared up at me like chicks in a nest. Each had been hand-labelled—make-up remover, body butter, shaving gel, dry shampoo—in silver marker. Lining the four walls of the case were elasticised pockets, one with band-aids, one with bobby pins, one with Hollywood tape, one with tweezers—all useful. Underneath the bottles were a concealer pen, tampons, a whiteboard marker and deodorant.

'To get you started again,' she beamed. 'It's still missing a few things, obviously.'

'Bettina, that is very thoughtful of you. Thank you. I will treasure this.'

'Yay! Two more!' She opened the bag.

I reached in and pulled out a slim, white envelope. *Liberty Australia Foundation*. Luke.

'He almost missed the boat. Didn't give it to me until the morning we left. Bet it's something amazing, like a gondola ride on the lake or Britney tickets—OMG, what if it's a ring?' She squeezed my hand.

'It's not going to be a ring.'

'You don't know that!'

I opened it and pulled out a ring—a key ring, to be precise. The rusty key attached to it looked sadder than I did.

'A vintage car?' squealed Bettina.

There was a note.

R,

Enclosed are:

* a copy of the note I left on the fridge, in case you go straight to the office when you land.
* Ethel's (the neighbour) contact details—she is prone to overfeeding, so don't leave the dogs with her too much longer, and my key, in case you need a spare.

Please remember to take the dogs to their appointment on Wednesday.

Not sure what else to say. See you soon, I guess.

Many happy returns.

L

Many happy returns? My eyes filled.

'OMFG, it's better than a vintage car, isn't it?' she swooned. 'Is it the key to a time capsule of your love? Or the key to a secret garden he planted for you in Provence?

Or a seaside cottage for two in Somethingborough in England or wherever you're from? Chez Harley-Stanhope. No, simpler. Ruby & Luke's. Too plain. Rulukeby's Manor?'

'Bettina?'

'What?'

'May I please have the last present?'

The brown paper parcel from Clem and Fran looked like a cubic hug. I tore it open to find a white Chloé box containing the huge Hepburnian sunglasses I'd coveted all season.

A badge with the number three and a handwritten zero was pinned to the card with the Hallmark message, HAPPY BIRTHDAY—YOU'RE A BIG GIRL NOW! Inside was a crayon drawing of a bug-eyed fugitive committing grand theft auto in a meteor shower.

Upon closer inspection, I surmised the fugitive might have been me in striped pyjamas, the bug-eyes my designer eyewear, the car my bed, and the meteor shower an abstract starry night.

Happy birthday, Aunty Wooby!

Mummy thought you could wear these when you go on hollow days with Luke.

I told Mummy you might go somewhere unsunny, like London. She said it doesn't matter because sometimes grown-ups need sunglasses even when there is no sun.

Lots of love,

Lady Clementine Gardner-Stanhope 1st (and her mother, Fran xxxx)

Never truer, I thought, and put them on.

Channelling deceased Democrats

Canberra was colder than Luke's birthday note when we touched down at the RAAF base on day two, year thirty. There had been another Oscar Franklin exclusive—this time of the backbench spleen-venting variety—so we went straight to Parliament House via a line-up of the worst newspaper headlines I'd seen in a while: FURTHER LEAK CRIPPLES HOBBLING MASTERS; BACKBENCHERS BITE BACK; PM'S DAYS NUMBERED.

'Der,' Bettina said. 'Everyone's days are numbered; we just don't know what the number is. I can't believe they're slamming him for that bit of paper. As if he wouldn't have lines prepared; he was at the White House for fruit's sake. If he got up there and went "ummmm" they'd fully slaughter him like Britney and lip-synch-gate. Seriously, the quality of journalism these days is terrible.'

We buzzed through security. 'I bet they're all jealous of Oscar Franklin though.'

'Why?'

'Well, a) he's hotter than Dubai, b) he's getting all the leaks. Do you think the backbenchers really said what he said they said? Is that—OMG, it is!'

'What?'

'Okay, don't look, because he'll totally know we're scoping him, but I'm pretty sure that's Cecil Berth.'

'It is.' I glanced up at him as he and Jack walked towards us.

'OMG, I knew it. He's *way* taller than he looks on TV. I started this Facebook page called The National Treasurer's A National Treasure—'

Cecil and I exchanged nods.

'Back from the States, I see, Roo,' he said.

'Evidently, Treasurer.'

'You off to the Fifedom?' asked Jack.

I nodded.

'Good luck in there, kiddo.' She winked. 'Your country appreciates your sacrifice.'

Bettina clutched my hand. 'Cecil Berth just called you Roo, Roo,' she whispered, her fingers trembling. 'What's the Fifedom?'

'It's what Jack calls Connie Fife's office.'

'Oh, fiefdom, Fifedom—I get it. Ha. Hang on, how come he knows where we're going?'

'Who?'

'Jack.'

'Jack's a she. And because she asked me to. They loathe each other and someone needed to tell Connie she can't proceed with this—'

She stopped dead beside a Sidney Nolan, her mouth agape. 'SHUT THE FRONT DOOR.'

'What?'

'It's a she?'

'Shhh. Keep walking. Bettina, *she* was at *Girls'* Club.'

'You can be a male feminist!'

'She was talking about sexual harassment in the workplace in the sixties!'

'Sor-ree. I was within touching distance of Senator Flight and Minister Fife and my heart was all thumpity thumpity. Plus, Adelina Pepper's scarf was in the way. And she has a boy's name. And a deep voice. So she's not a dude?'

'No!'

'Well, a bit of concealer wouldn't go astray,' said Bettina. 'And lipstick. Put your face on in the morning. Take it off in the night-time. That's what my nonna always says. And what's with the cross-dressing?'

'That's just Jack. She doesn't want to sexualise herself. She spent most of her youth fighting for women's rights.'

'She totally should have fought for the right to *be* a woman.'

'That generation had a different experience of the workplace, so she tones it down.'

'And turns it off.'

We turned a carpeted corner in the ministerial wing. 'We're here.'

'OMG,' Bettina said. 'I can't believe I'm going to shake hands with Connie Fife.'

'You just went to the White House, had a meeting with the first gentleman, got within a foot of the President and within an inch of an FBI file. The PM knows your name and you're on first-name basis with Shelly. Why does the Education Minister warrant an OMG?'

'You don't understand.' She sighed. 'I am her hugest fan under five foot four.' She pulled a piece of blotting paper from her purse and patted. 'I get shiny when I'm nervous. How do I look?'

I examined today's ensemble, a relatively demure navy-blue shift dress over topaz tights with patent navy brogues, giant aqua hoops and a plumed hairclip.

'Blue and feathery. Now, you remember our agreement?'

Bettina pouted. 'Shake hands, wait outside. No photos under any circumstances.'

Connie Fife, wearing more black than a stagehand, pushed through her office doors to greet us. 'Good to see you, Roo.'

'Minister, you'll remember Bettina Chu from Girls' Club.'

'Minister,' gushed Bettina, shaking Connie's hand, 'it's literally *the* biggest honour to meet you.'

'And you, Bettina. I've heard so much about the great work you're doing.'

'You have?'

'How are you post-White House?'

'OMG, that was *so* embarrassing.'

'*You* shouldn't be embarrassed,' she said. 'You were just doing your job, trying to protect the PM from his careless slip-up. I think it was admirable.'

'That means the world to me, Minister. I'm a passionate supporter of what you're doing with universities. I wrote an article about it for my blog.'

'That's very kind of you, Bettina. I'd love to read it.'

'*You* want to read *my* blog?'

'Yes. Very much. Now we had better do this meeting. Why don't you join us, Bettina?'

'I really shouldn't, Minister,' she said. 'Roo said I should just shake your hand and wait here.'

Facepalm.

Connie slapped me on the back. 'Well, this is my office and I'm inviting you to join us.'

We took opposing couches—Bettina on mine, Connie on the other.

'So what's this all about, Roo?'

'It's about your class size reduction scheme.'

'You're reducing class sizes?' asked Bettina. 'That's totally awesome.'

'Thank you, Bettina,' said Connie. 'We're announcing it today.'

'That's what I want to talk to you about,' I said. 'We can't really afford to be going out with an announcement like that right now, what with the latest instalment from Franklin. We need to stop perpetuating the news cycle.'

My BlackBerry vibrated against the coffee table.

I silenced it and continued. 'Sorry. As I was saying, I'm sure you'll appreciate the reasons for that given the sensitivity surrounding last week's Serve the Nation leak and this morning's development.'

'Then you're too sure of yourself,' she said. 'This is the third time PMO has asked us to reschedule the announcement.'

'And I know it's irritating, Minister, but these are circumstances beyond our control. These leaks change everything. You know that.'

'Look, Roo,' she said, her greasy hair in desperate need of dry shampoo, 'I know this must be about as enjoyable for the Prime Minister as a haemorrhoid for a jockey on Melbourne Cup Day.'

Bettina giggled. Connie continued. 'But I can't say I'm sympathetic. I was completely blindsided by last week's leak. Do you know how I found out about the PM's intention to scrap Serve the Nation?'

'No, and there was no intention to—'

'Guess.'

I shrugged.

'Are you any good at guessing, Bettina?'

I shot her a look that said if you do you are dead to me.

'The TV?'

'No, very close though.'

'The radio?'

'Ding, ding, ding! Bettina wins. It was my shower radio, Roo. I got soap in my eyes. So much for the Girls' Club. Three senior female government advisors—you, that feminazi bitch and Di—forgot to mention it to the female fucking Education Minister.'

'It caught us by surprise too.'

'It shouldn't have. You were all in on it. What kind of dimwitted dick canvasses cutting Serve the Nation in writing without consulting the Education Minister? It's no wonder backbenchers are furious.'

'If I may, Minister, we don't even know—'

Buzz. Buzz.

'Bettina, would you mind answering this? Take a message.'

Bettina hurried out of the room.

'As I was saying, we don't even know where the idea came from. It was one of thousands of stupid ideas bandied about between our office and Treasury in the lead-up to the budget. It was shut down almost as soon as it had surfaced—the email trail shows that. We're in as much of a pickle as you are, especially after this morning's mutterings. We understand that backbenchers are angry about this so called "leak" but we've been trying to get the message out that these funding cuts were never on the table.'

'Boo hoo, Roo. Every time my office is ready to announce something it's inconvenient for PMO.'

'I'm very sorry to interrupt,' said Bettina, tiptoeing towards me. 'It's urgent.'

'Who is it?'

'Ethel?'

'I'll call back.'

'She said it's an emergency.'

Connie's eyes narrowed. 'Take it. Bettina will hold the fort, won't you, Bettina?'

'Sure!'

I smiled apologetically and went outside to take the call.

'Ruby, love, it's Ethel Bannister, your neighbour from number forty-two. '

In case you have another neighbour called Ethel Bannister.

'Listen, pet, I know when we spoke this morning I said I could handle the dogs' vet appointment after the row between you and your man friend, you poor dear. And I'm usually very good with dogs what with my Jeffrey, but the thing is, Ruby, your pups just don't seem to respond to orders, love. I can't get them into the car. Did they go to obedience school?'

'Erm, no but that's fine, Ethel. I'll just cancel the appointment. Thanks so much for trying and for stepping in at the last minute.'

'I tried to cancel it for you, love. I rang them up and

said you'd be unable to make the appointment due to marital difficulties.'

Love thy neighbour.

'But they said it'd be a three-hundred-dollar cancellation fee.'

'That's okay.' I peered over my shoulder at Bettina and Connie who were posing for a photograph.

'Per dog.'

'Oh.'

'And that they'd charge it against the credit card you booked with.'

Luke's.

'Ethel, on second thoughts, I should be able to make it home. I'll be there in twenty. Thank you!'

I burst back into the Minister's office. 'Thanks for your time, Minister, and I'm sorry for stuffing you around. I will tell the PM that you intend to proceed with the announcement as planned.'

'I'm glad you've all come to your senses,' she said, glowing with victory.

We shook hands and I made my way to the door, but paused before opening it. 'Best of luck with the press conference,' I said. 'Hope they go easy on you.'

She chuckled. 'I'm announcing a scheme to reduce secondary-school class sizes in major cities, Roo. That's *good* news. Bettina agrees, don't you?'

Bettina nodded.

'I do too,' I said. 'So it's a pity tomorrow's coverage will be all about how the Education Minister avoided answering questions about Serve the Nation while trying to distract from it with a cynically-timed rehash of an election promise about class sizes. Come on, Bettina.'

'You rocked hard in there, Roo,' said Bettina as we walked back to the office.

I said nothing.

'Are you mad at me?'

'No.'

'Was it the photo?'

'No.'

'Was it that I came in to the meeting? The Minister said—'

'I just need to know that my intern is on my team.'

'I don't get it. She's a minister. Aren't we on the same team?'

'Politics is an individual sport.'

'Come on, lads!' I slapped my knees beside the open boot of our...my...the station wagon in the driveway.

JFK cowered under the front steps; The Widdler wagged his tail and ran in the opposite direction.

'I did try that,' said Ethel, watching from the fence in a floral apron.

'OMG, they're so cute,' said Bettina. 'But, eww, did they kill something?'

'Huh?' I looked at the pile of sheep remains near the front door. 'Ugh, my Uggs.'

'Best not to leave things like that lying around, pet,' said Ethel. 'My Jeffrey here used to chew all sorts of things when he was a pup, but he's a big boy now, aren't you Jeffrey? Obedience school was such a prudent investment.' The plump Doberman licked his balls.

'Thank you ever so much for looking after them while I was away. I'm sure I've taken up quite enough of your time.'

'Nonsense,' she said. 'I've got nothing to do while the washing machine finishes.'

I pursed my talentless lips together and blew a raspberry, dribbling down my white silk peasant top.

Luke can whistle, said my head.

I opened the packet of doggy treats. That got their attention. I created a path of snacks leading into the boot of the station wagon. 'This always works.'

'Watch this.' I got ready to close the boot.

On their hind legs they stood, front paws on the boot, and hoovered up the last of them with their long tongues before flopping in a sated heap on the driveway.

'That's why you're supposed to train them, I guess,' said Bettina.

'Luke trained them,' I said. 'They respond to Luke.'

'Maybe we could just get Luke on speakerphone?'

I searched for the vet's number on my BlackBerry.

'Dr Elliot Juniper's office,' said the woman in my earpiece.

'Yes, hello,' I said, as chirpy as I could muster. 'I wondered if it's at all possible for the vet to make a house call to my dogs.'

'Certainly. Are they patients of Dr Juniper's?'

'Yes. JFK and Widdler.'

'Was that your neighbour who called earlier about cancellation?'

'Yes, but—'

'I'm sorry to hear about your marital difficulties.'

Effing Ethel.

'Things have become rather urgent,' I said. 'It's an emergency, you see.'

'What's the emergency?'

'I can't get them into the car.'

'That's not an emergency.'

'Well, it is for me. How important is this vaccination thingy anyway? I know a lot of dog owners conscientiously object to vaccinations.'

'How do you feel about rabies?'

Snarky bitch.

I kept my cool. 'How much is it for a home visit?'

'The callout is six hundred dollars.'

You could buy a new dog with that.

'Per dog,' she added.

Two.

'Plus the cancellation fee of six hundred dollars for both dogs.'

'I'll see you soon.'

JFK turned his attention to puncturing the garden hose with his teeth while The Widdler rolled in Ugg fluff.

'Roo, I've dialled in to your conference call for you,' said Bettina, handing me my phone. 'Do you want to take it inside?'

I looked up at the empty house. 'No, I'll do it here. Can you take my suitcase in?'

She skipped up the front steps while I went into the garage for the leash. I clipped it to The Widdler's collar. JFK saw this as an opportunity to rub freedom in the face of his tethered brother—a sort of canine na-na-na-na-na. In a single leap, he cleared the fence and accelerated down the street. The Widdler took off after him, dragging me along.

'JFK,' I yelled. 'Come back!'

Shit. I was about to do a call about the latest leak while watching my dog take one on the neighbour's BMW.

'Oh dear, that's what's-his-name's from across the way. Better catch up with him, love.'

'Please record your name after the tone, then press hash.'

'Ruby Stanhope. Slow down, Widdles—bollocks—' Hash. Hold music. Phew.

JFK turned to face us with a wraparound smile. The Widdler surged, nearly dislocating my forearm from my elbow.

'Morning, kids,' said the Chief in my earpiece. 'Let's get started. The good news is that Roo managed to dissuade the EdMin from proceeding with her announcement today. The bad news is she's very pissed off about it and we still have no idea where these leaks are coming from—'

A motor rumbled in the distance, which didn't bode well. As it drew closer I prayed it was a lawn mower. Please, please don't be the postman.

I managed to tie The Widdler to a telephone post just in time to see the familiar satchel-laden motorbike whiz around the corner.

True to form, JFK yelped, then growled and galloped at speed in the opposite direction onto State Circle.

'John Fitzgerald Kennedy!'

The conference call went quiet in my ear. 'Roo?'

Crap. 'Sorry.' Car horns beeped as I skidded into the middle of the road.

The astute mute, said my head.

'Channelling deceased Democrats, Roo?' asked the press sec.

'Erm, not exactly. My dog is on the loose. I'm chasing him across—holy shit balls, how many lives do dogs have?'

'One.'

'I'll call—fuckity fuckington—back!'

I hung up and waved my arms to protect JFK, who had paused to sniff a road island. Cars swerved and screeched around us.

JFK dashed onto the footpath, almost knocking an old man from his mobility scooter and scattering his groceries across the path.

My phone rang. 'What, Bettina?'

'Did you walk to the vet?'

'No, I didn't walk to the fucking vet. JFK ran away and I'm running after him! Hang on a second,' I panted, picking up a dozen runaway oranges which had fallen from a crocheted shopping basket. 'I'm so sorry.'

'They're all bruised,' said the man. 'My wife was supposed to make marmalade with them for the church.'

'I'm sorry. I'll pay for them.'

'You should have that dog on a leash,' he said. 'I ought to report you to the police.'

'How much were the oranges?'

'Let me just get the receipt.'

'I don't have time! Were they more or less than ten dollars?'

'The young these days are so disrespectful. All those drugs and computer games. I will report you. What is your name?'

'Ru—Stooby Ranhope. Have a nice day!'

I followed JFK down the street. 'Bettina,' I said into my earpiece. 'The Widdler's tied to a pole somewhere near State Circle. Go pick him up and then come and get JFK and me.'

'Where?'

I looked around for a reference point just in time to see JFK squeeze through a gap in a big black gate behind an incoming car.

'Cock,' I said. 'Meet me at the South African High Commission.'

JFK's panting presence frenzied the guards.

I kicked off my wedges and ran up the bitumen hill in fishnets so torn they couldn't have caught a manta ray. 'Don't,' I heaved, 'shoot'—gasp—'my dog!'

JFK squatted to offload a stupendous, steaming deposit on the pristine lawn beside a white marquee, which housed an ice sculpture, and hatted and gloved ladies who had been enjoying tea and brownies.

Shit.

Members of a string quartet put down their bows. Teacups clattered. Brims lifted. Fascinators fluttered.

'Is this your dog?' said the brick of a man at the eight-foot cast-iron fence.

I grabbed his arm to prop myself up. 'Yes'—splutter—'he ran away'—cough—'on the way to the vet.'

'You poor dear,' said the tiny blonde lady, pacing towards me, 'our Rhodesian rudgebacks hate the vit.'

Good grief, Ruby, that's—

'Your Excellency, I'm terribly sorry to disturb your party.'

Bettina pulled up in the station wagon, popped the boot and whistled an ear-splitting command. JFK jumped in immediately. The Widdler was busy chewing the seatbelt. The only thing sheepish about him was his aura of Ugg.

I got out my credit card and phoned the vet to book a house call.

That's why they call them bullet points

There was a man sitting in the dark on my front step. The man wasn't Luke.

I separated my keys to form a makeshift knuckleduster. 'Can I help you?'

'Are you Ruby Stanhope?' he asked.

The sensor light blinded me. 'What's it to ya?'

Gangsta.

'I'm Elliot.' He stepped into the light. 'The vet.'

'The hot vet,' said my head.

No, I didn't.

Elliot shuffled. 'Did you just say, "the hot vet"?'

'Erm, no—I said, "the what vet". I don't remember making a vet appointment.'

'Today, after cancelling your appointment because you couldn't get the dogs in the car and something about marital—'

'Martial,' I said. 'Must have been a typo. I have martial

problems with my, er, sensei. Not *marital* problems. I'm not married!' I checked my watch trying not to drop the birthday roses Chief had given me after a half-hour bout of hair-related laughter. 4.27 a.m. Shit. 'Sorry, it's been one of those days.'

'I was starting to think you might not show.'

'Come in,' I said, climbing the stairs.

'I'm sorry about my receptionist,' he said. 'She can be a bit, what's the word?'

'Snarky?' I opened the door and switched on the lights.

He laughed. 'Yes, snarky. Of course I'm not going to charge you a cancellation fee for today.'

'Really?' I turned around to face him. 'That is, without a doubt, the best thing I have heard all day.' I promptly disintegrated. My tear ducts were monsoonal.

'Um, are you okay?'

'Yes,' I heaved. 'I'm not crying.'

The dogs went ballistic.

'Sit,' he said. They did.

'I'm sorry,' he said. 'I could come back another time.'

'No,' I heaved. 'I'm fine. It's just that my boyfriend proposed last week—'

'Congratulations.'

'And I said no because he was being a dick and then he left and now he's living with his ex-wife and son in Melbourne.'

'Oh. Uncongratulations.'

'And then I went to the US with work, which sucked balls, and yesterday was my birthday but it happened midair between time zones and now I'm thirty and alone with shit hair and a drab wardrobe.'

'Happy birthday for yesterday.'

'Happy?'

'Sorry. Obviously it's not a happy birthday. That was a reflex. When people say, "It was my birthday yesterday," you're supposed to say "happy birthday", so I did. Do you want me to, um, come back tomorrow?'

'No,' I said, putting the roses down on the spotless kitchen bench. 'Now's fine.'

I breathed and flapped my hands in front of my face. Salty tears continued to spew down my cheeks.

'I need a drink,' I said. 'Do you want a drink?'

'No thanks, I'm on call.'

'Oh my God!' I sobbed.

'What?'

'Now you think I'm hitting on you, don't you? I'm not. I swear. I just really need a drink. I'm not that kind of person! Oh crap, you think I'm that kind of person.'

'No, I don't think that at all,' he said.

'Promise?' I sniffed.

'I promise.'

'Good, because I'm really an old-fashioned prude.'

He laughed. 'I'm sure you are.'

'And even though you are impossibly tanned for someone who lives in Canberra and look like you've just stepped off a casting call for *The Farmer's Wife Needs a Lover*, I promise you I respect your professionalism.'

I didn't say that either.

'Um, okay.'

'That was really inappropriate, wasn't it? Don't answer that.'

'How about you get yourself a drink and I vaccinate your dogs?'

'Good idea.'

I ran into my ensuite.

There was a faint smell of disinfectant. It was hospital-grade clean. The whole house felt like a display home. Luke must have gone on one of his sanitation binges before he left, stripping it of every whiff of our former lives.

I switched on the lights.

Pull yourself togeth—Jiminy Cricket, you look like a chimney sweep.

I looked in the mirror. To say I had panda eyes was an insult to the species. I washed my face, and changed into jeans and a T-shirt.

Jeans and a T-shirt? Isn't that a bit familiar?

What do you want me to wear? A suit?

Maybe add a cardigan.

And slippers to make it casual.

Slippers?

Bare feet, then.

Your toenails look mouldy.

Okay, socks.

Good call.

'Sorry about that,' I said, sliding across the super-slippery floors towards the wine rack. Pinot would make me weepy again. I reached for a medicinal Médoc instead.

'No worries,' he called from the living room.

On the fridge, under a three-dimensional fridge magnet of Big Ben was a typed note.

- Addressed forwarding envelopes in drawer for my mail
- Power bill under this magnet—overdue
- *Julie & Julia* needs to go back to Blockbuster by tomorrow, *Lawrence of Arabia* by Sunday
- Vet appointment on Wednesday at 11

Ouch. That's why they call them bullet points, I thought. I poured myself a glass and gulped.

'Lovely dogs you have,' Elliot called out. 'Who named them?'

'My aunt.' I went into the living room. He'd covered the floor with a drop cloth and was patting The Widdler. 'Her dog, Pansy, gave birth to three pups. She could only keep one and she gave JFK and The Widdler to us. As a pup, JFK liked to give long speeches from the footstool and Widdles, well, widdled everywhere.'

'Cute.'

I crouched down beside JFK and patted him. 'How are they looking?'

'They're healthy. The Widdler could probably watch what he's eating a bit. JFK seems fine.' He held JFK's gums up with his fingers. 'They'll both need their teeth cleaned within the next six months or so. This is just their annual booster.'

'How can I help?' I asked, looking at the syringe.

'Just keep really calm and give JFK a good pat while I give Widdles his shot.'

Widdles flinched a little but then forgot about it when Elliot gave him his treat. JFK whimpered, true to form, and as a result got two treats, which appeased him.

'Thank you,' I said, as Elliot packed up. 'And listen, I'm really sorry about earlier. I'm not usually that neurotic.'

'No worries, mate. Seriously, I was a wreck on my thirtieth too.'

'I am a wreck, aren't I?'

'Yep.' He smiled and folded the drop cloth. The dogs wagged their tails and panted, anticipating his departure.

'Sit,' he said.

They sat.

'How did you do that?'

'With authority,' he said. 'Like this: sit. Don't molly-coddle them. You're not doing them any favours if you do. What do you do for a living?'

'I work in the Prime Minister's Office. I'm an advisor.'

'Does he listen to you?'

'Yes.'

'How do you do it?'

'I have to know what I'm talking about, I guess.'

'You're unequivocal.'

'Yeah, I am.'

'Well, mate, if you can tell the Prime Minister what to do, you can get your dogs to sit.'

'Elliot,' I breathed with an index finger extended. I snort-laughed at my own joke.

'Huh?'

'Sorry, you probably get that all the time.'

'Get what?'

I did it again. He looked blank.

'ET? Elliot? Never mind.' I took another sip of my wine for courage. 'Listen, as nice as the thought is of spending my first night as a thirty-year-old snacking on stale Cheezels with dogs who don't listen to me, I could really use some company; just a friend. I promise I won't go all neurotic on you again.'

He looked at me with espresso eyes. 'How stale are your Cheezels?'

I went to the pantry and pulled out the open box.

He put one in his mouth. 'There's still crunch.'

'Excellent.' I poured him a glass of red. 'I may even order some pizza.'

'Now you're talking,' he said, taking it. 'Cheers—to Cheezels and better birthdays.'

'Cheers.'

Elliot and I finished the Cheezels, two bottles of wine and three pizzas. We watched TV until the infomercials started. We laughed and talked about everything but politics, until he told me he didn't vote.

'You're not a Kiwi, are you?'

'No,' he laughed. 'I'm just not interested.'

'I'm English.'

'You're kidding.'

'Ha ha,' I said. 'But it means I can't vote here which is so irritating because I'm far more interested in Australian politics than I am in British.'

'Why's that?'

'I was an investment banker before I came to Australia. I knew nothing about politics.'

'What changed?'

'Circumstance. I met Luke.' I swallowed. 'He was Chief of Staff to Max. He offered me a job, I joined the campaign, had a great time and stayed.'

'So you didn't choose to work for this party or this politician, it just happened.'

'Yes.'

'Right.' He picked up his glass from the coffee table. 'What?'

'Don't you think it's a bit, I dunno, meaningless, latching onto the first politician who offers you a job? I mean, did you think about what he stood for?'

'Yes,' I said, mildly offended. 'And there are things we do that I disagree with. I'm certainly not that pleased with where the government's headed at the moment. We've made serious mistakes and some days it's hard to get up in the morning.'

'So stop.'

'No.'

'Why not?'

'I don't know.' I topped up our glasses. 'Why are you a vet?'

'I wanted to be a jockey.' He was slurring a bit. 'But I'm too fucking tall.'

I laughed.

'So I learned everything I could about horses and became a vet. I love animals and this is a way of making money and helping them. Last year, I bought a property out at Yass and one day I'm going to own and train a racehorse and he's going to win the Melbourne Cup.'

'You're quite sure of yourself.' I yawned.

'Yep. I've even picked out a name for him.'

'What?'

'Donkey.'

'You can't call a racehorse donkey!'

'Says the owner of JFK and Widdles.'

I laughed and closed my eyes. The room span.

'I should go,' he said, standing up.

'You're not going to drive.'

'No, I'll call a cab.'

'I'll call one for you.' I stood up. Alcohol and jet lag saturated my brain cells.

'Welcome to Capital Cabs. Would you like to book a taxi?'

'Yesss,' I slurred.

'If so, say yes, if—'

'Ye-esss.'

'I'm sorry, I'm having trouble understanding—'

'I said yes, you comprehensive fuckwit.'

Elliot laughed.

I hung up. 'Look, it's not worth it. Just stay here.'

'I don't think that's wise, Ruby.'

'I meant in the guest room.'

'Are you sure you can resist my impossible tan?'

'Certain,' I smiled. 'Where do you get it done?'

'What?'

'Your spray tan,' I said, showing him to the guest room.

'Very funny.'

I rubbed my tired, sore eyes.

'Good night, birthday girl,' he said, kissing my cheek. 'You'll be right.'

The dogs barked. A floorboard creaked. My door opened.

Elliot appeared, bare-chested.

'Ruby,' he whispered.

'Mmmm?'

'There's someone in the house. Are you expecting anyone?'

'What time is it?'

'Shhh. Seven.'

'Oh fuck, I'm late for work.'

'Did you not hear me? Someone's here.'

I clutched my head, threw on a robe and followed him into the kitchen, trying not to stare at the horseshoe tattoo on his right shoulderblade.

'Here,' I whispered, fumbling in the utensil drawer for a knife. Then we saw a figure reflected in the fridge's stainless steel door.

Don't just stand there, said my head.

'Halt,' I growled, lunging with my weapon. 'Who goes there?'

Halt, who goes there? Seriously?

'Christ, you almost scared the baby out of me!'

The lights came on to reveal Debs in all her pregnant splendour. The white cord from her iPhone earphones wound its way into the structured black-leather tote slung over her shoulder.

'I'm *sorry?*'

'No harm done.'

'I'm not sorry!'

'You just said you were.'

'Perhaps you didn't pick up on the incredulity in my rising inflection.'

'Who's she?'

'My aunt's missus, Debs.'

'Who's he?'

'Elliot.'

'Hel-lo, Elliot.'

'Hello.'

'Did you really just say halt?'

'She did,' said Elliot.

'What would you have said to a home invader?'

'Probably something like, "If you don't get the fuck out of my house I will lop off your family jewels with a pair of rusty secateurs, sauté them in a knob of salted butter and make you watch as I spoon-feed them to my bull terriers." But I'm just improvising.'

A surge of envy and wrath paralysed my vocal chords.

'I'll put the kettle on,' said Elliot.

'What's with the whisk?' asked Debs.

I looked down at the ridiculous weapon in my grip.

'Hoping to beat your attacker into stiff peaks?'

'It was dark!' I shouted.

'Was it dark when Joh Bailey did that to your hair?'

'*How* and *why* are you in my house?'

'The spare key was under the doormat—very original—and I texted you. I need a place to stay.'

I checked my BlackBerry for unread messages. 'You mean this one, sent at 5 a.m.?' I showed her my screen.

Happy b'day for yesterday, chook. See you soon. Mum's the word. D

'That's the one.' She rifled through my pantry. 'Got any cashews?'

'No.'

'How about Barbeque Shapes?'

'No. Why is mum the word?'

'I don't want anyone to freak out.' She put a jar of peanut butter on the bench. 'Cheezels?'

'All out,' said Elliot.

She raised an eyebrow.

I slammed the pantry door. 'Debs, does Aunt Daphne even know you're here?'

'She knows I'm away on business,' she said, dipping her finger into the jar.

I picked up the portable phone.

'What are you doing?'

'She needs to know where you are.'

'I'm not a baby!'

'No, but you're acting like one and you're having one, which is enough for me.'

Elliot rinsed a few mugs. 'Anyone for a cuppa?'

'Yes, please,' said Debs.

'Debs, I'm serious.'

She spared the spread. 'Don't call her now, she'll freak out. I told her I'm in Perth with a mining client.'

I ignored her.

She clutched her stomach.

'What?' I asked.

'Nothing.' She doubled over.

'What is it?'

'I'm fine.'

I put my hand on her back. 'Is everything okay?'

She shrieked with glee as she snatched the phone from my hand and scampered down the hallway with it.

'Debs!' I ran after her. 'This is *so* immature. Give it back!'

'Can't catch me!' She slid into the living room on slippery socks and hid behind the piano.

'Fine, I'll just use my BlackBerry.'

'No!' she squealed, charging towards me. We landed in a heap on the couch.

'Let me put it this way,' she said. 'If you tell her I'm here, I'll tell her who else is here.'

'Shhhhh.' I blushed. 'He's just a friend.'

'Like a *buddy*?' She winked.

'No, like a *friend*. He's the vet.'

'I usually pay our vet in cash.'

'Deborah!'

'What?'

'Even if I did let you stay,' I said, 'Stan will find out and then we'll both be in trouble.'

'I said my Perth client was particular about confidentiality, which he accepted, but he still wanted to book my flights, so I said I was going by private jet. Then he and the Italian stallion insisted on driving me to the airport in their banana-yellow Mini Pooper. I had to bribe a media-mogul mate, with box seats to the grand final, into letting me board his plane at Tullamarine for half an hour so I could wave them off the tarmac. Then I got a commercial flight.'

'Either of you have milk?' Elliot yelled out from the kitchen.

'Yep, but not until the little one's out.'

'I meant, do you take milk in your tea?'

'Oh. Yes. And sugar.' She lowered her voice. 'He's a keeper.'

'Tea's on the bench,' he yelled. 'I'm going to have a shower.'

'Okay! There's a towel in there for you.'

At least she waited for the tap to turn on before she started laughing.

'He's just a friend!'

'If I had friends like that I'd be a very straight woman.'

'Look, I was lonely last night and I needed company. Shit. That didn't come out right. We just talked.'

'Whatever. No judgment, lady. Listen. Don't blow my cover, please.' She tucked her feet underneath her. 'I'm thirty-one weeks in—this is the last week Daph will let me travel. I had to get out of there. And Daph isn't too happy with you at the moment, anyway, Ducks. The only call I'd be making to her is a grovelling one.'

I considered it. 'When—not if—Daphne finds out, I want you to leave me out of it. I can't afford to be done for aiding and abetting.'

'It's just for a couple of days and I'll stay out of your terribly cut hair, I promise. I can feed the pups and cook.'

'You can't cook.'

'True, but I order a very authentic Pad Thai.'

'Deal.'

She went quiet. 'Um, re the Luke thing, are you, y'know?'

'Fine. I don't really want to talk about it.'

'Can I just ask one question?'

I groaned. 'What?'

'Was it the ring? Because—er—he probably put a lot of thought into it.'

'No,' I said, smiling. 'The ring was exquisite.' My smile dissipated.

'Thank poop.' Her shoulders dropped with relief.

We sat in silence, the sound of running water in the background. I checked my emails.

Morning, Roo!

See below—there's been another leak.

Oscar Franklin's blog has something about the delayed class-size announcement coming as a result of pressure from PMO.

Also, I got a call from Mike the mail guy. Unsolicited. He said he had some info for me but I told him I wasn't interested.

Toodles, Bettina xoxoxo

'I have to go to work,' I said.

'Luke's not doing too well,' Debs blurted.

'I said I don't want to talk about it.'

'You can't just runaway and hide, chickadee,' she said.

'Because you're doing such a great job of facing up to your own personal problems right now?'

'I know, but—'

'Listen to me. I. Do. Not. Want. To. Talk. About. Luke. If you ask me again I will not only tell the angry mob in Melbourne where you are, but also that while you were here you won the ACT regional women's weight-lifting competition. I'll say that you built up your strength by taking steroids and eating nothing but beef carpaccio with blue cheese dressing and unwashed rocket every day for a week and that you celebrated your new title with an afternoon of bungee-jumping and tequila slammers, followed by a hangover recovery involving a triple-shot macchiato and soft-boiled eggs.'

Her eyes widened. 'Okay, okay.'

'I'm not finished. I will then see to it personally that you serve out the rest of your pregnancy at a Tasmanian BlackBerry-free health farm with a strict diet of buckwheat porridge, dandelion-root tea and mashed yam and a daily routine of compulsory counselling, yogalates, group hugs and folk choir, for which I will nominate you as first tambourinist. Understood?'

JFK whimpered.

'Excellent. Make yourself at home. I'm going to get ready for work.'

'Banana and praline muffin,' said Bettina, putting the home-baked cake on my desk. 'And a latte.'

'Do you sleep?' I kept typing.

'Sometimes.' She applied wet shine lipgloss. 'So, did you get my email?'

'About the Oscar Franklin leak?'

'And the other thing.'

'Other thing?'

'Postal Mike.' She re-tied the polka-dot bow at the nape of her neck. 'Told him I was totally uninterested.'

I took a bite of the muffin. 'This is amazing.'

'I know, right?' She hovered above my desk like the animated blue bird in *Zip-a-Dee-Doo-Dah*.

I stopped typing. 'What is it?'

'If you like, I could just get the information from Mike to put your mind at ease.'

'My mind is at ease.'

'Okay.'

Hover, hover.

'It doesn't look at ease.'

'It is.'

'Why don't you want to know? Aren't you the least bit curious about what he discovered?'

'No. Go do some work.'

'Okay, okay. Sheesh.'

The bat phone lit up.

'Roo, where are you?' Chief said.

'Just outside,' I waved Bettina away.

'Can I see you in my office, please?'

Her skin was grey. I shut the door.

'There's been another one.' She passed me an envelope. I opened it. Same font. Different words.

Happy anniversary.

'Turn it over.'

I know.

She sighed. 'Today's the day we—you know.'

Ick.

'I went back through all my old diaries and found it. There was a party for a retiring senator. We all went—

everyone was there. We all got shit-faced and ended up at Green Square.'

'But who would know? I mean, were either of you, erm, demonstrative?' I tried not to think about it.

'No. I only told my sister and she wouldn't have told anyone. I know that.'

'What if she told her husband or a girlfriend or—?'

'She said she'd forgotten all about it because there were so many stories like it.' She smacked her forehead.

'Holy heck, who else did you...?'

'Ruby!'

'Sorry. Did Max tell anyone?'

She nodded. 'Shelly knows. He said he told her before they got married. To think all these years have passed and she's never mentioned it or hated me for it or objected to my role.'

'Well, that's fine then,' I said. 'No. A young MP has a consensual one-night stand with a junior press sec ten years ago. Young MP confesses to his fiancée. They marry and have a baby and live happily ever after. The end.'

'That's not how this world works, Roo. The young MP becomes the Prime Minister and he bombs in the polls. The junior press sec becomes his Chief of Staff. There's a big, sordid story in that and whoever's doing this knows it.'

'As your friend, Di, I'm telling you again: you must show the police. They're trained to protect you and the PM.'

'I can't take that risk. We just need to find who's doing it and stop them.'

'Hmmm.' I stroked my chin. 'Who could possible have a vendetta against the Prime Minister? We're not going to be able to do this without a few tools.'

'What?'

'*Law & Order* theme music, police tape and one of those fancy purple sperm-finder lights,' I said.

'Fuck off with the sarcasm.'

'What? You know it's ridiculous.'

'Can you at least put some thought into it?'

'Fine.'

Her door opened after a quick, urgent knock.

'What is it, Bettina?'

'Chief, Roo, there's something you need to see.'

'What?'

'Mick O'Donoghue's making a speech. It's about the PM. None of the networks are covering it, but Anastasia Ng is live-tweeting it.'

We huddled around Bettina's monitor and watched.

@Stasing: Former PM says fear for party is that if we keep settling for the safe guy, we'll never get anything done.

'The safe guy?'

@Stasing: O'Donoghue says Masters incapable of implementing a single original idea. Can he grow in job? Possibly. Is time running out? Definitely.

'What the fuck?' said Chief. 'Did anyone know about this?'

'No,' I said. 'I knew he was speaking but it was going to be about the EU.'

Chief raged. 'Is the whole fucking world out to get us?' She slammed her door.

My phone buzzed.

Thanks for Cheezels. Debs is cool. So are you. Let me know if you're free for coffee on the weekend. Elliot

A school of endorphins swam like merry minnows

through my blood stream. Cold latte in hand, I grabbed my faded-black duffle coat and stepped out into the chilly air to draft a reply.

Thanks for a fun night, mate—

Back-space.

—buddy—

Clear.

Splendid to have made your platonic acquaintance.

No.

Any chance you'd be up for a rebound fling in about a fortnight when I know for sure that I'm as single as a dingle? If I could ogle you in the interim, preferably shirtless, that would be great.

My head interrupted me. *Ruby, what are you doing?* No idea.

Well, can you find out before you do it, please?

I took a seat on a bench, shut my eyes and watched the dappled light through my eyelids until it was interrupted by a shadow.

'Mind if I join you?'

Jack's dog tags mirrored the trees above.

I sat up and moved over. 'Please.'

Her lighter struggled in the wind. She struck it a few times before inhaling. 'The US was a bit of a clusterfuck. And not just your intern's army crawl.' Smoke seeped through a tiny gap in the corner of her mouth, drifting towards me. 'And now the O'Donoghue speech. I saw the transcript. Bit of a low blow.'

I waved the smoke away. 'Tell me about it. And bloody Fife's office leaked the conversation we had yesterday.'

'She's such a whiny little bitch. Anyway, it's nowhere near as big a story as the one we'd have had if she proceeded with the class-size announcement. Well done for talking her out of it.'

'Thanks.'

Another puff. 'You look contemplative, honey.'

I nodded. 'It's Luke. He—he wants more than I want to give.'

'I'm twice your age, pumpkin. Hear me. Don't put all your eggs in one bastard. Meet interesting people and, when they no longer interest you, throw them back into the ocean. If you're looking for a man who'll let your career cast a shadow over his, you'll wear your eyes out. Even good men can't turn off their egos.'

'My father was an investment banker and my mother's a judge. They've been married thirty-five years.'

'It's different when your man's as successful as you are, but Luke quit. He wasn't as good at this job as you are.' Her glasses darkened as the sun came out from under a cloud.

'That's a little harsh, he led us out of Opposition into government.'

'Government's where the real work begins. Government is marriage, campaigning is courtship. Anyway, my point is that for women, balance is a myth. You're going to have to make a choice.'

'Can I ask you something?'

The smoke zigzagged when she nodded.

'You chose work, right?'

'Yep.'

'Do you think you'll regret that?'

She considered it. 'No more than I would regret the

opposite. Sometimes I think about my mum. I remember her in her pinny, hair in rollers, my youngest brother on one hip as she flipped rissoles in the pan my dad bought her for Christmas. He was never there, always away on tours of duty, but his portrait hung above the piano.

'We were there with Dad when he died. At the funeral, the church was packed. The commandant gave the eulogy. He listed every battle, every medal.

'My mum went suddenly. After all that lonely, thankless work for others, she died on her own. My uncle's eulogy said she was a good wife and mother, renowned for her melting moments.' She took a final drag. 'I don't want to be remembered for supporting someone that mattered; I want to be the one that mattered.'

My phone buzzed.

Roo, are you coming tomorrow night? The network said you haven't RSVP'd. Oscar

'I've got to go,' I said, leaving her to stamp out her cigarette.

In the corridor, I sent three texts.

Oscar, I'll be there. Looking forward to catching up. Ruby

Thanks for your company last night, Elliot. A bit hectic at work at the moment. Will let you know re weekend. Ruby

Bettina, go talk to Mike from postal. Ruby.

Waxing lyrical

'Cocktail party,' I said to my open wardrobe, as if it might be a voice-activated stylist.

JFK licked the moisturiser off my leg.

I re-read the invitation aloud. 'Oscar Franklin invites Ruby Stanhope, open brackets, plus one, close brackets—

Open brackets, minus one, close brackets, mocked my head.

'—to a cocktail party celebrating the launch of *24/11* at Axis, National Museum of Australia—'

Where you belong.

'Date—'

None.

'Time—'

To get your watch fixed.

'RSVP—'

Or even Match.com. Try both.

I grabbed three dresses—a pleated black Burberry, new

blue Kate Spade and nude one-shoulder Rachel Gilbert—and, in towel and turban, went to seek Debs' advice.

On my couch she channel-surfed, her skin thick with face mask, a Cheezel on each finger. 'I went to uni with her. Bit of a psycho.'

'Who?'

'Connie Fife—ow!' She bit through Cheezel to flesh.

I stood in front of the TV to get her attention. 'Which frock?'

She studied the options. 'Why not just wrap your underarm hair around your body, Rapunzel? You'll at least get a mini-dress out of it and I guarantee no one else will be wearing the same thing.'

I peered at the fuzz. 'It's not that bad...'

'No, it's much worse than bad. You could plait it and tie your evening purse to it so you don't have to carry it. Or you could chop it off and sell it to a wig-maker. Or maybe wear the strapless number and knot the hair from both pits behind your neck to turn it into a halter.'

'Bother.'

I went in search of the DIY wax kit I had bought at the chemist but had never found time to use.

Nail polish remover. Acetone-free nail polish remover. Nail polish removal wipes. There it was in a cardboard box with a photograph of the smoothest leg known to man—probably many men.

I ran into the kitchen, hurled the plastic tub into the microwave and crossed nail polish remover off the shopping list on the fridge. Five minutes ought to do it, I thought.

'What are you doing?' asked Debs, coming into the kitchen.

'I read a magazine with tips for time-poor women. Waxing is better for the skin under your arms than shaving and it takes longer to grow back. And this one's organic.'

'Can't be more organic than your armpits,' she said. 'Want help?'

I handed her a little booklet from inside the box. 'Just read me this while I heat it up.' I used one of the nail polish remover wipes to rid myself of the remnants of my last manicure, which now looked like a fragmented map of Micronesia.

Debs put on her cat's-eye reading glasses and cleared her throat. 'Waxing is the simplest, most effective means of hair removal—'

'Blah, blah, get to the point.'

'Here we go. Step one, cleanse and dry the area in question.'

'Already done.'

'Okay, step two. Heat up the wax. Step three. Test on a small patch of skin. If your skin looks normal after twenty-four hours it's safe to proceed.'

'As if anyone ever does that. Anyway, my version of normal is furry.'

'Good point. When the wax has melted, coat the spatula in a thin layer and apply to the desired area. Smooth the cotton strip over the wax in the direction of the hair growth. Hold the skin taut and swiftly pull the strip to remove the hair.'

'There weren't any cotton strips in the box,' I said.

'Maybe use an old hanky?'

'Good thinking.'

The microwave finished beeping. I opened it. My hands took turns holding the wax pot as I skidded across the polished floors towards my room.

'For underarms, dust the area with talcum power first,' said Debs as I sped past her. 'Not suitable for sensitive—'

I hung up my towel in the ensuite and went to Luke's smalls drawer and pulled out a white hanky embroidered with his initials. That'll do, I thought, and opened the wax pot.

With my left hand I dipped the thin wooden spatula in the hot amber wax and pulled it out, letting the excess dribble away. I stuck my arm in the air and smeared wax over the fluffy tuft of my right pit. It didn't seem like enough, so I put a bit more on to be sure. Perhaps a little much; it oozed down my side.

My phone rang. Private number. It could be Max, I thought. Or Elliot. Or Luke. Shit, what if it's Elliot? Shittier, what if it's Luke?

I tried to answer it with my left hand but the spatula had stuck between my index and middle fingers, so I answered it with my nose and cradled the phone between ear and shoulder.

'Erm—hello?'

'Ruby,' said Fran, 'why didn't you tell me?'

'The caller ID said you were a private number. One second. Just hold—I'm putting you on speaker.'

I turned on the tap with my left elbow to try to unstick the spatula. Instead, the cold water set the wax hard, gluing the spatula between my middle and index fingers. I had to get the wax under my arm off before it dried. I lifted the hanky to my right pit, accidentally dunking it into the wax pot on the way.

'Bollocks.'

The syrup drizzled off it in a tacky trail down my

boob and up my right arm. Slick with wax, the hanky stuck to my wrist.

'Sorry, Fran—donkey bollocks.'

'Donkey bollocks, indeed,' said Fran. 'You were a right bitch to Aunt Daphne on the phone, Ruby.'

'Whoopsy daisies.'

'And now Debs is off gallivanting with some West Australian mining magnate.'

'Erm—now's not a great time. I'll call you back.'

'Liar. You've been avoiding me for days, Ruby.'

Weren't you supposed to use the talc first?

Shit. I aimed the open talc bottle towards my right armpit and squeezed. My lungs flailed as a jet stream of snowy powder shot up my nose and into my mouth. I gasped.

'Don't be dramatic. I just need to know how you are,' said Fran, her tone impatient.

'Fine.' I coughed. The powder had settled in perfect V-formation on my sticky boob.

'Nobody is "fine" at the end of a two-year relationship, Ruby.'

I turned my attention to the handkerchief crusted onto my wrist. With my left hand welded to the spatula, I took its monogrammed corner between my teeth.

On three, said my head. *One, two, two-and-a-half—*

I pulled, ripping a small colony of forearm hairs out with it. 'Ouch!' Looking down at the angry red cluster of empty follicles, I saw firsthand the effects of deforestation without community consultation.

'What?'

'That weally hurt.' I tried to spit out the hanky now dangling from my lip.

'If it hurts *you*, Ruby, can you imagine what Luke must be going through?'

'Wisten, Fwan,' I said, 'I apweciate the call, but I'm getting weddy to go to a wather swanky party so I can't chat wight now.' The white veil dangling from my mouth flapped with every word.

'Don't stiff-upper-lip me, Ruby,' she shouted. 'I'm your sister.'

I yanked at the hanky with the only unsticky finger on my left hand. The force split my chapped pout. Blood pooled and seeped through the white cotton.

Stripped of her innocence, my head lamented.

'What happened?'

'He pwoposed, and...' I used both hands to peel the messy fabric dangling from my mouth. I sniffled.

'I know,' she soothed. 'These things are terribly difficult. It's important not to bottle up your feelings.'

The soft skin of my right inner arm met the dribbled wax. I felt it sticking. 'I've compwetely cocked it up.'

'We all make mistakes, darling,' said Fran. 'But it's not too late.'

Oh, but it was. My left hand had frozen in a permanent Vulcan salute so convincing even the most dexterous Trekkies would envy me. My right arm was fixed to my side. I tried to wriggle free of the fast-coagulating treacle like a bug caught in a spider web.

'Ah can't move ma arm,' I said.

'Your arm?'

'Ah can't waise ma arm. It's gwued to ma wibcage. And ma wips are stuck togever.'

'Good Lord, you're having a stroke! Stay calm. I'll call an ambulance.'

'No stwoke, no ambuwance,' I said. 'Debs! Debs!'

'Debs is in Perth, Ruby. You've lost the plot. Sit down. Breathe. You're going to be okay. I'll get help.'

Bare, but for my towel-turban, I hobbled out of the bathroom and used my knee to bang on the bedroom door. 'Debs!' I screamed. 'Debowah!'

'What?' She barged through the door, bowling me over. 'Holy poopamole!'

'Awert your eyes!' I said, holding up my left hand to protect my modesty.

She reciprocated. 'Live long and prosper, Commander Spock.'

'Hiwarious.'

'Yes, it is,' she said, throwing my towel over me. 'Let me just get my camera.'

Fran's muffled voice emanated from my phone. 'Ruby, are you okay? I heard a crash. Is someone there with you? Was that a man?'

'Is someone on the phone?' whispered Debs.

'Fwan.'

'Who's there with you?' asked Fran.

'I'm not here,' mouthed Debs, her eyes wide.

'Nobody,' I said. 'I need to go now, Fwan.' I ended the call with my nose.

Debs pulled me off the floor and ripped the hanky off my lip. I felt it split again. 'Ouch!'

'You just outed me!'

'You just removed a layer of my skin, so I think we're even!'

'No, we're not. She's going to call Daph and then I'll be screwed and not the good kind of screwed.' She paced around my bedroom.

'My arm is stuck to my side!' I moaned. 'My lip makes me look like I've been playing spin the bottle with the cast of *Twilight*.' I looked at the clock radio. 'And I'm already ten minutes late for a glamorous party full of TV people and a man I have a, er, history with.'

Her eyes narrowed. 'Not Oscar bloody Franklin?'

'It's not what you think. I'm just doing my job.'

'Your job blows.'

'That was below the belt.'

'Ha!' She laughed.

'I wasn't trying to be funny. Are you going to help me or not?'

Sticky lips sink ships

Forty minutes later Debs dropped me off at the National Museum in the dog-hair-encrusted station wagon.

Paparazzi loitered in the dark, flashing their wares at incoming starlets.

'How's my make-up?'

She winced. 'I've created a Munster.'

'Has my lip stopped bleeding?'

Her jaw had dropped. '*Who* is *that*?'

I shut the mirror and looked out the window in time to see a mammarily gifted blonde giraffe strutting down the red carpet. Covered in bronze splotches, she was camouflaged and ready for the jungles of Africa—or birdcages of Flemington. So extreme was her altitude that the poor thing couldn't find a dress for the occasion long enough to cover her bits. This must have been cumbersome, but she pulled it off. Her neck was easily two feet long. Silver-tasselled earrings the length of my shins shimmied well above her collarbone. A male human in a midnight-blue suit approached her from behind.

Zookeeper?

It was Oscar. The artificial teeth in his artificial smile gleamed in the artificial light.

He wrapped a strapping arm around the creature's waist, which was so tiny he could have encircled it twice over. Photographers clicked, lighting up the night sky. The inter-species couple posed for each camera, rotating like a freestanding fan. Then Oscar stared in our direction, his eyes flickering with recognition.

'Drive around the block,' I said.

Debs turned the key in the ignition.

'Hurry.'

'Ruby!' He came towards the car, leaving the giraffe to fend for itself.

The snappers followed Oscar, forming a scrum around the station wagon.

'Get out of the car, Ruby,' said Debs through gritted teeth.

'No.'

'Get out of the pooping car right now.'

'No,' I clutched at the seat with my fingernails. 'I won't do it.'

Oscar opened the passenger-side door. 'I *knew* it was you,' he said, offering me an arm.

'Hello, Oscar.' I swivelled out of the passenger seat, put both Choos on the bitumen and stepped out.

Debs sped off.

For a moment, the flashes stopped. Perhaps the photographers needed to adjust their lenses on account of my luminosity.

They recommenced.

'Love your new look—especially the glove.' Oscar breathed into my ear, posing for the cameras. 'Very eighties rocker.'

A lens zoomed towards me. 'Can I get your name?' asked the man behind it. 'We like to get it right for the captions.'

'I'm nobody,' I said.

'She's being modest,' said Oscar. 'It's Ruby Stanhope. S-T-A-N-H-O-P-E. She's the PM's advisor.'

'G'day, Roo,' said one of the snappers, angling his camera up at me. 'I didn't recognise you in all that get-up.'

'Hi, Gary.'

Oscar shepherded me away. 'Let me introduce you to Winnie.'

Whinny.

'Where's your man?' he asked as we walked away from the cameras.

'Prior engagement,' I said as I made eye contact with the Winnie's navel.

'Winnie Ralph, this is Ruby Stanhope. Winnie, as I'm sure you know, is a model-cum-actress,' Oscar said. 'And Ruby works for the Prime Minister.'

'Charmed.' She held out her right hand.

Shaking it was impossible, given the limited trajectory of my right arm, so I opted for air kisses instead. Even on tippy-toes I could barely reach her neck and managed to get smacked in the face by the chainmail dangling from her earlobes.

'Who did your make-up?' She stooped to my level. 'Vampire chic is very fashion forward.'

'A Melbourne-based artist by the name of Debs.'

'Can I have her number?'

'I'm sure she'd love that.'

'And that cut! I haven't seen anything like that outside of New York. Who's the artist?'

'Koto San at—'

'Onsen Fugiku! I've always wanted to work with him.'

I turned to Oscar. 'Is there somewhere we can talk privately?' Winnie pouted.

'I like the sound of that. Let's find a quiet corner. There's some things I want to talk to you about as well.'

We walked in.

'Don't you want to check your cape?' asked Oscar as we passed the cloakroom.

'No thanks, I'm a bit chilly.'

'Sure? They've set up the braziers.'

'Never surer.'

The deck groaned under the weight of Oscar's guest-list. Combed-over editor at the *Tasmanian* Blobby Roberts leered at a waitress with a tray of foie gras. The *National*'s new Editor-in-Chief ran opera-length pearls between her fingers like rosaries while pretending to listen to an ambitious backbencher. Lobbyists languished on the outer perimeter, gossip columnists cooed at the epicentre.

'Oscar,' Winnie called, and pulled him into the mass of people.

'Just give me a second, Roo,' he said, holding my gaze. 'Don't move.'

No doubt seething about her network's decision to put Oscar at the helm of its digital flagship, Anastasia Ng, in a jade-silk cheongsam, sipped lime and soda at the bar. Notoriously shortsighted, she made the perfect small-talk companion.

'Anastasia.' I could hold my red wine, but couldn't bring it to my mouth. 'How's your day been?'

'Better than yours.' She puzzled over my bouffant. 'The O'Donoghue speech yesterday seemed to come out of nowhere.'

'That's just Mick,' I said. 'I think we're on the same table at the ball.'

'Terrific. Haven't seen Luke in ages. Is he coming?'

'Um, well, he's very busy—what did you think of the Girls' Club?'

'Interesting,' she said. 'I don't know how long it will last, but I'm keen to enjoy it while it does. Feminism always gets the better of women. We can't help but peck each other to pieces. Speak of the devil. I'm going to get another drink.'

Jack paced towards us in a double-breasted tuxedo, no shirt and silver brogues. Her bob was so sharp it looked like it had been styled by a samurai.

'Ruby, you look hot.'

Is she coming onto you?

'Thanks.'

'No, I meant you're sweating, sweetie.'

'Oh.'

She looked down at the wine glass and clutch in my grip. 'You've got your hands full. Here, I'll help you with your coat.'

'Thank you, but I'd prefer you didn't.'

'You're really burning up.' She undid the cashmere sash on my cape.

'No—'

I sloshed wine on my mitten, trying to stop her. But the cape fell open. The damage was done.

The one-shouldered nude number had been the only dress I could get into, what with my right arm still plastered to my ribcage. Globules of hardened yellow wax squelched out from my right pit. It looked like an old man's ear under a microscope. Sweaty foundation could no longer mask my cherry-red, Hitleresque, hairless mo. My bald forearm had turned purple paisley. The taupe angora mitten, which Debs suggested would be a romantic take on MJ's moonwalk glove, looked even more ridiculous than the sticky hand it hid. Well, not quite.

Ladies whispered behind evening purses. Diary-page busybodies closed in. Jack stood back.

Then Oscar threw his jacket over my shoulders. 'Let's get some air,' he said, leaving Winnie pouting in his wake. We walked back out onto the street, where the photographers were packing up. The moonlight made each gumtree's silver bark shimmer.

'Roo, is everything okay at home?' he asked, staring at my split lip. 'You're not yourself.'

'Yes,' I said, before realising what he was implying. 'No. It was self-inflicted. I was trying to—never mind.'

He pushed the hair away from my face. 'A lot of us care about you. I certainly do.'

'I'm fine—just a little grooming accident.' I wished I could remove his hands from my shoulders. 'I've had a bad week. I turned thirty. And Luke and I broke up. In the reverse order.'

'I'm sorry to hear that.'

A possum shrieked in the trees above us. The sobering smell of eucalyptus reminded me of my purpose. 'You said you wanted to talk to me. I appreciate it. It's been an awful few weeks.'

'Yes.' He looked into my eyes. 'I want to tell you something.'

'You can trust me,' I said. 'I know this is a minefield.'

'It's been a long time.' He ran his fingers through his hair. 'I know things didn't work out so well last time, but I still think about you. I think we'd be good together, Roo.'

Do not compute. Do not compute.

'Say again?'

'Hear me out. I'm glad you've ended things with Harley. He wasn't right for you. I mean, a think tank? You're the strategic communications director to the Prime Minister. I'm about to take on the most important anchor gig in politics. It makes sense; you know that. We're hot together. Did you see the way the cameras went nuts for us tonight?' His hands moved up my arms, skimmed my shoulders, tilted my head towards his, and pulled me into a kiss.

'Oscar!' I spat him out and pushed him away. 'What do you think you're doing?'

'I thought—'

'You thought what?'

'Your mouth was open.'

'That's how I look when I'm dumbfounded. It's not an invitation to snog.'

'But you broke up with Harley.'

'See above.'

He ran his fingers through his hair then restyled it. 'What did you think I was going to tell you?'

'I—'

'Wait. You thought I was going to give away my source!'

'No, I—'

'Call me vain, sure, that's my job. But unethical?'

'You are unethical! You went through my BlackBerry

while I was asleep in your bed!'

'Get off your fucking high horse. You were about to take advantage of my feelings for you to get the down-low on my sources.'

'Feelings? Feeling that we look hot together and that Canberra needs a power couple, you mean?'

'Yes.'

I squirmed free of his jacket and stomped on it when it hit the ground. I stopped a passing cab.

'You just stomped on Zegna!'

I shrugged and slammed the door.

Handfuls of snowflakes glowed gold then pink as my taxi slowed at the traffic lights. They kissed the windscreen, melting on impact. I composed a text to Luke:

Can we talk?

But I didn't send it.

Cyclone Daphne

Having spent most of the night between chatroom and bathroom seeking wax-removal methodologies and applying them, I was not in the mood to be woken with a newspaper in my face. I could still smell peanut butter on my skin.

'Evacuate,' said Debs. 'Cyclone Daphne is about to hit Canberra. I feel it in my lady loins.'

'Go away.' My lids were sealed.

'Your shenanigans have earned us front-page notoriety. Well, front page of the *Busy & Body* section, which is the only part of the Saturday papers your blessed aunt reads before she gets to the sumo Sudoku.'

I opened one eye and waited for my pupil to shrink. Three snapshots were spread across the bottom of the page. Oscar helping Dracula's fuck buddy out of a car.

No, that's you.

Oscar's attempted snog in grainy night-vision.

Is that tongue?

Me, standing beside the US President.

Nothing mellow about that yellow.

Debs pointed at the first photograph. 'Look at me.'

I squinted. 'Your face is obscured by my cape and your bump is the size of a butterfly's penis.'

'That butterfly must be hung like a pterodactyl.'

My heart used my sternum as a trampoline. Humiliation curdled with panic in the back of my throat. 'I can't read it,' I said, pulling the covers over my head.

'Allow me.' Debs shook the crease from the papers and cleared her throat.

THE ELEVENTH HOUR

Life & Style was ready to go to press with a story about last night's *24/11* launch party when a series of game-changing shots were filed.

The network's anchor, fox-trotter and *Sunday Roast* host, Oscar Franklin, arrived with enviable arm candy in the form of Winifred Ralph, only to be photographed minutes later canoodling, then quarrelling with, questionably attired prime ministerial advisor Ruby Stanhope.

Stanhope, thirty, shares a Canberra residence with the PM's former Chief of Staff, Luke Harley, CEO of Liberty Australia.

The Capital couple, seen together a fortnight ago at an opera fundraiser for his foundation, have been an item since the last election.

Franklin's blog has published several government leaks in as many weeks, sparking panic within government ranks about the identity of the source.

Debs' phone rang. 'Poop! It's her.'

'Take it,' I said. 'She's probably just checking up on you.'

'Darling, how are... I miss you too... yes, sorry, I meant to call back but I was doing my pelvic floor stretches...'

She left me to self-soothe.

The text to Luke floated in the purgatory of my drafts folder. Can. We. Talk. Three of the simplest words in the English language, banded together to form a message of hope.

But this morning they would have meant something else: desperation. He would have seen the pictures; he would think the worst.

I stared at my phone, willing it to ring, for the wonky-eyed photograph that I'd assigned to his number to pop up. His silence stung like chilli in a paper cut. Clearly, he didn't care, what with his hot pots and fresh berries.

It's over.

My phone beeped. It wasn't him.

Want to grab dinner tonight? Elliot

Yes—

Back-space.

Sure.

Send.

Buzz.

8? I'll pick you up.

Then it rang. Chief.

'It's not as bad as you think,' I said.

'How so?'

'It's in *Busy & Body*, Chief. It'll go away.'

'What is?'

'Ah, what were you ringing about?'

'The poll.'

'What poll?'

'Check your email much? We've been sent the results of tomorrow's Southpoll. We're down three points in the two-party preferred.'

'As in, three *more* points?'

'Correct. If Australia went to the ballot box tomorrow, Adelina Pepper would become PM.'

I used my fingers to count. 'With fifty-nine per cent of the vote?'

'Yep. But wait for the steak knives. They've tested Max against alternative leaders.'

'Like Bartlet and Dumbledore?'

'No, real alternatives, like Cecil Berth. He got thirty points to Max's thirty-eight.'

'Get out. Why?'

'Pollsters don't ask helpful questions like that, but the fact that they're testing it at all is not good.'

'But Cecil's a former investment banker. I'm the only affable former investment banker I know. Also, his name is Cecil. Campaign slogan: Special Cecil—your friendly neighbourhood investment banker. Perhaps we should release that photograph of Cecil beating the toddler at snakes and ladders.'

'Not helpful, Roo.'

'Have you told Max?'

'I thought maybe you could.'

'Me?'

'Aren't you going around to The Lodge for the *Woman's Life* covershot?'

I checked my hand. 'Oh, yeah.'

'By the way, how was last night? Did Oscar give you any info about the leaks?'

'Um—no.'

She sighed. 'It was a long shot. What were you saying about *Busy & Body*?' I heard the rustle of newspapers at the other end of the line.

'A teeny-tiny tidbit at the bottom of the page—'

'Fuck me.'

'As I mentioned, it's not as bad as it looks.'

'That's good,' she said, 'because it looks fucking atrocious. Why are you in drag?'

'I was trying to get information out of him about the leaks.'

'Was the information written in braille on his tonsils?'

'It was one-way tongue. Total misunderstanding.'

'This office has enough to deal with at the moment without staffers being the scandal, Roo.'

'You can talk! Sorry. That was out of line.'

'Forget it.'

'Everyone will think I'm the source, won't they?'

She was silent.

'Chief?'

'I'm nodding.'

'What should I do?'

'I'm thinking.' She stopped. 'Luke must be ropeable. He hates that guy.'

'We broke up.'

'Shit.' There was a long pause. 'I'm sure it's salvagable, Roo. Did you explain what happened?'

'It's not because of this. It happened the night before I left for New York.'

'That was a week ago. Why didn't you tell me?

'You have a lot on your plate.'

'You need to take some leave, Roo.'

'No, thanks. Navel-gazing just makes you realise how fat you are. Anyway, you can't afford to be a woman down at the moment.'

The doorbell rang. Debs burst into my room wheeling an overstuffed suitcase. 'Should've listened to my lady loins,' she said, zipping manically.

'Speak later, Chief.' I fastened my robe. 'What are you doing?'

'Get rid of them,' she said, stepping into my walk-in robe.

'Who?'

'Shhhh!' She shut the door.

Ding-dong.

I went to the front door, JFK and Widdles scrambling behind me, and peered through the peephole.

My aunt's kind, blinking, grey-blue eye grew larger as she attempted to defy the one-way lens. I ducked.

She had discovered Debs' whereabouts and I was complicit. There was nothing to do but wait for Karma's bitch-slap. I closed my eyes, braced and opened the door.

'Surprise!'

The dogs panted.

I opened one eye. Behind Daphne's billowing, bejewelled kaftan stood Fran and Clem, their faces full of joy.

Fran's hair was longer and a few shades lighter than her Burberry trench, and far less structured. Clem, however, was completely different. There were fewer teeth to her smile. Gone were the ribbed tights and gumboots—she wore a red T-shirt, blue jeans and canvas sneakers.

'Clem! Fran! Daphne! How, erm, splendid!'

Where 'splendid' equals 'mind-fucked' to the power of ten.

'Happy birthday, Aunty Wooby!' A much taller Clem wrapped her arms around my stomach, staring up at me—the last time I'd seen her she'd just made it to my hips, and my hair had made it to my shoulders.

I kissed the gap between her two plaits. Fran and Daphne joined the embrace.

'She didn't know, Mummy,' said Clem, pushing past me. 'I told you I didn't give it away.'

'When did you get here?' I asked, taking a suitcase.

'We surprised Aunt Daphne in Melbourne yesterday,' said Fran. 'That's where I was calling from.'

'It was Luke's idea,' said Daphne, and I knew I was forgiven.

'Really?' I couldn't help the smile.

Fran and Daphne exchanged worried looks.

'He booked it months ago,' Fran rushed in, 'and didn't—change anything.'

'Oh.'

'We went in first class!' said Clem. 'They gave us lip balm and ginger beer and moustachioed nuts!'

'Pistachios, sweetheart,' said Fran. 'What in God's name have you done to your arm? I'm not asking about your hair.'

I looked down at the purple scar and raised rash. 'Allergies.'

'To what?'

'Questions. Where's Debs?'

'Debs is in Perth, poor thing,' said Daph. 'I only just got through to her. She sounded very upset to have missed out. I must call her back, actually. We were cut off.'

'They're two hours behind in the West,' I said, spying Debs' phone on the hallstand. 'Why don't we call later?'

'Of course,' she said. 'No wonder she sounded so bamboozled. I probably woke her.'

'We wanted to be here when you got back from New York but Lu—um—the consensus was you'd be busy at work, so we decided the weekend would be best.'

'We're going to cook you a birthday dinner,' said Daphne.

'That's very sweet, but I'm afraid you've caught me off-guard. The place is a disgrace. Why don't I put the kettle on?'

'I'll do that,' Daphne said, putting the empty Cheezels packet in the bin. 'We're here to help.'

'Yes, we are,' said Clem, playing chopsticks on the piano.

'You won't even know we're here,' said Fran.

'Listen,' I said. 'It's a glorious day. I have to go to The Lodge to supervise a photo shoot, but I could see if we could all go. How does that sound?'

'Lovely,' said Fran, brushing her hair with her fingers.

'I'll get changed and then we'll have a cup of tea and go,' I said. 'Wait here. Don't move a muscle.'

I slammed the bedroom door and opened my wardrobe to find Debs cowering under a cream pashmina.

'Have they gone?' she whispered urgently.

'No, they haven't bloody gone. Why didn't you tell me?'

'You were on the phone and I was trying to pack.'

'So? You could've said, "Excuse me, Ruby, your fucking family is at the door and given I'm not supposed to be here, perhaps you and I could conduct a quick planning session before you let them in."'

'You should have listened to my lady loins.'

'If you weren't carrying my infant cousin right now I'd

kick you in the lady loins,' I said, squeezing into my jeans.

'Calm down.'

'I cannot calm down because I've just promised I'll take them all to the Prime Minister's house. Fuck knows how I'm going to pull that off, but it was the only thing I could think of. Hand me that jacket.'

She obliged.

'Meanwhile, *you* are going to pack all of your belongings. Everything. Think of this as a crime scene—a single pube could get us both convicted.'

'Not likely—just had a Brazilian.'

'Overshare. Pashmina.'

She handed me the scarf. 'Wowsers, that waxing injury isn't waning at all, is it?'

I put the jacket on. 'Then you will go to the airport and get on the next plane to Melbourne and call Daphne. Tell her you came home early to surprise her. And we will never speak of this again. Clear?'

'Yes'm.'

'Ruby?' said Daphne from the other side of my bedroom door.

Panic contorted Debs' face. She whipped the scarf off my neck and leapt back into the closet.

'Can I come in?' Daphne.

Debs shook her head so hard I thought it might snap off its axis.

'Erm—I'll be out in a second.'

'I was hoping to have a moment alone.'

'Hold on, I'm dressing.'

'It's too risky,' Debs breathed from the closet.

I closed the door on her. 'Come in!'

Daphne came in with JFK in tow. He was beating his

white tail happily against her black leggings.

'This is a beautiful room,' she said, handing me a cup of tea.

'Thanks. We—I—love it.'

She cocked her head to one side and twirled the blister pearl in her ear. 'I wanted to talk about our phone call the other day.'

'I'm sorry, Aunt Daphne.'

'No, I'm sorry.'

'Unnecessary but wonderful. We're both sorry. Sorted. Shall we go?'

'I'm not finished,' she said, dusting the dog hair from my window seat. 'I've been anxious about Debs. She has the emotional intelligence of a dung beetle.'

'I know.'

There was a thud from the cupboard.

JFK's head jerked towards it. Daphne turned.

'Ow!' I clutched my foot. 'I stubbed my toe on the bed.'

'Shall I get ice?'

'No, it's fine. I mean, yes, probably a good idea.'

'Can I tell you something first?'

I checked my watch. 4.27 a.m. Shit.

'It'll only take a second.'

She clutched my hands as I sat beside her on the bed. 'We're having a boy, Ruby,' she said, her eyes glistening. 'We had the ultrasound lady write it down and put it in an envelope.' She sniffed. 'We weren't sure if we wanted to know or not and then, with Debs away, I just couldn't wait. I hope she won't be too angry with me. A baby boy. Isn't that the most magnificent thing you ever heard?' Tears filled her smile lines.

I hugged her tight. 'The most,' I said, inhaling the fresh

bread smell that lingers in every baker's pores. 'The most, Aunt Daphne.'

JFK sniffed the gap between my wardrobe door and carpet.

'I know I'm overbearing. I hope she knows I'd give my right arm to be the oven carrying our bun.'

'Debs can be an arsehole,' I said.

'I know, but she's my arsehole.' She wiped her eyes. 'Anyway, it feels good to tell you. I've been bursting for weeks.'

I blotted her cheeks with my sleeves. 'Champagne tonight.' JFK barked and head-butted the closet as I ushered my aunt out the door. 'Can you grab two bottles from the cellar and put them in the fridge? I'll just be a second.'

'Ruby, darling? Aunt Daphne?'

Fran. Crap. 'I'll be out in a minute.'

'Can I come in? What are you two whispering about?'

I opened the door. JFK whimpered at the closet.

'Poor darling,' said Fran. 'He must be missing Luke.'

'Fran, I don't think Ruby wants to talk about it,' said Daphne.

'Well, let's not be coy about this. Their split is likely to have an impact on the dogs.' More barking.

'What's happening, Aunty Wooby?' asked Clem, from the hallway.

'I, erm—I need to ask Mummy something.'

'What's wrong with JFK?' *Why is he barking like that? Ruby!*

'Um, perhaps he can smell one of Luke's ties.' I leaned against the closet, patting JFK with my foot. 'Um, Fran.' I held her hands. 'Will you be my date for the Midwinter

Ball? It's a masquerade next Tuesday at Parliament House and I couldn't bear going alone.'

'Of course.'

'Wonderful.' I ushered them all to the door and out of it. 'I'll just be a second.'

'Is masquerade like Gatorade?' Clem asked as they walked back into the kitchen.

'No, darling. It's a ball you wear masks to.'

'You can come out of the closet now,' I whispered, opening it.

Debs sat cross-legged on top of her suitcase, fingers interlocked over her bump. 'A baby bloke.' She bit her bottom lip. 'Kind of cool.'

'The coolest.' I offered my hand to help her up. 'Have a safe flight, Debs.'

'Ta, kiddo.'

Orange makes a hash of things

'Name?'

'Ruby Stanhope.' I flashed my staff pass. 'They're expecting us.'

He ticked me off his clipboard. 'And your passengers?'

'I'm Ruby's aunt, Daphne Partridge. Lovely to meet you, officer.'

'Who's in the back?'

'Francesca Stanhope, barrister-at-law, and this is my daughter—'

'Clementine Genevieve Gardner-Stanhope,' said Clem in a big voice. 'Londoner.'

'I'm going to need to see some ID.'

Fran flipped her passport. 'I haven't been carded since my twenties.'

Two ticks later, the black bollards sank into the ground, the gates opened and we crunched over the rose-lined gravel drive.

As we rounded the corner, Daphne's eyes widened, just as mine had the first time I saw that bed of low-lying lavender sloping downhill onto a huge, sprawling lawn. I drove around Abigail's bike, its wheel still spinning, near topiary cumquats at the portico entrance to the old cream home. We parked and made our way to the back door.

Fergus greeted us in chef whites and a striped apron, his head balder than Debs' privates. He owed me a favour after an incident involving suckling pig and a vegetarian ambassador.

'Ruby, my love! I saw the papers. Are you okay?'

'Extremely okay,' I cut in. 'The okayest person in Canberra.'

Fran studied me. 'What's in the paper, Ruby?'

'The usual anti-government faff,' I said. 'You know, politics. Fergus, I'd like you to meet Daphne, my aunt, Fran, my sister, and my niece, Clementine.'

'Welcome to The Lodge,' he said, shaking their hands. 'You're Daphne of *Daphne's Dough* in St Kilda. I can't tell you how much I admire the consistency of your brioche.'

Daphne smiled. 'Keep your flour in the freezer.'

'Genius.' He led them away. 'Ruby says you're a green thumb, Daphne. Shall we leave her to do her thing while I show you what we're doing with the veggie garden?'

'I'd love that.'

'Thanks Fergus,' I called out.

'My pleasure,' he said. 'The PM's in his study. He's expecting you. And there's a young lass waiting in the staffroom.'

'Who?'

'I don't know. I think she might be a children's television presenter.'

Orange. That was the first word that popped into my head when I saw Bettina in the otherwise-subdued staff-room, decked out in bike shorts, a tank top and a cap, each so bright they'd make a vat of Fanta cringe.

She read my expression. 'I was halfway through a relay for the blind when you called, so I left the race and ran straight here.'

'If I had known you were in a race...'

'Fun run or Lodge?' She used her hands as imaginary scales. 'Fun run or Lodge? Lodge wins, hands down!'

'Great. Listen, we have to do a cover shoot for *Australian Woman's Life* with the PM, Shelly and their daughter, Abigail.'

'Get. Out.'

'And the photographer will be here any minute with her make-up artist and stylist. I need you to greet them, make them feel welcome and show them in to the morning room to set up. The staff here will help. I have to brief the PM on an opinion poll.'

'Roger that. PS: I had a word with Mike.'

'And?'

'He said there was another one which arrived yesterday, postmarked about six months ago from a sorting centre in Queanbeyan.'

'And?'

'He rang his Queanbeyan contact, who said if it had gone missing between the point of postmark and the point of delivery, it would have been recorded.'

'So?'

'So the postmark given to that stamp was not given to

that envelope. In other words, the stamp has been re-used.'

'Well, that doesn't help us.'

'Does so.'

'How?'

'Because if all the other envelopes carry an outdated postmark from Queanbeyan, they've all been sent by someone who regularly receives or has access to mail which has been sorted by the Queanbeyan centre.'

'Great. So we're looking for a Canberra resident.'

'We're looking for someone with regular access to Mike's mailroom—because if they haven't ended up there via post, they've ended up there by personal delivery.'

'So it's someone inside the building?'

'Yes, or with frequent access to it.'

'Bettina, do you know how many people live in Canberra?'

'About three hundred and forty thousand in non-sitting weeks.'

'And how many of those are public servants?'

'Zillions.'

'And how many of the zillions have access to the internal post system, not to mention those who can and do visit Parliament House?'

'A quarter of a zillion. But still, we've narrowed it down a bit.'

'True. We've narrowed it down to a quarter of a zillion.'

'Whatevs. The only two Canberrans I'm interested in are you and the dream fox.'

'Huh?'

'Oscar Franklin? The pash?'

'It wasn't a pash.'

'Does that mean you and Luke are over?'

'We broke up last week.'

'Well, no wonder you've been wearing your cranky pants. OMG, the rusty key. I'm so sorry, Roo. I thought it was the key to his heart. Why didn't you tell me?'

'Because it's none of your business.'

'So are you and the dream fox—'

'No.'

'Roger *that*.' She winked.

I stomped down the long, grey-linoleum kitchen and charged through the swinging doors into the dining room, or at least would have if the doors hadn't smashed into something and rebounded into my face with two ugly crunches and a thud.

There was a distinctly male 'bugger' on the other side of the door.

'Are you all right?'

'No.'

My nose un-concertinaed. 'On three I will open the door,' I shouted. 'Stand clear. One, two, three—cock!'

There, on the floor, was the bloody Prime Minister, his head between his legs, crimsoning the carpet.

'Ruby,' he said.

My head muttered incoherent scraps from the decade-old first aid course collecting dust in the corner of my memory.

Elevate. You can't elevate a nose. 'Prime Minister, *please put your nose up on this miniature ottoman.' Apply pressure. Surely blunt trauma to the face was pressure enough? Check your blind spot. Wrong course.*

'Ice,' said Max, with more than the usual Australian twang. 'I need ice.'

'Capital idea.' I shot back into the kitchen and dug my

229

hands into the icemaker. 'Hold tight,' I yelled, the cubes sticking to my fingers.

Solid work, Edward Freezerhands.

I backed through the doors, dropped to my knees beside him and laid my frostbitten fingers on his face.

Builder's crack, observed the eyes in the back of my head.

'Sorry, PM.'

'Ruby, you're dropping ice in my lap.'

'Bother.'

Bettina sprang through the doors like tangerine lightning. 'OMFG!' She sprang out again.

'What was that?'

'Bettina.'

'Why is she orange?'

'Fun run to help blind people.'

'Well, it worked.'

'Shield your eyes. She's coming back.'

'Stand clear,' said Bettina, brandishing an icepack, gloves and cloth. 'What happened?'

'I opened the door into his face.'

'Did you hear a snap, Prime Minister?'

'No.'

'Do you feel sick or dizzy?'

'No. No.'

She got within an inch of his grill. 'It doesn't look any different to how it looks on TV—it's not crooked and I can't see any bruising yet. Sir, you're in safe hands.' Bettina snapped on the rubber gloves. 'I volunteered with Médecins Sans Frontières.'

He twitched as she applied pressure. 'MSF does incredible work,' he said, nasally. 'Where were you based, Bettina?'

'Darfur—just the legal team. OMG, can I tweet that you know my name?'

'No,' I said.

'Hey, that reminds me, you're a hash-tag, Roo.'

Mayday, mayday.

Max grinned through the pain. 'What's she done now?'

'After the photo of Roo and the dream fox in the papers this morning, someone was like, "is that tongue?" and everyone agreed it was, so then the debate became #whosetongueisitanyway? It's trending at number seven nationally.'

There's something wrong with the ejection seat.

'A dream fox? Luke will be thrilled,' said Max, holding the icepack to his face.

'It wasn't Luke. It—'

'Bettina, thanks for your help, but I think the photographer's here.'

'My bad,' she said, dejected. 'Just keep the ice on your nose, PM. I'll leave you two to discuss the poll.'

'Poll?'

I nodded. 'It's out tomorrow.'

'C'mon,' he said, his knees creaking as he got to his feet.

I followed Max into the study, a corner room lined with bookshelves, opening out onto the wisteria-covered courtyard. Apricot roses in a green glass jar propped up an unframed photograph of Shelly and Abigail feeding the ducks at Lake Burley Griffin. The dwindling fire crackled and popped.

He kicked off his flip-flops and sat on the sofa beside it. 'What poll?'

'It's not great,' I said, sitting opposite him. 'They're fifty-nine.'

'To our forty-one?'

'Yes.'

'That's the worst shit sandwich I've ever tasted. Is it the worst in history?'

'Well—'

'Oh God. It is.'

'And—' I hesitated.

'I can take it.'

'They tested you against alternative leaders.'

'Who?'

'Cecil and three others.'

'I think I preferred the smack in the face.'

'Support for him was negligible—thirty points.'

'And me?'

'Thirty-eight. The picture of health.'

'Ouch.'

'It's not ideal to be compared to others, no, but you are the standout candidate.'

'No shit. Has Cecil said anything?'

'I spoke to Jack on the way here. The Treasurer won't be commenting.'

'What should I do?'

This must be the advisory part of being an advisor.

'I think you should just keep doing your job. We've had an unlucky couple of weeks—with the leak and—'

Blackmail.

'—other stuff. Stay positive. You're on *Sunday Roast* tomorrow night. People will see you and they'll remember who they voted for.'

'You think they've forgotten who they voted for.'

Dig up.

'That's not what I meant.'

'Sometimes I don't know why I do this, Roo.' He scrunched a few sheets of newspaper and added them to the flames. 'I seem to spend more time trying to convince everyone I'm the guy for the job than I spend *doing* it.

'Every second of every day is a performance review. A guy quips something clever on Twitter about my nasal hair, it gets retweeted five hundred times and I have to be briefed just in case I'm asked about it at a press conference.

'Then I have to be seen to laugh off the attack on my nasal hair like it's not personal. "No worries, Australia," I'm supposed to say. "Feel free to make fun of my untidy tanglies—that's what I'm here for." If I trim it, I'm too sensitive to criticism. If I let it grow, I'm defiant. If I appear ever so slightly offended to wake up to up-nostril shots on breakfast television, let alone complain about them, I'm hot-tempered. "It's part and parcel of public life," they say.' He flipped the icepack. 'My daughter says I'm an embarrassment because a) I'm her dad, b) I'm on TV and c) I have no idea who Saxon Gist is.'

'Vibe.'

'Whatever. And my wife—' He sighed. 'Let's just say it's tough on relationships.'

'I know, PM.'

'I make about a twentieth of what the average mining CEO makes and I'm meant to apologise for it. You probably out-earned me as an investment banker and I bet nobody picked on your nose.'

'I did,' I said. 'But I've been up-nostrilled too. Once I tried to fix a broken camera mid-video-conference and broadcast a close-up of parsley stuck between my teeth to the Toyota board, but I suppose that was more unintentional self-portraiture.'

He smiled. 'How's the bruising?'

'Minimal puffiness. Nothing the make-up artist can't fix.'

Later, a made-up Max put his arm around a made-up Shelly in their rearranged living room under searing studio lights.

The make-up artist taped down Max's disobedient collar and powdered his sweaty brow.

'Lobal warming,' he said.

'Very punny,' said Shelly.

'Prime Minister,' said the photographer, 'now just touch Shelly's right cheek with your left hand, and relax. No, relax with your hand on her cheek, and look into her— yes! Very natural. Right there—yes! Yes! Yes!'

'Happy to be of service,' said Shelly, through gritted teeth.

Bettina, who had changed into magenta spray-on jeans, beckoned me outside.

'Roo, it was unprofessional of me to raise that in front of the PM. I'm sorry.' She handed me a bottle of water and a sandwich. 'But I set up Google alerts so you can keep an eye on the hash-tag.'

'Thanks. I think,' I said, crumbs cascading down my chest. 'What did I miss?'

'Your aunt, sister and niece have gone to Fyshwick markets with Fergus to pick up groceries for dinner.'

'Anything else?'

'Are you on Facebook?'

'No. I'd better get back in there, Bettina. They're about to start the interview.'

'Um, it's just that—'

'Can it wait?'

234

She hesitated.

'Hold that thought,' I said, chewing the crusts. 'I'll be back. Thanks for the sandwich.'

The photographer was packing up when I went back in. He showed me a gorgeous shot of Max looking into Shelly's adoring eyes.

'I'd buy that magazine,' I said, taking a seat beside the first couple on the interview couch. I tested my dictaphone.

'Sorry I'm late,' said a small lady, hurrying into the room. 'Jocelyn Drew,' she said, shaking our hands.

'Great to put a face to the name, Jocelyn,' I said. 'Let me introduce you to Max and Shelly Masters.'

'It's an honour,' she said.

Max and Shelly smiled and shook her hand.

'Now,' she said, 'I'm a bit nervous, but I think we've got some good questions.'

'Looking forward to it,' said Max.

I pressed record.

'I was disappointed to hear your daughter was unable to join us,' she said.

'Me too,' said Max. 'Abba has an assignment due on Monday. Grade 10. Would you want to go back there?'

'I wouldn't,' said Shelly.

'Nor would I,' said Jocelyn. 'But Abigail's Facebook status says—let me find it.' She pulled out her phone. 'Quote, "Got out of stupid photo shoot with parentals. Thank fuck. Do I look like Marcia Brady to you?"'

Shelly's face fell.

Max blinked. Twice. 'As I said, grade 10. Who would want to go back there?'

'She seems to have a very active social life. Lots of parties, sometimes with friends of drinking age. As parents of a child in the spotlight, how do you police that?'

'What were you doing on my daughter's Facebook page?' There was a distinct tremor in Shelly's voice.

'She accepted me as a friend,' said Jocelyn.

'Really? She accepted Jocelyn Drew, journalist, as a friend?'

'I'm Jozzy Drew on Facebook, but yes.'

'Is your profession listed?'

'No.' Jocelyn looked her straight in the face.

'It's okay, Shell,' said Max.

'No, it's not okay, Max. Do you have children, Jozzy?'

'No.'

'That's probably a very good thing.' She stood up. 'Excuse me.'

'Shell,' said Max.

She shot him a scathing look as she left.

'I might be able to negotiate a bilateral,' he said, 'but parenting a teenager takes real talent.'

The interview went for an hour and didn't get any better.

'I'm so sorry, PM,' I said when she'd left. 'I had no idea.'

'That was shit, Roo,' he said, climbing the stairs. 'We were totally blindsided in there. Tell Di to call me when she can.'

I stormed into the staffroom where Bettina was drinking coffee. 'How did it go?' she asked, pouring me one.

I tried to contain the explosion within.

'Roo?'

'Did you know about Abigail's Facebook status update? Yes or no?'

'Yes, but—'

'And you didn't tell me?'

'I tried to.'

'I was caught off-guard. So were the Prime Minister and his wife. Now we have to go into damage control. Don't let it happen again.'

Her face flushed dark pink. 'Roger that.'

Lumpy gravy

'Hooray! Aunty Wooby's home.'

Clem was wearing my saffron scarf as a turban. It was so huge it engulfed her eyes. She leaped on me as I walked through the door. It was a strangulating but welcome hug after the long afternoon on the phone with magazine editors, making deals to get Abigail out of the shit.

'That tickles!' She shrieked as I strummed her stomach in time with Van Morrison's *Brown Eyed Girl*. 'Put me down!'

Her skinny legs clung to my waist as we walked through to the kitchen, where a big blue and white vase of irises graced the bench.

'You're very late, you know, Aunty Wooby.'

'I know, I'm sorry. I had to go to the office.'

'Why?'

'I had to fix something.'

'What?'

'A young girl said something silly on Facebook.'

'Was it a lie?'

'No.'

'What was it?'

'Unhelpful.'

'Mummy won't let me go on Facebook. She says only big girls are allowed to ruin their reputations.'

'Your mummy's a sensible lady,' I said, putting her down. 'It smells delicious in here. What have you lot been up to?'

'We went to the market and then we came home and I shelled the peas.'

'I hate shelling peas,' I said, peeling the aluminium foil off the roast potatoes to steal one.

'Me too—they're so green.' Clem stole a potato too. 'Then Daphne made Yorkshire puds and birthday cake— oops, I'm not supposed to tell you that. Then Mummy made roast beef and Elliot made gravy.'

'Who?'

'Don't talk with your mouth full.'

I swallowed half a potato whole. 'Who made the gravy?' I coughed.

'Elliot.'

'What do you mean "Elliot"?'

Her turban slipped when I lifted her onto the bench. 'Elliot came to pick you up but I said you weren't here and Aunt Daphne said we were having a birthday dinner and he looked sad and Aunt Daphne said he was welcome to join us and he said he didn't want to propose and Mummy said he wouldn't be proposing.'

Elliot?

I looked at my watch. 4.27 a.m. 'Shit!'

'Mummy!' Clem slid off the bench and skipped into the living room. 'She said "shit"!'

'Who did, darling?'

'Aunty Wooby.'

I peered into the living room to find Elliot sitting on my couch eating cheese with my aunt.

'Language, Ruby!' said Fran, weaving into the kitchen with a half-empty champagne flute. She breathed into my ear. 'Dishhhhy, very dishy.'

'Fran, you're off your tits,' I whispered.

'I am not.'

'Yes, you are.'

'No, you're not.'

'What?'

'Shut up. *I'm* trying to interrogate *you*.'

'Keep your voice down,' I said.

'Ruby,' she slurred, 'your partner of two years proposed to you less than a week ago.'

'No, it was'—I counted my fingers—'eight days ago.'

'Okay, so your partner of two years proposed to you eight days ago. You turned him down. He left and now there's a very fine-looking man in your living room ready to take you to dinner.'

'It's dinner. People eat.'

'Are you or are you not shagging him?' She slapped her hand on the bench. 'Answer the question!'

'He's my vet.'

'In my lifetime, I've had three guinea pigs, two rabbits and a parakeet—all of whom sadly passed—and not once met a hot vet, let alone had one bring me flowers.'

'Flowers?'

She stroked the underside of an iris. 'Aren't they

spectacular? He says they're from his horse stud in a faraway place called Yass.' She giggled.

'What?'

'Stud.' Gigglier still. 'My point is, he picked you flowers. Men don't pick flowers—they buy them.'

'You're reading too much into this.'

'I am not. I'm your sister. We shared a flat, remember? You have that look on your face.'

'What look?'

'The "today is for doing, tomorrow is for thinking" look.'

'That's absurd. You're trollied and I'm not listening to another word until you've eaten some carbs.' I shoved a potato in her mouth.

'Am I interrupting something?' said Elliot. He greeted me then leaned against the doorframe in jeans and a crew-neck black wool jumper. The Widdler licked his hand. Lucky dog.

'No,' I said, wobbly-kneed from a single kiss on the cheek. 'Listen, I'm terribly sorry about all this. Could I borrow you for just a quick second?'

Fran smirked and topped up her champagne, as I grabbed Elliot's hand, dragged him into the laundry and shut the door.

The laundry was not a room I used with any regularity, so I hadn't a clue where the light was. I fumbled for the switch, sending a peg basket clattering to the tiled floor.

He laughed. 'Are all the women in your family charming and nuts?'

'Yes,' I said. 'Shit. I can't find the light.'

'I find it helpful to turn a light on before I enter a dark room and shut the door.'

'I don't know where it is.' I snatched a pair of knickers off the clotheshorse and shoved them in my back pocket. 'Thank you for the flowers.'

'You're welcome. You don't know where your laundry light is?'

'No, I only use it during the day.' A broken nail snagged on my jumper as I brushed past him. 'I'm caught.'

He unhooked it.

'You didn't mention anything about Debs, did you?'

'No, but I almost did.'

'Thank God. Daphne doesn't know she was here.'

'I gathered that.'

'I'm so sorry for the mix-up. With my family arriving I confused the timing of our, ah, our...'

'Date.'

I found the switch. In the light, I could see the certainty in his face matched his tone.

'Well, maybe...meeting or rendezvous? Rendezvous is wrong. Too—something. Appointment? Yes, appointment.'

'I don't mind what you want to call it,' he said, unfazed. 'I just wanted to grab dinner because I think you're cool. Dinner appointment. Dinner date. Dinner rendezvous. Or just dinner. Whatever.'

'Excellent.' I punched his arm.

'Ow,' he said, rubbing it. 'What was that?'

'A convivial slap?'

'Ruby, if you don't want me to be here, I can—'

'No, it's not that.'

Look at those lashes, said my body. *And aren't they the most kissable earlobes you ever did see?*

'I get it,' he said. 'You just came out of a relationship.

You're not ready for anything else. I'm not putting the moves on.'

'Oh.'

Sigh.

He laughed. 'Now you look disappointed.'

'Just a bit.'

'How about this: I would like to put the moves on—'

Yay!

'—but I won't until you let me know it's time.'

All systems go.

'Right. Is there a special put-the-moves-on sign for that?'

'Signs can be cumbersome. How about a password?'

There was a knock at the door. 'The gravy's getting lumpy, Aunty Wooby!'

'That works,' said Elliot.

'Lumpy gravy it is.'

'Um'—he opened the door—'your grundies are in your pocket.'

'Right. Yes.' I scrunched them into a ball, threw them over my shoulder and turned out the light.

Later, with sated bellies, we sat around the fire trying to make room for cake. Elliot played snap with Clem and Fran on the floor. The Widdler saw this as an opportunity to show off his ability to shake hands. Daphne dog-eared pages of *Gourmet Traveller*. I sat behind Fran, braiding her hair while we debated the key ingredient of a mint julep.

'Fran, it's vodka,' I said.

'Rum.'

'Vodka.'

'It's white rum, Ruby.' Fran yawned.

'How could it be rum? Then it'd be a mojito.'

'You're both wrong,' said Daphne. 'It's bourbon.'

'Bourbon makes me sick,' said Fran.

'Snap,' said Elliot.

'Hey,' said Clem, 'that was a three and a queen!'

'I meant, "Snap, bourbon makes me sick too." Can't stand the smell of it.'

'Me neither.' Fran lowered her head, making me lose my grip on several pivotal strands.

'Mummy and Elliot, you're not paying attent—SNAP!' Ding-dong.

JFK's ears pricked up. He raced his brother to the door.

'Are you expecting anyone?' Daphne closed her magazine.

4.27 a.m. Shit. 'What time is it?'

'After ten.'

I abandoned Fran's braid and went to the door.

On the other side of the peephole stood the Chief, looking dishevelled.

I opened the door. 'Need cake?'

'Like you wouldn't believe.' She followed me through to the living room.

'Chief, I think you've met my aunt Daphne, my sister Fran and my niece—'

'Clementine Genevieve Gardner-Stanhope, how could I forget.'

'This is Elliot. Elliot, meet Di, my boss.'

'Pleasure,' he said, standing to shake her hand.

'She needs cake,' I said.

'Here's one I prepared earlier,' said Daphne. She lifted the dome off a duck-egg-blue cake stand to reveal a layered Victoria sponge filled with strawberries, jam and cream.

'Oh my,' said Chief.

I couldn't tell whether she was salivating over Victoria or Elliot.

'Chief and I will make tea,' I said, leading her into the kitchen.

'So what's up?' I asked, rinsing the kettle.

'I got another one this afternoon.'

I flicked the tap off. 'What this time?'

'Same format, but with a quote.' She took the milk out of the fridge. 'It says, "Saw him in the corridors today. Bit awkward."'

'What's that?'

'I've been over and over it in my mind. I think it's an email from me to my sister. I rang her today and she can't be sure either. It sounds like me, doesn't it?'

I nodded.

She swallowed. 'Roo, I can't sleep.'

'Sleepless in Canberra doesn't have quite the same ring to it.'

'What a shit week,' she said. 'Crap polls, leaks, threats, Abigail on Facebook and then *Sunday Roast* tomorrow night.'

'Cake, ladies,' yelled Elliot.

'Tea's almost done,' I called back. 'We won't be a second.'

'*Who* is *he*?' whispered Di.

'Elliot.'

'Where did he come from? I didn't know they made men like that anymore.'

'He's my vet.' I spooned tea-leaves into the pot. 'What?'

'Nothing,' she said, looking a bit sad. 'It's none of my business.'

'Go on, say it.'

'Don't give up on Luke,' she said, filling the creamer.

'Not you too. He's the one who gave up. He hasn't even called.'

'Have you called him?'

'I know you're his friend, but he hasn't been himself for a long time.'

'Nor have you, Roo. This kind of work is tough on relationships. Anyway, I'm here for both of you. All I'm saying is, try not to bury yourself in work. You might end up like...'

'Jack?'

She nodded.

'Plenty of men make the choices she's made and it doesn't make them any less of a man.'

'I've known her a long time, Roo. She used to be my boss.'

'Aunty Wooby,' said Clem, hands on hips. 'Hurry up!'

'Coming! Your boss?'

Chief took the tea tray. 'When she was Connie Fife's Chief of Staff.'

'You worked for Connie Fife? *She* worked for Connie Fife?'

'Years ago. When I was just starting out.'

The living room was dark but for the candle-lit cake and crackling fire. It was a gutsy if discordant rendition of *Happy Birthday* backed up by canine doo-wops.

Clem's excited eyes sparkled in anticipation, Elliot's skin glowed amber in the candlelight, Fran filmed it with her camera phone.

'Make a wish, Aunty Wooby!'

'May I make two?'

'Yes, but you mustn't tell us or they won't come true.'

I wished for more nights like this; for weeks less like this.

Whoosh.

Hip hip hooray.

'The lights won't come back on.'

'Must have blown a fuse.'

'Nope, they're all out.'

'The rest of the street is fine.'

'Have you paid your power bill?'

Shit.

Sunday Roast

I woke up to the Southpoll figures all over the Sunday papers. They were uniformly foul.

RE-BERTH? said one. *PEPPER RUBS SALT IN PM'S WOUNDS*, said another.

But it was *The Gallery*, a weekly panel chat show, that really got my hackles up.

'We have some footage of Cecil Berth on his morning jog.'

They cut to footage of Cecil, in a PM's XII Cricket Team T-shirt, running in the shadow of the bridge at Milson's Point.

'Morning, fellas,' he says between puffs.

'Treasurer,' says a suit-clad journalist, chasing after him. 'Treasurer, what do you make of this morning's poll?'

'Haven't seen it,' he says, running faster.

'It makes you a strong contender for the leadership.'

'Guys, can't you see I'm running?'

That, of course, sailed straight to the top of the TV bulletin. Jack rang within a matter of minutes.

'Roo, honey, I'm so sorry. I know how this looks.'

'It looks like Cecil made a joke about running for the leadership, Jack.'

'He's kicking himself, really, Roo. He jogged around the corner and rang me to fess up. Is there any way we could get him a quick call with the PM? He really wants to apologise.'

'The PM has a full schedule this morning and prep for the *Sunday Roast* prerecord this afternoon, but I'll tell him the Treasurer's keen to have a word.'

'Tell him Cecil was just trying to avoid fanning the flame. He even took a different route for his morning run to get out of saying anything. He fucked up and didn't mean anything by it. We won't be commenting on this or any other poll.'

'Thanks for the call, Jack.'

Outside, in the berry-free garden, Daphne had prepared a picnic of sorts on the front lawn. Two mismatched throws pegged together formed a rug for our Sunday feast—oven-fresh focaccia, home-made coleslaw and roast chicken.

Clem did cartwheels around the yard. In her bathing suit, Fran did the crossword on a beach towel, sweltering in the eighteen-degree heat.

'Hello, darling,' said Daphne, passing me a plate and napkin. She dusted the grass off the sunny patch of the rug for me to sit on. 'Try some of this Polish dip I bought at the deli this morning.'

'Thanks, but I'm a bit over polls at the minute,' I said. She laughed.

'You know, it's taken me two years but I think I've acclimatised.' I sat down beside her. 'I'm wearing a jacket and Fran's working on her tan.'

'I told you it would happen.' She carved me the drumstick. 'Elliot's nice.'

'Yes,' I said. 'He is.'

'He seems to like you.'

I pretended to study the salad. 'I guess.'

'Do you like him?'

'As you said, he's nice.'

She sighed. 'You know exactly what I mean.'

'Things with Luke haven't been great for a long time.'

'So Elliot's not Luke and therefore he interests you?'

'I didn't mean it like—look, Elliot and I aren't an item, if that's what you're implying.'

'Yet,' she said.

'Yes, yet. Who knows? I'm a young, recently single woman. I work hard in a stressful job. When I come home I need support—someone to lean on. What I got from Luke was at best melancholy, at worst criticism. Do you know he proposed on condition that I quit my job? Why is it that you all seem to be in the Luke camp?'

She looked forlorn. 'I'm firmly in Camp Ruby, but I just want to make sure you know that life is more than work.'

'Which is why I want the non-work bits to be fun.' I put my sunglasses on and got up, knees cracking. 'I have to get ready for work.'

'Where's Aunty Wooby going?' Clem smoothed down her hair with a grassy hand.

'She has to go to work, darling,' said Fran.

'But it's Sunday.'

Daphne laughed. 'Some people have to work on Sunday.

The Prime Minister is going to be on television.'

'Can I go on the television too? Please?'

'It's okay by me if it's okay by Ruby,' said Fran.

'I'll be working, Clem,' I said, 'and you wouldn't be on the television, you'd be at a studio where someone else is on the television. Why don't you stay here with Mummy and Aunt Daphne instead? I'm sure they have fun plans for the afternoon.'

'No,' said Fran, 'no fun plans for me.'

Daphne smiled. 'I was just going to keep knitting—I'm making something for the baby.'

'Knitting makes me itchy,' said Clem. 'I want to come with you. Please? I'll be on my best behaviour.' She sat on the picnic rug with plaintive eyes and a button nose that twitched every time she said, 'Please, Aunty Wooby.'

'Okay.'

'Hooray!' She got up and did a few more cartwheels. Shit.

'Quickly run and have a bath. We have to leave in half an hour.'

Inside, I prepped for battle. I picked a bold-shouldered black pantsuit, cream silk shell top and nothing but a lick of mascara for luck. I slicked my hair back into a low pony, smeared on some colourless lip balm and stepped into the simplest, low-heeled black court shoe in my wardrobe.

I looked fierce. I looked tough. I looked like someone you wouldn't want to mess with.

Clem had a different approach. She wore an eggplant corduroy pinafore over striped tights with an embroidered denim jacket. Daphne blow-dried her hair so that her natural curls were so plump and glossy they looked like glazed pastry.

'You look lovely, Clementine,' said Fran, taking photos of her little girl. 'So do you, Ruby. Very, what's the word?'

'Professional,' said Daphne.

'Thanks,' I said. 'Come on, Clem. Let's go.'

'I'll wave to you, Mummy,' she said, running out the door behind me.

'I *love* your outfit,' said Bettina and handed me the brief.

'Thanks,' Clem and I chorused.

'I meant Clementine's,' she said. 'Not that you look— you look fierce without make-up on. I hope you're not nervous about seeing the dream fox again. Speaking of make-up, you'll never guess who I saw on my run this morning?'

My head spun. 'Who?'

'Guess.'

'No.'

'Fine. I saw Connie Fife. She was walking her beagles.'

'Excellent. I'm thrilled for you.'

'With that other woman. The staffer. What's her name?'

'I don't know. Listen, I don't have time for this, I have to brief the PM now. Can you keep an eye on my phone and take messages?'

'Sure. I'll come get you if there's anything urgent?'

'No.'

'Nothing at all? What about a cyclone?'

'In Canberra? No, nothing's more urgent than this. Just take messages.'

'Got it.'

'And can you take Clem into the green room and then bring her up to the studio before we record?'

'The *green* room? Yuck. I *hate* green.'

'It's not actually green,' said Bettina. 'That's just the name of it.'

'Oh, you mean like blue BlackBerries?'

'Totally.'

'Or like car keys?'

'Huh?'

'You know, car key green. I like your nails, by the way. I have a knapsack that colour.'

'Me too. Don't you think it's like the colour you get when you mix a purple highlighter with a pink one?'

'Yes! I love highlighters. Mummy only uses yellow.'

'Boring. I'll show you my pencil case, if you like.'

'This room isn't green at all!'

I left the kindred spirits to discuss their stationery and found the PM in the dressing room being preened by a woman with supercharged hair.

'You've thinned out since I last saw you, PM, that's for sure.' She spritzed him with hairspray. 'But it doesn't look as bad in person as it does on TV. Must be the studio lights, do you reckon?'

Max's eyes narrowed.

'Erm,' I said, 'the PM has to take a call before the sound guy comes in. Would you mind giving us a moment?'

'Sure, love. I'll touch him up when you come out.'

'Thanks ever so much.' I shut the door behind her.

'Good call,' Max said, plucking the tissues from his collar. 'I'm not sure how much more of her honesty I could've taken without commenting on her halitosis.'

'I'd have gone for the chin hair,' I said. 'It's every vain woman's jugular.'

He smiled, but it wasn't a laugh. 'I've got a bad feeling about this, Roo.'

'You look fine.'

'No, not my hair; the show. With the poll this morning it feels like my Sunday's already well and truly roasted.'

'They're people, PM. By the time this goes to air tonight, they'll just want to see you having a chat while they eat their Red Rooster family packs. Just be yourself.'

'Be myself? Okay.' He made eye contact with my reflection. 'I shouldn't have promised the impossible, but I didn't know how tough it would be and I should have.

'I shouldn't have thought it'd be easy to get school-leavers into community service without people rorting the system. I long to change my position on marriage equality but I'll be crucified by the Christian lobby.

'I wish I had better news for the country than the hard slog ahead. I'm glad Cecil's a good treasurer but today's poll is a kick in the guts, even though some days I don't even like me.' He swivelled to face me. 'Still think I should be myself?'

'You know what I meant, PM.'

'You meant don't be myself.'

There was a knock at the door.

'I have to mike you, Prime Minister,' said a freckled boy with hair the colour of carrot cake. He turned to me. 'And the EP says you have to go and take your seat.'

'Can't I wait here?'

'Sure, but he said something about your niece. She's in a corner seat in the front row.'

'Nobody puts Clem in the corner,' said Max. 'Go.'

'Thanks. Break a leg, PM. You'll be great.'

Clem waved with excitement when she saw me emerge from backstage. I sat down beside her.

'Ladies and gentlemen,' said the effervescent warm-up

guy, '*Sunday Roast* will be recording in five. But first, I'd like to introduce our host. He's hotter than Szechuan pepper and sharper than a cleaver. Make some noise for Oscar Franklin!'

Gay men swooned, straight women whistled. The straight men in the audience puffed out their chests as Oscar moseyed on set, pausing to sign autographs.

Taking a seat at the *Sunday Roast* dining table— complete with napkins, crockery and cutlery—he winked and flashed a meringue-white smile at the crowd. He saw me, flared his nostrils and brushed down his Zegna.

'Right,' said the floor manager, 'let's go in ten, nine, eight seven—' He signed the rest of the countdown with his fingers.

Music. Emphatic applause, Clem's the loudest.

The camera panned to Oscar.

'Good evening, Australia, I'm Oscar Franklin, welcome to *Sunday Roast.*'

The audience clapped and hooted.

'Joining us at the dinner table tonight is a man fifty-three per cent of you backed at the ballot box two years ago but only twenty-eight per cent of you would today.'

What utter tosh! Fifty-three is the two-party preferred vote. The other is the current primary.

'Will he be a one-term wonder? Here for a chat about the nation's biggest gig is Max Masters, Prime Minister of Australia!'

Despite the nonsensical introduction, Max exhaled and stepped into the light, smiling and waving at the audience. Even in smart casual he was statesmanlike—precision-cut dark jacket, open-collared wide-checked shirt, shoes shiny as molasses.

Some audience members booed, others clapped. Clem and I were among a small handful of cheerers.

'Well, will you?'

'Will I what?'

'Will you be a one-term wonder? And don't say that's up to the people of Australia.'

'I hope not. I love my job, I love being in a position to make the country a better place. But that's up to the people of Australia, Oscar.'

Oscar rolled his eyes. 'Booooooo,' said a man in the third row.

It got a lot worse. I watched in horror as Oscar decimated my boss. It was as if the audience had decided to hate him.

'So, what do you make of Cecil Berth's comments today?'

'There's a reason I chose him as my running mate,' said Max.

I laughed. Nobody else did.

A phone rang. I turned to scowl at the culprit. It was Clem.

'It's my gnocchi,' she whispered. 'Mummy is calling.'

I snatched it and turned it off.

'One of our viewers, Thomas, sent in a question. He asks: are you as disappointed with yourself as we are?'

The audience laughed. I didn't. I almost cried.

Max stammered. 'I—I always think there are things I could do better, but I stand by this government's record.'

'Well, let's have a look at your report card, shall we? Corrupt ministers, policy failures, leaks—'

'You'd know more than me about the latter, Oscar.'

By the end of it Max shook hands with the front row

of the audience and disappeared into the dressing room, slamming the door behind him.

'Roo!' said Bettina.

'Not now,' I said.

'But Roo, it's really urgent.'

'Bettina!'

'PM,' I said as I walked in the door.

He sat, crumpled, in a chair. 'What?'

I didn't have anything to say. There wasn't anything to say.

'Are you okay?'

'Not really,' he said. 'I'm going home.'

'All right,' I said. 'I'll get the car.'

The flag fluttered as they drove off. I wandered back into the green room, where Clem was doing a handstand.

'Roo,' said Bettina, pulling me aside. 'Something's happened.'

'What?' I said, filthy with myself.

'It's Debs, your aunt's—'

'I know who Debs is.'

'She called. She's had some complications. They have to induce the baby. Fran and Daphne have flown to Melbourne.'

'What? When?'

'Just after you went into the studio. Debs called and I explained you were busy—'

'You did what?'

'You said—'

'Shoosh.' I dialled Debs. 'This is Deborah Llewellyn...'

Daphne. 'The mobile telephone you are calling is switched...'

Fran. 'Leave me a message after the...'

There was a message in my inbox. Luke. A chill scaled the length of my spine, vertebra by vertebra, like rungs on a ladder. I clicked on it.

Debs is in labour. We're at St Vincent's. No phones allowed in here. Daphne's en route. Text when you get to Melbourne. L

'I'm sure everything will be okay.'

I shrugged her hand off my shoulder. 'And how in the name of cock would you know that, Bettina?'

'I'm sorry, I was just trying to help.'

'You failed. You un-helped. Like the time you tried to help by eavesdropping on a conversation between the Chief and I.'

'The Chief and me.'

'Or the time you twittered about the PM's manicure.'

'Tweeted.'

'Or the time you tried to help by sucking up to Connie Fife when I was trying to deliver a very difficult message on behalf of the Prime Minister.'

'We're on the same team!'

'Or the time you tried to exercise subtlety while retrieving a piece of paper from between the lecterns of the US President and the Australian Prime Minister.'

'You told me to!'

'I didn't tell you to be a nosy, well-meaning ning-nong who can't help but be a walking clusterfuck. '

'Aunty Wooby!' Clem said.

'Shoosh, Clem.' I couldn't bear the look on her face. 'We're going to the airport.'

When there's a Will

'Ladies and gentlemen, welcome to Melbourne, where the time is a quarter past nine and it's a cool thirteen degrees. If your mobile phone is within reach...'

Mine was already on; it had been since we took off and Clem hadn't been happy about it.

'You're not supposed to have your phone on, Aunty Wooby.'

'It's fine, Clem.'

'I listened to the captain and she said it's not fine.'

'I fly a lot. Trust me.'

'Um, actually, I prefer to trust the pilot.'

'Clem.'

'She said it will interfere with the navigational equipment.'

'It won't. Look. I have no signal up here anyway.'

'Can I turn mine on then?'

'No.'

'Why not?'

'I'll give you my Mint Slice if you don't ask anymore questions.'

'What's a Mint Slice?'

I showed her.

'I told you, I hate green. You didn't listen to the pilot and you don't listen to me.'

As I got our things together and buttoned Clem's jacket I refreshed my email one more time.

Dear ones,

Will Llewellyn Partridge was born at eight o'clock tonight.

Mothers and baby a bit shocked but doing okay.

Will weighs a fighting 1.8 kilos (just under four pounds for those of you playing at home) which is a good effort for a bun pulled out of the oven well before the timer was due to go off.

All our love,

Daphne & Debs

I looked up at the red FASTEN SEATBELT sign. Ping, it went, and I sprang out of my seat, pulling Clem past the scrum of dawdling passengers, all sucking teeth at my rudeness, and past the singsong farewell of the flight attendants. I didn't care. Not one bit. We needed a cab. Now.

'Ladies don't run, Aunty Wooby.' Clem put her hands on her hips and stood still.

'The baby has been born.'

She ran to catch up with me. 'Hip hip hooray! Is it a boy or a girl?'

'A boy.'

'Oh well.'

I scanned the terminal for the nearest exit. This way. No luggage. That way. No—Luke?

Luke.

He looked awful: ten-day growth, a dryer-shrunken polo shirt, wonky pleated chinos. He held his hand out.

Relief skipped through my arteries.

Clem ran ahead. 'Luke!' She wrapped her arms around his legs.

'Hi, Clem. How was your flight?'

'Mostly good. Also I went on the television and I have a new boy cousin. Is Dan here?'

'No, he's at home.'

'Who's home?'

'My—his mummy's home.'

'Oh.'

'Let me take that.' He pointed at my bag. No eye contact.

'I've got it,' I said. 'You didn't have to come.'

'Daphne asked me to so, yes, I had to.'

'How are they?'

'As well as can be expected.'

'I'll call Daphne.'

'They're not allowed phones in there.'

'We weren't allowed phones on the plane, but—'

'Clem.'

Silence.

'What's the baby's name?' asked Clem.

'Will,' said Luke.

'I like that name. There's a boy in my class called Will. He has a trampoline.'

As Clem and Luke nattered, I followed in silence past

a cherubic toddler with an over-chewed teething ring pointing at the tarmac. 'Plane, Poppy!' he said to the old man holding him up by his overalls. 'Poppy, Poppy, plane.' Past a Japanese exchange student who met her banner-waving welcoming committee with a bow and nervous giggle. Past teary teenage sweethearts farewelling each other over a Happy Meal.

All the while, questions coursed through my head—about Debs, about the baby, about us—but none of them sounded right, so it wasn't until we got to the car park that I said, 'Will's a strong name.' I heard my voice; it sounded nervous.

Luke nodded, unlocked the doors and buckled Clem into the back. The car smelled of him, like rain on topsoil and dry-cleaned suits.

The seatbelt jammed. I tugged hard, frustrated. It wouldn't budge. Car park ticket between his teeth, Luke leaned over and pulled gently. It slid with ease. I buckled it.

He reversed. The radio announcer's voice crackled and whined incomprehensibly until we'd passed through the boom gate into the open air.

'...Opposition Leader Adelina Pepper told her party's national conference in Sydney today she would oppose measures to...'

Luke channel-surfed. Silhouetted birds flapped past wispy clouds backlit in the dark sky.

'Hey, I like that song,' said Clem.

He switched it back and turned it up.

She closed her eyes and sang along. 'My snail's a frayed vagina, in a little old boat to find you...'

We need air.

I loosened my strangulating pashmina and fumbled

with the electronic window. It was child-locked. Luke flicked a driver's-side switch and opened a rear window. Cold air blasted our eyes and ears. It built to a roar on the freeway.

'What's with your hair?' he yelled above it.

'What's with your stubble?'

'I'm growing a beard, but at least mine's on my chin.'

'You couldn't grow a beard if you tried.'

'Did you burn your arm?'

My waxing wound was darker today. 'I went rock climbing with my friends.'

Clem sang, 'Ain't nothin' gonna break my pride, nobody's gonna mow me down...'

'You climbed a rock? Where?'

Bollocks.

'Rocks. Plural. Canberra.'

'Where in Canberra?'

'The road behind was rocky, but now you're playin' hockey...' Clem strummed her air-guitar.

'Black Mountain.'

'Looks serious. Did you have it checked out?'

'I'm quite capable of looking after myself.'

'Oh no, I've got to keep on grooving...'

I watched a plane rise out the window. Its wheels tucked into the fuselage before it disappeared behind a cloud.

'How about another song, Clem.'

'Maybe I could lend you my iPod?' asked Luke. 'What kind of music do you like?'

'Beyonce, John Lennon...'

I found *Imagine* on Luke's iPod and handed it back to her. She put the headphones in and clicked her fingers. I took a deep breath and waited.

'I can't believe you hid Debs in Canberra,' said Luke.

'Don't you *dare* suggest that had anything to do with what happened.'

'I didn't.'

'You were about to.'

'No, I wasn't, I just don't think it's responsible harbouring a heavily pregnant woman when her partner—your aunt—thinks she's on the other side of the country. Don't worry, I covered for you.'

'Debs is her own person, Luke. Everyone was telling her what to do and she needed a place to escape to. I can relate to that.'

'I saw yesterday's paper. Nice.'

'He tried to kiss me—it was a misunderstanding.'

'Standing alone with Oscar Franklin in the dark and wearing his jacket is easily misunderstood.'

'I thought he was going to give me a hint about the leak. He got the wrong impression. You couldn't possibly think I—'

He mumbled something.

'I can't hear you!'

'I SAID—'

My ears popped when he put the window up.

'—WHATEVER.'

'Huh?' Clem took out an earphone.

'Nothing,' I said.

She put the earphones back in.

'How's *Bella*?'

How are Bella's berries?

'She's at a nursing conference in Brisbane. I'm looking after Dan. It's been on the cards for weeks. You'd have known that if you—God, I promised myself I wouldn't do this. Let's just drop it, okay?'

'...sneezy if you fly...'

'No, let's not drop it,' I said. 'I don't know why you proposed to me. I think you should marry Bella.'

'Bella? I've already been married to Bella. You're being a knob.'

'No, I'm not; it makes perfect sense. Don't feel obliged to marry me just because we're an item.'

'Obliged?'

'Yes, obliged. It's clear that you don't actually like me. And I don't have a berry garden.'

'Berry garden?'

'Yes, I have no berry garden and no time for berry gardens.'

'Good. If I wanted a berry garden I'd have planted one. Let's just drop it.'

'No, let's not drop it,' I said. 'Let's, erm, pick it up. We had an argument about the gender of the Japanese prime minister. You were defensive. You said some hurtful things. Then you proposed on the condition that I quit my job. I declined, so you fled.'

'Interesting synopsis.' He scratched the scruffy stubble on his chin.

'...imagine there's no gum trees...'

Streetlights flickered outside the Queen Victoria Market. I could smell jam donuts.

'...livin' life in peas, yoo-hoo-oo-oo-oo...'

'I'll just say it,' he said.

'Please.'

He swerved around a pothole. 'You've stopped being Ruby, Ruby. The job has embittered you. I wanted to take you away from it so you could remember yourself.

There was kindness and patience in you. You used to hope. That's what made you beautiful.'

I rolled my eyes. 'What bollocks. There's a fine line between hope and naivety, Luke. Take my new intern for example. She's paper smart, but she's a baby. She swoons in Question Time. It's puppy love. Politics will break her heart and she'll be tougher for it. She'll grow up, she'll get real. We all do.'

'God, you're condescending.' We pulled up outside the hospital. 'There's nothing smart about being cynical, Ruby.'

'...I hope Sunday you'll join us...'

'I appreciate the lift,' I said, gathering my things. 'And thank you for being there for my family today. Come on, Clem'

'I did it for Debs,' he said, reaching into the backseat for my briefcase. 'Tell Daphne I'll stop by tomorrow.'

'Mummy! Mummy!'

Fran staggered down the fluorescent-lit corridor towards us. 'You're here!' she said, embracing us both.

'Did you see me on the television?'

'You were magnificent, darling.'

'What happened?' I asked.

'Daphne and I were at home when Bettina called.'

'She called you?'

'Yes. She said there was an emergency at Melbourne Airport and that we should go to Melbourne. We were confused at first because Debs was supposed to be in Perth, but Luke—who was with her in the ambulance—explained she'd come home early. We couldn't get through to you. Bettina said you couldn't be contacted. We just had to get on the plane.'

Clem yawned.

'How about I take you to the hotel, Clementine.'

'I want to see the baby.'

'He's sleeping now. You can meet him tomorrow. Is that okay?'

She rubbed her eyes. 'Okay.'

'We'll see you at the hotel, Ruby. I've booked a room for you. I'll text the details.'

'Clem?'

She looked up at me with tired eyes.

'Sorry I've been such a grumble bum.'

'That's okay.' She kissed me goodnight. 'One time, Samantha Fingleton said I was too dumb to play with her dollhouse. You were like that, but meaner.'

'I'm sorry.'

'No, not to me. To Bettina. She's nice.'

'You don't understand, Clem.'

'Yes, I do. Goodnight, Aunty Wooby.'

The maternity ward nurse's station was empty, so I accosted the tea lady, whose rose-gold brooch-watch swung with every step.

'Down the hall on your left, pet.'

'Do I just knock?'

She winked and patted me on the small of my back. 'She won't bite.'

She doesn't know Debs.

Tentative, I knocked twice on the door and stepped back.

'Who is it?' Debs' voice was so weak it was almost unrecognisable.

'Me.'

Debs was alone, propped up on pillows, staring at the

curtained window. 'Hey.' The narrow path of a single tear ended at the corner of her mouth. She quashed it with her tongue. 'Thanks for coming.'

'I didn't think this could happen to you,' I said, my eyes welling.

'Me neither, kiddo.' She squeezed my hand. 'We're all vulnerable, I guess. Especially when we think we aren't.'

I sat in the chair beside her. My head had prepared me based on the only precedent it had. When Clem was born, there were so many roses the hospital ran out of vases. Fran had been flushed with happy hormones, Mark beaming with pride. Daddy bought Veuve Grande Dame of Fran's vintage. We drank it from plastic cups, each taking turns nursing the newest member of our family.

This was different.

'What happened?' I asked, handing her a tissue.

'It's been a bit of an ordeal. After you left, I packed and went to the airport but there were no flights; so I hired a car, drove to Sydney and checked into a day spa. Fuck that facial was orgasmic. Then this arvo I flew to Melbourne. I was feeling a bit funky, but I thought that might have had something to do with the psyllium husk they used in the spa food. Then, just before we landed, I started bleeding. I told the hosties. They called an ambulance to meet us on the tarmac. Almost shat myself with fear because a) I thought I might lose him'—another tear—'and b) Daph was going to be angry as a rash.

'Then I called your mobile and that nice little lollipop who works for you answered and told me you were unreachable, so I rang Luke. He came straight over. I told him about my Capital getaway. He said he'd sort it out. He lied to Daphne's face that I'd flown home early because I was homesick for her'—an actual sob—'I haven't had a case of the guilts like this since I dobbed in Sister Mary-Constantine for playing poker with the gardeners.'

'Don't beat yourself up, Debs. It doesn't matter.' I handed her a fresh tissue.

'Suffice to say, that man is my fucking hero, kiddo.'

'It was good of him to come,' I said, still aching from our fight.

'That's what you say if someone drops off a casserole when your goldfish dies. I bawled my pooping eyes out when they told me the baby had to come out. Luke let me punch him, which was nice. Then, when they cut me open, he stood there like a pooping trooper in his blue scrubs. He even held a tissue when I blew my nose, and recorded the whole thing on his phone so Daph could see it.

'And when they took him out of me—which felt like someone rummaging around in my briefcase, by the way— Luke insisted that they let me see him before they took him away because I couldn't move, which was genius because I'm too weak to go into the NICU right now.

'The thing that struck me is that it was a baby—like a proper person. He even has elbows! Not that I expected to have an elbowless child with unbendable arms, but they are the most perfect elbows in human history.

'The doctor said, "There's will in him." Hence his name. And then they took him away from me. Luke promised me he would go with Will while they sewed me up. He sat there until Daph and Fran arrived. That's when he went to get you from the airport. Anyway, go see Will, and give Daph a kiss for me.'

I followed the signs to the NICU and washed my hands

at the door like they do on *House* in a basin under an enormous Anne Geddes poster.

'You must be Ruby,' said a cheery nurse. He opened the door. 'Welcome to the NICU!'

'Shhhhhhhhhh,' I said.

'Heavens,' he said, 'why would I want to be quiet in here? Their parents will sue me when they take them home. We keep the radio on all day for a reason, blossom. Now, would you like to meet Will?'

Tiny pink people lay in two rows of humidicribs like seedlings in a greenhouse. Some were swaddled pastel bundles, others yawning, stretching sun-bakers. They were all individual and yet somehow in sync, with staccato heartbeats like stanzas to a sonnet.

Daphne was sitting at a corner crib, her hand reaching through a sleeved hole. The tip of her pinky rested in the palm of Will's hand, overwhelming it. His long, articulated fingers flexed when he yawned. I could see what Debs meant about his elbows. They were edible, as were his knees. Will was the length of a sheet of A4. The scrunchy disposable nappy fastened just below his nipples.

'Don't they make smaller nappies for newborns?' I asked, still whispering.

'That's the pre-term size,' said the nurse. 'He'll grow into them.'

'Will he make it?'

'Nine in ten babies born at thirty-two weeks survive. Most of them have very healthy, long lives. We just have to look after him for a bit—give him time to concentrate on growing. Growing is exhausting work for little ones. They can double their body weight in a week.'

'What are the tubes for?'

'We have him on a CPAP machine—his lungs didn't expect to have to work for a few more weeks, so we're helping them boot up. Doctor says he'll probably come off that within forty-eight hours. The other one's an IV.'

Daphne beckoned me over. Her navy linen pants had crumpled into a concertina around her middle. Her cheeks were damp where her powder had been. I thanked the nurse and approached the crib.

'Will, this is your cousin, Ruby. Ruby, meet Will.'

'Hello,' I whispered.

'You should at least shake hands.' She vacated the chair.

I sat in it and reached in and touched the arch of his foot with my index finger.

He flinched, blinked and squinted under the bright lights.

My other arm reached over his crib to shade his eyes.

Then they opened, those mysterious dark eyes. Nobody would believe me, but for a fleeting moment we held each other's gaze.

Despite everything he had endured in his first two hours, Will Llewellyn Partridge already had the courage of optimism.

And if he could live that way, so could I.

Dear dairy

The front-page photographs of Max's roasting were bigger news than Debs' right breast, and that was saying something.

'Cheeses, this is good,' she said from her hospital bed, smearing Camembert onto a slice of pear. 'All those people who sent flowers are dead to me. Ruby's cheese platter is now the benchmark post-birth gift. Hold the phone: is that Maggie Beer pâté? Thank you, pheasant! And Daph, there's quince paste!'

'It's very thoughtful, Ruby—look at that. It's twelve and I haven't eaten.' Daphne looked exhausted after a long morning spent dashing between mother and baby.

'Kiddo.' Debs stopped mid-chew. 'No offence, but can you stop staring at my tits?'

The crumb of a water cracker lodged itself in my uvula. 'I'm not sure I can,' I said, coughing to clear it. 'You're being milked.'

'Well, would you look at that?' She feigned shock and stared at the breast pump attached to her boob.

'I'm sorry,' I said. 'It's a bit distracting. I've never seen a human producing and eating dairy simultaneously.'

'Is it dairy when it's human?' asked Debs.

'It's dairy when it's goat and sheep, so I don't see why it wouldn't apply to humans,' said Daphne, moving to the edge of the bed. 'Debs' milk is worth its weight in gold for Will. He's too little to suckle, so they feed it to him through a nasal tube.'

'Is it uncomfortable?'

'Hurts like buggery, I imagine,' said Debs, sucking the red bit out of a green olive. 'But this feels pooping normal after that nurse who came in yesterday. She was like a fluffer on a porno. "Hi, I'm here to get you going," she says, and takes my boobs between her fingers, just behind the nipple. Then she starts milking me while chatting away about the situation in Yemen and the weekend weather report. Fuck, it hurt. You should've seen Daph's face. Nice enough girl, but I was like, "Steady on, sweetheart—you haven't even bought me a—" Ruby!'

'I'm sorry, it's mesmerising.' I covered my eyes.

'It's all right, I'm done anyway. Twenty minutes on each tit and all I've got to show for it's a thimbleful.'

'The doctor said it'll take some time to build up volume,' said Daphne. 'Your body wasn't ready to be a source of sustenance so soon, ravishing as you are.' She kissed her.

Sitting there, their tired eyes muddled with anxiety and joy, these new parents were as any might be, which is why that morning's shopping expedition to Bonnets and Booties had been so upsetting.

An antique teddy on a rocking horse guarded the door

of the chic Prahran bubby boutique when I got there at half past nine. Visiting hours at the hospital didn't start till eleven.

I went straight to the neonatal section, where pink bonnets were half the size of my palm and T-shirts would fit my feet as snug as socks. In the end, I picked a suite of seven day-of-the-week beanie and bootie sets and the plushest cashmere nursing wrap for Debs.

'Excuse me,' I said to the too-tanned shop assistant, 'will these fit a premmy baby?'

'Depends,' she said, whistling her 's'. 'How much does the little one weigh?'

'Just under two kilograms.'

'They should fit. If not today, then next week. Do you know the circumference of his head?'

'No, but would a photograph help?'

She lowered leopard-print glasses from her forehead to her nose as I pulled up the photograph Daphne had sent that morning on my BlackBerry.

'Here he is,' I said. 'This is their first family portrait. Will was born yesterday at thirty-two weeks. Debs finally got to hold his hand this morning, so everyone's a bit emotional. Isn't he spectacular?'

'Very early.' Her nostrils flared. 'Which one's the mother?'

'They both are, but Debs here gave birth. Daphne's my aunt.'

She let her glasses fall and dangle around her neck on their rose-gold chain. 'I guess that's what happens when you play with nature.'

She did not just say that.

My credit card bounced off the counter and hit the floor

somewhere near my jaw. I picked it up. 'How *dare* you!'

Prams U-turned towards us. The sudden attention darkened her cheeks. 'Don't take it personally,' she said.

'If you had even one per cent of my cousin's body weight in grey matter between those over-bronzed ears you'd know his pre-term birth has nothing to do with the sexuality of his parents.' I leaned closer. 'Perhaps you should sue your solarium to recover damages for cerebral evaporation.'

'No need to get nasty,' she said. 'I just don't think you should interfere with God's plan. It's unnatural. Things are bound to go wrong.'

'That is the stupidest thing I've ever heard and I listen to a lot of talkback radio. If you believe that God is the giver of life, as I do, then Will is His creation.'

'I'm just saying, he's premature and that probably has something to do with the whole test tube thing.'

'How do you explain pre-term births of married heterosexual couples? Or miscarriages, for that matter?'

She lowered her voice. 'Everyone's entitled to their own opinion.'

'Yes, and I'm of the opinion that you're a twit, and I don't mean a witty Tweeter. You will not find two people more loving of their child than my aunts. Will was wanted. It took more than a shandy and a quick shag to get Debs pregnant, but God blessed them with the ability to conceive as quickly as they did and they thank him everyday for it. We all do.'

'Fine,' she said, shaken. 'Do you want to buy these or not?'

'I'd prefer to make love to a staple gun than to support your business.'

I stormed out of the shop and into the deli next door. I ordered a coffee while they made up Debs' cheese platter and took a seat by the open window, pretending to read the newspaper while my blood reduced to a simmer.

Over the top of the broadsheet I spotted one of the aerodynamic prams wheeling past me.

'You were awesome in there,' said the dad driving it.

'Sorry about that—I haven't had enough sleep.' I smiled into the pram where long black eyelashes peeped out from under a red beanie.

'You should sleep less all the time,' he said. 'What you said made so much sense. Go into politics. I'd vote for you.'

'I *am* in politics.' My hands still shook from the adrenaline rush. 'I work for the PM.'

He looked away. 'He doesn't have your kind of passion. He tempers everything. Sorry. I just wanted to thank you for telling the old goat off.'

'Well, thanks, but I can promise you, I learned what I care about because of Max Masters.'

'He doesn't, you know, say what he thinks. But they're all like that, aren't they? There's a bad poll and they say there's only one poll that matters, but they must feel like stabbing themselves in the eyeball with a chopstick. It's like he's faking it or something. Tiptoeing.'

He is.

Senator Flight closed the curtains against the chatter and the darkening sky outside, then came back to her seat. 'Ladies, ladies, I know the ball is tomorrow night—wait till you see my frock—but I call this second meeting of the Girls' Club to order.' She banged her gavel. 'You will have received the very thorough minutes from our last meeting thanks to Bettina Chu. Bettina, why don't you stand up.'

I scanned the committee room for brights.

'Bettina sends her apologies,' said Chief.

'Mid-season Smiggle sale?' I asked.

Chief shook her head. 'She resigned.'

The air-conditioning seemed to stop.

'She gave notice this morning,' said Chief, 'but asked if she could leave immediately to commence a paralegal role in Brisbane.'

'A paralegal role?' asked Connie Fife. 'Shame. She was a bright spark.'

'That's a real pity,' said the Senator. 'Thanks to Bettina in absentia. Ruby, would you mind taking the minutes?'

I found my voice. 'Just a minute, Senator,' I said. 'Did she say why, Chief?'

'We'll discuss it later, Roo.'

'I'd like to hear why,' said Anastasia Ng.

'You know I can't talk about human resources issues,' said Chief. 'Sorry to disrupt the meeting. Please continue, Senator.'

'Good riddance,' I said. 'She was all froth, no coffee.'

'That's a bit harsh,' said a rookie journo up the back. 'I was rushing to a press conference and out of paper last week and she gave me'—she rummaged through her handbag and pulled out an apple-green spiral notepad—'this. How sweet is that?'

'I have a scarf that colour,' said Adelina Pepper.

Approving nods and murmurs.

'Don't get me wrong,' I said. 'She's nice with a capital N, but not all that bright—and I'm not referring to her wardrobe.'

'Not all that bright?' the Senator asked. 'Have you read these minutes? She developed a communications strategy, letterhead options and a charter for the Girls' Club, which I was about to move we adopt.'

'She's not dumb,' I said. 'It's just that she's so bloody chirpy. And emphatic. Every second word is "totally" and once I counted ninety-four "OMGs" in a day.'

'OMG?' asked Adelina.

'Oh my gosh in Catholic,' said a voice at the back.

'She gave my press sec a tin of this magical stuff,' said Connie. 'Now she spritzes me when she does my make-up for press conferences and it somehow gives my hair body—'

'Dry shampoo,' said Adelina.

'That's it!' said Connie. 'Incredible.'

'People,' I said. 'Her kindness is not in doubt here. And her knowledge of stationery and beauty products is second to none, but she wasn't going to be able to hack it in this building. Reality disappoints her. And she doesn't sleep, she bakes muffins and time capsules every moment of her internship and she keeps trying to go above and beyond her role, which makes my eye twitch, and she made me wear a yellow dress—' I put down my wine glass. 'Bollocks. What have I done?'

The claw

The doorbell didn't ding-dong. It didn't even brrring.

Instead, it went, la la la; la la la la la, and I couldn't get it out of my head.

La la la; la la la la la.

It was twenty-four degrees on the Gold Coast. Skateboarders hung their hoodies on palm trees as they practised in the cul-de-sac of Seabreeze Drive in the Regal Robina Estate.

I pressed it again. La la la; la la la la la. No answer.

La la la—make it stop—la la la la la.

I decided to write a note. True to form, there was a green gingham notepad and contrasting mauve marker stuck to the shocking puce door, the only non-white door in the Gold Coast gated community.

Dear Bettina, I wrote, inadvertently spiralling, not dotting, the i. *Your flatmate said you'd be here so I flew up to apologise in person, but nobody was hom—*

The marker squiggled off the notepad and onto the glossy door as it opened.

'Are you Ruby?' asked a woman in a silk tunic with an oriental lily motif.

'Hello, you must be Mrs Chu.'

She slammed the door in my face.

La la la; la la la la la.

'Leave or I'll turn on the sprinklers,' she yelled over a yapping dog.

'Um, is Bettina there?'

'No.'

'Really?'

'Yes.'

'Do you know where she is?'

'Yes.'

'Can you tell me, please?'

'No. Did your parents not love you enough to play Twenty Questions during long car trips?'

'We played I Spy,' I said. 'Please tell me where she is. She won't take my calls so I flew up from Canberra to ask her to reconsider.'

The rattle of latches sounded promising.

A dog smaller than a fish you'd have to kiss and throw back growled at me as I followed its owner down the white marble hallway.

'Barbara,' Mrs Chu said, sternly. The growling ceased. 'Take a seat and I'll fix us a cool drink.'

I sat on a cling-wrapped couch opposite a trophy cabinet so full its shelves sagged in the middle. Homemade scrapbooks towered four feet above the coffee table next to a hot-glue gun which itself was bedazzled.

Mrs Chu returned with a mirrored tray and a pair

of highball glasses covered in hand-painted daisies. She poured me a glass.

'Thanks, it's lovely,' I lied. The cordial had the sugar content of fairy floss. I tried to ignore the feeling of my teeth corroding. 'Are these all Bettina's?' I gestured towards the trophies.

'Every single one.' The glass door sprang open when she pushed it. 'Bettina's always been into everything. Spellathons, Jump Rope for Heart, swing dancing, singing eisteddfods, Huffing Awareness Week, Toastmasters, baton-twirling, debating, the 40 Hour Famine, hurdles, tae kwon doe, Movember—you know, the usual.'

'She has so much energy.'

'Which is why it kills her father and me to see her like this. Do you have any idea how excited she was when they told her she got the internship?'

'I think so,' I said, remembering her first day.

'No, I don't think you do. Politics is her dream, Ruby. For her, it's the opportunity to make a difference, to change people's lives, to do something that matters. It only took you a week to do what even Knut's death couldn't: you broke her spirit. A pod of six dolphins swam past us when we were walking on the beach this morning. Bettina didn't even try to sonar them. "They won't hear me, Mum," she said. It was heartbreaking. I took her to the Smiggle sale to cheer her up. And do you know what she bought, Ruby?'

I shook my head.

'A lined, white notepad and a black biro.' She fiddled with the heavy, gold crucifix around her neck the same way her daughter did. 'What were you thinking, trampling on a young girl's dreams like that?'

'Mrs Chu, I know Bettina's upset. I'm here to apologise to her and plead with her to come back. She shouldn't throw her career away just because I'm a bitch. And I'm not a bitch. I'm really not, I've just been a little lost. If you could tell me where she is I could explain that to her.'

She pressed her lips together and closed her eyes. Sugared-almond pink eye shadow had creased on her lids. 'I will tell you where she is. But'—she pointed a long, red fingernail at me—'if I hear that you've caused her any more grief, I'll find you. I know where you live.' She picked up the hot-glue gun.

'Understood.'

'One adult, please.'

'Coupons or vouchers?' asked the lady under the visor.

'No.'

'Okay, that's seventy-four dollars.'

'Ha!'

'What?'

'I thought you said seventy-four dollars.'

'I did.'

'What about a student?'

'Can I see your student ID?'

'I left it at home.'

'You'll have to pay adult admission then.'

'Right. How much is it for an adult who doesn't want to go on any rides? I get terrible vertigo and spinning makes me—'

'Seventy-four dollars.'

I handed her my card.

'Welcome to Dreamworld,' she said. 'Savings or credit?'

Bettina was exactly where her mother said she would be. 'When she's numb she goes there to feel alive and find a bit of peace.'

The Claw didn't strike me as an ideal environment for existential reflection.

Nine storeys high, strapped to a giant, swinging, tangerine pendulum, Bettina hurtled through the air. In case going side to side wasn't life-affirming enough, the seating at the base of the pendulum spun counter-clockwise—a kind of carousel on steroids—while a subwoofer belted out Lady Gaga's *Bad Romance*.

As it slowed from seventy-five kilometres an hour to thirty I got a glimpse of Bettina's face. G-force aside, it was expressionless. No screams, no fear, no delight. Not even a raised brow. She just sat there, unamused, legs dangling above and below her, depending on the beast's trajectory.

'Just one?' asked the ride operator, a man old enough to know better.

'No, no, no,' I shouted above the noise, turning away to avoid watching it spin. 'I'm just waiting for my friend.'

'Her?'

'Yes.'

'She's not getting off.'

'What do you mean?'

'This is her eleventh ride.'

'Surely it's better for her to have a rest.'

'There's no one else here,' he said. 'It's a Tuesday morning. She's got a season pass—she can stay there all day if she wants to.'

'Bettina,' I shouted from behind the barrier when it stopped. 'Bettina!'

'What?'

'Come off so we can talk.'

'OMG, I quit already. Go away.'

'Come on,' I said. 'I want to apologise. Please.'

'What? I can't hear you.'

The operator unlocked the barrier. 'Are you getting on or not?'

'No, just hold the ride for a second,' I said. 'I need to talk to her.'

'No can do. You're either on the ride or you're nowhere near it. What's it going to be?'

I stared at Bettina's black Capri pants and beige zip-up cardigan. She yawned.

'Fine,' I said, 'but make it slow.'

The harness locked into place.

'What are you doing here?' Bettina barely turned her head.

'I'm here to apolo—' we started spinning '—gise.'

'It's not your fault, Roo,' she yelled above the noise, unfazed by the merger of our internal organs.

Ruby, said my head. *I think I fell off.*

'Yes, it is my fault,' I shouted. 'I've been a complete twat—holy shit balls, what is happening—aaaaaargh!'

Bettina yawned as the pendulum tossed us upside-down, I think.

'I shouldn't have taken the job,' she said. 'People warned me it was going to be tough and I was like, "Can't be tougher than Darfur," but at least you can make a difference in Darfur.'

Tears of shock ran over my eyebrows and down my forehead. 'You can make a difference in Canberra too—which way is up? I think I dropped my eyeballs!'

'I just couldn't cope with all the anger and the bitterness,' she said. 'It's like the Freemasons for defeatists. BYO sarcasm. Secret password: that's just the way it is.'

Why am I the only one screaming?

'I'm like, why don't we aim to close the gap in life expectancy for indigenous people by 2020? "Ha ha, Bettina. You don't understand. It's too hard. That's just the way it is." Okay, well let's make media more accountable! "Can't do that—you're so naive—that's just the way it is." I want university to be free for all school leavers. "You're hilarious. OMG, you were serious? Sweetie, that's just the way it is." Why are we focusing all of our energy on doing each other over? "See above." I don't want to end up like one of you, Roo. I want to be me. I want to change the world.'

'I just vomited in my mouth,' I shouted and shut my eyes.

'See what I mean?'

'No, I literally just vomited in my mouth. There was vomit in my mouth. I now know why they say better out than in.'

'Oh, sorry, I'm just so used to it. This is my safe place.'

'Bettinaaaaaaargh! Sorry. Bettina. I am terribly afrAID of heights and get nauseous just watching gymnastICS. But I left CanberrAAAAAAAA to fly here—FARK—and get on this MONSTER machine to tell you—I'M GOING TO DIE IN AN AMUSEMENT PARK—I need you.'

The Claw slowed.

'You need me?'

'Not just because you're the most oooorganised, punctual, professional I have eveeeeer worked with but also because you *believe* in something. You are a neon-pink buoy of optimism in a pinstriped ocean. You are precious. That's why I've been such a bitch. I'm jealous of you.'

We stopped spinning, but the world didn't.

'You're jealous of *me*?' She smiled. 'Get. Out.'

'I intend to,' I said.

Harnesses sprung open.

I wiped the drool and tears from my chest and forehead, checked to see I hadn't fallen victim to incontinence, stood up and fell down again.

'You okay?' Bettina squatted beside me.

'Mmm hmm.' The ground was so nice beneath my cheek.

'It was nice of you to come all this way, Roo. I guess I could give it another go.' She yanked me off the ground.

'Everything's still spinning, Bettina.' I clutched her arm. 'We'd better get back to Canberra if we're going to make it in time for the ball.'

'The ball?'

'The Midwinter Ball. It's tonight. It's—'

'Only the biggest black-tie event on the parliamentary calendar!' Her eyes snuffed out as quickly as they lit up. 'Oh well. I guess I could go next year.'

'I got you a ticket this morning. My sister Fran's coming too.'

She grabbed my hands. 'OMFG—what are you wearing? What am I going to wear? OMG!'

'I've got an idea. It's a surprise.'

'I love surprises.' She put on a pair of black Ray-Bans. I stared.

'These are my funeral sunnies,' she said. 'Don't knock them.'

'Right. I'm quite proud of myself for not being sick,'

I said as we passed a group of Japanese tourists posing for photographs.

'You look a bit pale still,' she said. 'Maybe you're hungry. I don't know about you, but I could *so* murder a couple of cheeseburgers and a strawberry shake right now.'

Bluuuuuuurrrrrrrgh.

Balls

I reverse-parked into a small bay beside a skip in the industrial park. Bettina and Fran held their noses as I pressed the intercom next to an unmarked, tinted-glass door between Pujari's Plumbing and Canberra Roller Doors.

'You rang?'

'Is Martha in?'

'For whom?'

'Ruby, Fran and Bettina.'

'Miss Ruby Stanhope. *Entrez.*'

The door popped open.

'Ooh,' said Fran.

'OMG,' said Bettina.

Burgundy velvet flocked paper covered the walls of the chandelier-lit room. Rack upon rack of clothes led to the centerpiece: a huge, freestanding, antique, gilt-edged mirror. Nina Simone smoothed over the scratches in the spinning vinyl.

'Welcome to my boudoir, sweets,' she called out from the back of the store. 'Just powdering my nose.'

When he was Arthur, he was the best shoe repairman in town. But when Martha was in, she ran Canberra's finest vintage boutique—by appointment only, of course.

'Darling,' she said, dashing over to air-kiss me. She was wearing a sheer black robe hemmed with pink ostrich-feathers. 'Divine to see you.' She flicked black hair over her shoulders.

I stated the obvious. 'You look fabulous.'

'I know.' She stared at my hair and batted inch-long falsies. '*Quelle catastrophe!* You must tell me who did that to you and what you want me to do to them. Now, who do we have here?'

'Bettina Chu,' I said. 'This girl works colour like nobody else, present company excepted.'

'Pleased to meet you, Martha.'

'Charmed.' She removed the band from Bettina's pony-tail and fluffed her hair. 'Better. Much better. And this one?'

'This is Fran, my sister.'

'Francesca of deadbeat ex-husband and delightful daughter fame,' she said. 'I feel like I know you already. How can I help, ladies?'

'The Midwinter Ball tonight. It's a masquerade this year, so we want something a bit—'

'Mysterious,' said Martha. She pursed matte-red lips and closed her gel-lined eyes. 'Come,' she said, her feathers fluttering as she put us in three separate taffeta-curtained change rooms. 'Martha will look after you. I've just the thing.'

A long, hair-free arm reached through the curtains

with a glass of champagne. I downed it.

'Bettina,' I heard her saying, 'you will put this on.'

'But—'

'Trust me, sweetness.'

'Okay,' squeaked Bettina.

'Francesca, you will wear this. And you, Miss Ruby Stanhope, will wear this.'

'I will?'

'You will. Step into the heels provided and tell me when you're ready. Drum roll please, maestro.'

'Ready.'

'Ready.'

'Ready.'

Martha tore back our curtains.

'It's official,' she said. 'I am gifted.'

And she was. We gazed at ourselves in the mirror. Breathtaking.

'Shall I tell you about the gowns?'

We nodded, awestruck.

'You, Miss Chu, are rocking a cobalt-sequined mini-dress. I like to think Liz Taylor left it in her hotel room on a 1978 stopover in Hong Kong and then a Qantas hostie found it, brought it home and left it to her grand-daughter who had no taste and sold it to me in 2001 at her garage sale in Fyshwick.'

'My mum was a hostie!'

'I can see it in your wrists.'

'Hang on, Elizabeth Taylor wore this dress?'

'We can't know for sure, but it's plausible. Anyway, I rescued it and replaced all the missing sequins. It's cap-sleeved, slash-necked at the front and—spin'

Bettina turned around.

'—low at the back, but not tramp-stamp low. We can't have you looking cheap.

'Francesca, this is a raspberry, single-shouldered, pleated toga gown with original silver-rope waist belt. This dress came with instructions: it must be worn with chandelier earrings. Voila et voila. It was first modelled by Sofia Loren between films, but she grew too fat for it and it has now found its natural habitat here on planet Fran. I love a happy ending; believe me, I've had plenty.

'Which brings me to you, Miss Ruby.' Martha cleared her throat. 'This is almost certainly the dress Grace Kelly wore in *To Catch a Thief*. Some museum in Hollywood claims to have it. Alas, they were swindled—because I have it. The old film they used made the gown appear white; but as you see, it's the palest of pale pinks, like the innermost petals of spring's first peony.'

I twirled.

'I counted eighteen separate pieces of the finest chiffon, draped diagonally across the strapless, sweetheart bodice. Its waist sits just below the final rib in your cage, with a tiny, delicate chiffon bow, before cascading to the floor in all its gossamer glory. This is not a dress to die for. No, no. This, my dear, is the dress to live for.'

'We'll take them,' I said, whipping out my credit card.

At half past six, in the PMO bathrooms, Bettina presented Fran and I with a box each. 'Open them.'

The ribbons slipped their knots. We opened the boxes. Inside, white-feathered masks with diamante-lined eyeholes lay on tissue paper.

'They're stunning.' I said, stroking the long, thick feathers.

'Where did you find them?' Fran said.

'Craft is kind of my thing.' She opened her evening purse. Hers was blue lace with black sequins.

The Great Hall at Parliament House had been transformed. Rotating digital patterns were beamed onto a giant white mask centre-stage. Long metallic sashes streamed from the high ceiling, stopping just above the centre of each of the hundred tables. Tea candles lit each place card.

Men in tuxes cut dashing figures, their tired faces hidden. Cecil Berth wore a mask plastered in Monopoly money. Connie Fife teetered on platform shoes, her full, black skirt rustled past us; her mask was a muted-gold butterfly. Senator Flight wore cornflower-blue and waved at us with a broad, ostrich-feathered fan. The floor was already rolling with stray pearls, sequins and glitter.

Chief joined us in a red bandage dress, her only mask her perfectly applied make-up. 'Nice diamantes, ladies. Can I talk to you for a second, Roo?'

'Sure.' We moved a little way apart from Fran and Bettina. 'What's up?'

'It's happened again. This time they sent the emails. They're all printed, all from me.'

'Show me.'

We drew behind a potted palm and she pulled a few sheets of paper out of her purse. 'They're embarrassing.'

'This is your Parliament House email address,' I said.

She looked at it. 'I didn't even notice.'

'Do you mind if I hold onto them? It could be one of the IT guys. I'll look into it tomorr—'

There, over her shoulder, was the giraffe wearing a brocade napkin. Cameras flashed; so did she. But that wasn't what caught my eye. On her left arm in Oscar's place was someone resembling none other than—

'Oh look, it's Luke,' said Fran.

Chief followed my line of sight. 'Balls.'

He was wearing a bow tie, vest and mask in satin with a green and orange print. Awful.

A waiter tried to pass me. I snatched two glasses of champagne from his tray and knocked them back like tequila slammers.

'*What* is *he* doing *here* with *her*?' I paced over to the seating-plan board.

Chief pointed to a circle with ten chairs.

Liberty Australia Foundation. Table 18

Host: Luke Harley, CEO.

Guests: Winifred Ralph...

'I'm going to be sick.'

'No,' said Fran. 'You're going to walk over there, smile and greet them. Be mature, Ruby.'

'I can't do that. Not without a date.'

'I'm your date.'

'You're my sister! I thought it'd be poor form to bring a male this soon after we broke up. I have an idea.'

I ran back to the office, texting on the way.

Lumpy Gravy.

Elliot replied:

Place and time?

Parliament House. Now. Wear tuxedo.

A pause.

As in now now? That's not much notice for black tie.

Is there another kind of now?

Twenty minutes later, pre-dinner drinks were over and I was standing at the marble foyer to Parliament House, losing hope.

'Go on in, love,' said the security guy. 'I'll send him in when he gets here.'

'I'll just give it a few more minutes.'

And there he was. Dreamy, debonair Elliot strode through security in a tux, minus black tie and kissed my cheek.

'You look gorgeous, gorgeous,' he said. 'Like a goddess in disguise or something.' He handed me a box containing a bow tie.

'Thanks,' I said. 'So do you.'

'I wasn't really going for the goddess look,' he said, sitting so that I could read his collar, 'but I'll take the compliment.'

'Thanks for coming.' I pulled the tie out of the box, ran the stiff silk through my fingers. 'I'm sorry for the late notice.'

'Yeah, what's that about? I still smell like dog.'

Dog by Calvin Klein, said my body.

'Well—erm—I didn't realise we were supposed to bring dates and then I saw—erm—that everyone else was so I thought I'd see if you were free.'

'Hmmm,' he said.

I straightened his tie and bit the dry-cleaning tag off his cuff with my teeth.

'Come on,' I said, taking him by the hand and leading him in. 'They're about to start.'

'Woah, is that your sister?'

I introduced him to the people at our table—Anastasia Ng as Catwoman and her husband Hugh, Bettina, some mining CEO, wearing top hat and tails—and then scanned the room for Luke and the giraffe.

At the next table, Chief pointed towards the far corner. I saw the full head of highlights. Seated, she was at least ten centimetres taller than him.

Ha!

'Ladies and gentlemen,' said Oscar, his dinner jacket shinier than his hair, 'welcome to the sixteenth annual Midwinter Ball, the perfect place to network with the politterati and raise money for a good cause. This year we're going to do things a little differently. Tonight, under the safety of those masks, we're going to ditch speeches for the dance floor.

'Here's where it gets interesting. On each table, attached to the sashes, you will find stickers naming each of our wonderful sponsors. Each table must nominate one couple to compete in a dance-off. The stickers are for the gentleman's back.

'I'm delighted to announce that leading us on the dance floor tonight will be none other than Prime Minister Max Masters and Adelina Pepper, Leader of the Opposition. They are great sports and have auctioned this dance for fifty thousand dollars, which will go towards multiple sclerosis research.'

Everybody hooted.

Max stood with Shelly, who was wearing a crystal bindi. They laughed and waved. Adelina posed with her husband, in a leopard-print silk scarf with two holes cut into it—a Hermes Zorro.

'I'm going to leave you to decide who among you will participate. There are no excuses, no exceptions—we're all here to have a good time and raise money for charity. Go!'

The giraffe used long fingernails to smooth the sticker onto Luke's back.

'I nominate Roo and Elliot,' said Bettina.

'Seconded,' said Anastasia.

'I'm game if you are,' said Elliot.

Could I dance? Not really. Would I dance? Hell, yes.

'Turn around,' I said, smacking the Drill Metal sticker to his jacket.

'Now,' said Oscar. 'I'd like to call the Prime Minister and his alternative to the dance floor. And if I could give the Opposition leader a word of advice—the PM has two left feet. PM, try not to trip this time. Give it up for Maxelina!'

The lights dimmed. A spotlight shone on the couple. The jazz band played *Can't We Be Friends*. Max led, Adelina didn't really follow. Both were excellent sports.

Oscar approached our table in the middle of the dance. 'Roo,' he said, shaking my hand, his eyes unreadable through a black-suede mask.

'Oscar,' I said, 'this is my, erm—friend, Elliot.'

'Elliot—?'

'Juniper,' said Fran.

'It is?' I looked at him. 'It is!'

'Oscar Franklin,' said Oscar, shaking his hand. 'What do you do, Elliot?'

'I'm a vet,' he said. 'You?'

Oscar laughed before realising Elliot had no idea who he was.

'Oscar's a television presenter.'

'Journalist,' Oscar corrected, and resumed scanning the table. He stopped at Bettina, who had lowered her blue-lace mask and was staring at him with her big, beautiful eyes from across the table. Her skin was singing. Long black gloves stopped just above her elbows. She was, without a doubt, the belle of the ball.

'Roo, I was wondering whether you could introduce me to your friend.'

I shook my head.

Anastasia groaned. Loudly. Fran rolled her eyes.

'Which friend?'

'That one.'

I sighed. 'Oscar Franklin, meet Bettina Chu. Oscar is from the Eleven Network. Bettina is a highly intelligent, way-out-of-your-league intern from PMO. She's twenty-two.'

Bettina kicked me under the table.

'Bettina,' he said. 'I love your dress. Is it vintage?'

'Yes,' she said, her posture tall. 'It was Elizabeth Taylor's, I'm told.'

'You look better in it, I'm sure. Tell me, Bettina, do you like to dance?'

She nodded. 'I learned how to salsa with underprivileged kids in Venezuela.'

Of course she did.

'Well, you're in luck. Salsa is my specialty. I'm on a television program. I don't know if you've heard of it...'

'*Celebrity Dancefloor*? I watch it every single week!'

'I'm supposed to dance with someone but, as MC, I don't have a table. Would you do me the honour?'

She took his hand, her blue gown purpling as they moved into the pink spotlight. He puffed out his chest.

'Are they proper ballroom shoes?' asked Fran, spotting the steady, well-worn heels as Bettina pointed and flexed. 'She's really very good.'

Bettina looked into Oscar's eyes; Oscar looked into the audience. She mesmerised us all; he was mesmerised by his reflection in the mirror ball. We clapped as she extended her leg over his shoulder, pointing her toe so that the arch of her foot looked like a crescent. Before the applause had a chance to crescendo, Oscar lifted her from the waist, high above his head, but our cheers became gasps when Bettina splayed her long, gloved arms into a balletic arch above her head and her legs into an airborne arabesque. When the music drew to a close she was upside down, her legs scissored around Oscar's neck, her fingers grazing the floor. We cheered on our feet. She smiled and curtsied gracefully; he stepped in front of her and bowed.

'That guy's a knob,' said Elliot as Bettina made her way back to the table.

'Back in a minute. Fran, why don't you stay here with Elliot? Ballroom Betty and I are going to freshen up.'

'O. M. F. G. Oscar Franklin just danced with me! Not the best dance of my life—his counting's all off—but he said I looked more beautiful than Elizabeth Taylor! She was beautiful. Oscar Franklin thinks I'm beautifuller than the most beautiful woman in Hollywood!' Bettina stared at herself in the bathroom mirror as though her reflection was entirely new to her.

'Oscar Franklin is a Player. Capital P.' I pulled my lipstick out of my sequined evening bag.

Flush. 'You would know,' said a voice. A stall door opened.

'Winnie.' My jaw tightened. 'Good to see you.'

She edged me out of the way and positioned herself in front of the mirror. 'Don't think I didn't see you two pashing in the paper.'

'Believe me, it was unsolicited.'

She ducked to powder her nose. 'God, if it was just you, Renee—'

'Ruby.'

'—I could've forgiven it. But with that bitter bitch? I walked in on them. Gross. Later, ladies—I'm due on the dance floor with another one of your former flames, but this one's a keeper.'

If I could've reached her, I would have punched her in the face.

'That was Winnie Ralph!' said Bettina as we hurried back. 'What a night!'

'Listen, Bettina, about Oscar. You're a grown woman. Do what you like. But it's buyer beware.'

When Elliot led me to the dance floor, everyone stared, especially Luke. Not that I was looking at him. I wasn't. I was looking at Elliot like every other red-blooded straight woman and gay man; but if I had been looking at Luke, I'm sure he would have been looking at me.

'Ready?' asked Elliot, holding me.

'Bring it.'

'Wow, you're really taking the competition thing seriously.'

'It's for charity,' I said. 'Charity is always serious.'

'Of course, but maybe just relax a bit.'

The music started. A waltz. *Moon River.*

1, 2, 3; 1 2 3; 123

'Um, Ruby,' said Elliot, 'it's not a race—we win if we keep in time with the beat, not beat the beat.'

'Right,' I said, slowing down a notch.

'Hey.' He kissed my hand as I scanned the room. 'Just follow my lead.'

We moved past Oscar and Bettina. 'Don't feel like you need to lift your game because you're dancing with me,' I heard him say through a showman's smile.

'It's okay,' she said, holding herself beautifully. 'I've danced with amateurs before.'

Shelly stared at me over Max's shoulder, then at Luke and back at me. Her bindi rose with her questioning look. I guided Elliot away from them. He was a decent partner, except he wanted to talk all the time. 'I was thinking we could grab some dinner sometime next—'

'Watch where you're going, Ruby!'

I had accidentally elbowed Connie, who was dancing with her husband. She lifted her butterfly.

'Sorry, Minister.'

'Ruby, are you trying to steer me?' asked Elliot, shouting over the music.

'Not at all,' I said, 'but maybe we should move over that way a bit.'

'What's over there? Oh, I get it.'

'You do?'

'Yeah, I'm a fan of Winnie Ralph too. I'm sure she'd sign an autograph for you later. Hey, I reckon I know the guy with her. He looks familiar.'

I turned on my heel and twirled him.

'That was unconventional,' he said. 'By the way, Franny told me about the baby. Will's a lovely name.'

We were about to pass Luke. 'Maybe you should dip me.'

'You don't dip in a waltz.'

'I don't think it matters really,' I said. 'It's an interpretive waltz.'

Dry-cleaning. Rain on top-soil. I followed my nose. We

brushed shoulders. He knew it. I knew it. My pulse grew erratic, arrhythmic, clashing with the waltz.

'Roo,' said Luke.

'Luke. What a coincidence.' I sucked in my stomach. 'Didn't know you were here.'

'Right.'

'Luke?' said Elliot. 'Hang on.'

'Come on, Luke,' said Winnie, and twirled away. He shimmied after her.

Elliot stopped. He let go of me, holding only my hand. 'What's going on?'

'Keep going,' I urged, grabbing him close. 'Everyone's looking at us.'

'Luke. He's brought the dogs in before. Luke. Right.'

'Yes.' I kicked up my right leg and dipped myself.

'Fuck!' He grabbed his lower back. 'That really hurt.'

'Concentrate,' I said. 'We need to lift our game.'

'Lift your own game,' he said. 'I don't want to be here.'

'Don't be a pussy, we've only just started. Don't you want to win? Think of the children.'

'Children don't get multiple sclerosis.'

I grinned and did the Nutbush to fill the stillness. 'Join me!'

'I was okay with being an afterthought, but an afterthought and a revenge date?'

'How about you lift me over your head then I'll stand on your shoulders and we can—'

'You're not listening, Ruby. I'm going.'

Moon River faded out. 'Well done, everybody,' said Oscar. 'Now, could the following teams resume their seats. Drill Metal—'

People clapped and cheered as the spotlight focused on us.

Elliot started walking away.

'Elliot!' I went after him. The spotlight followed.

'Go away,' he said, ripping off his bow tie.

'Elliot, you're lovely and I—'

'Go. Away.'

Fran pushed through the crowd after him.

I caught a glimpse of orange and green. 'Looks like you're going to need a new vet.'

'So the dogs are mine then?' I retorted.

'You never told me you have dogs,' said Winnie.

Luke ignored her. 'I figured with the rate you're moving through men you'll probably need some form of constant companionship. Oscar and Elliot in one week. Moving through the vowels are we? All you need now is an Igor, an Angus and an Ulrich, unless you count Y too. Perhaps a Yuri?'

'It's good that you could make it tonight,' I said, 'what with your incredibly hectic schedule. Did you have any meetings last week? Change printer cartridges? Important phone calls?'

'Yes, as a matter of fact. I had a phone call from Blockbuster. They said you still haven't returned *Lawrence of Arabia*.'

'It's a long film!'

'Luke, honey,' Winnie broke in, 'We have to dance.'

'Yes, Luke, honey, you and your clip-on bow tie are wanted on the dance floor.' Up close I could see that the green and orange print was a cumquat tree.

'I'll be over to get my other bow tie and the rest of my things next week. But now, I'm going to dance with this exquisite woman.'

'Salsa begins in five, dancers,' Oscar said into the

microphone. 'Grab your partners and get ready to put some arse into it. Are you having fun, Belinda?' He shoved the microphone in Bettina's face, looking to the crowd.

'It's Be*ttin*a,' she said, seizing the mike and removing her mask. 'And OMG, no, I'm not having fun. No frickin' way. If I had to choose between dancing with you and dancing with a shopping trolley with a dodgy wheel, I'd take the shopping trolley. Any day.'

Oscar stormed off the dance floor. Jack, of all people, hurried after him, in a swish of black silk.

Women's voices whooped and whistled their appreciation. Half of the Girls' Club gave her a standing ovation. All I could manage was a proud nod.

'Come on, darling,' said Fran, when she found me, a huge tuxedo jacket over her ballgown. 'Let's take you home.'

Ding-dong

My doorbell rang at 4.27 a.m.

I opened it.

Bettina stood there in a peacock-print pea coat, with two litre bottles of Fanta and straws.

'It's night-time.'

'You have to listen to this.' She handed me a Fanta, and pushed past me into the kitchen.

'Now?'

'You're going to freak.'

'I don't want to freak. I'm tired.'

'Listen.' She flipped open her laptop and pressed play on an audio file. Max's voice filled the room.

'How long have you been working here, Jim?'

'Bit over three months. I'm on a sound-engineering apprenticeship, trying to get some savings together; you know how it is.'

'Good on you. What are you saving for?'

'If you asked yesterday I would have told you I was saving for a ring, one of those proper diamond ones. I done my research. Colour. Clarity. Carat. Cut. Figure I need to work another eight months before I can get it. That's if you asked me yesterday.'

'But not now?'

'Nah.' A sigh. 'Not now. Now I may as well get a new car or something.'

'Oh. What happened?'

'She comes home from work and she's all tired and straight into the Tim Tams and she goes, "I don't want kids." Like, "Hi, babe, how was your day? Did you pay the phone bill? By the way, no kids, thanks. Want Subway for tea?"'

'What did you say?'

'Nothing.'

'Nothing?'

'Yeah, well, what am I supposed to say? The girl doesn't want kids, that's her call. Not my place to tell her otherwise. So I just took the rubbish out, got in the car, got myself a kebab and went over to me brother's.'

'You idiot,' laughed Max.

'Steady on.'

'What if she was saying it because she wanted to figure out what you thought about kids?'

'Dude, if she wanted to know what I thought she would have said, "What do you think about having kids?"'

'It doesn't work like that, mate. People don't always say what they're thinking.'

'I do.'

'No, you didn't say, "I really want to have kids with you some day," did you?'

'Nah, but—'

'Take my advice. Go get a packet of Tim Tams, get her favourite DVD, cook dinner and explain yourself to her.'

Silence. 'I can't cook.'

'You'll figure something out.'

'Righto. Yeah. Thanks. Shit, we better get you out there—'

The audio stopped.

'It's viral,' said Bettina.

'How viral?'

'Two hundred thousand likes on Facebook, five hundred thousand retweets and already a remix of it on YouTube. It's the sound guy from *Sunday Roast*. Said he accidentally recorded it and wanted to share it with people so they know Max is a decent bloke. He proposed to his girlfriend—hid the ring in a packet of Tim Tams. She said yes. It's early in the day, but it's on every news site in the country.'

'It's too personal, the Prime Minister dishing out love advice.'

'Nuh uh. It's real. This is the Max you and I know. Now the whole country knows him.'

'Seriously?'

She nodded. 'Mind if I time capsule here?'

'Yes.' I wrapped my robe tight around me and plunged my freezing hands into deep pockets.

'C'mon Roo, it's one those moments. The future needs to know.'

'Fine, but keep your voice down. Fran's sleeping.'

I put the kettle on.

'Good morning fair-weather, future fairies, today's the day the government turns around, I'm sure of it. You guys are like, "Der, Bettina, Max Masters stayed in office until he died, was cryogenically frozen and defrosted for a twenty-ninth term in office in 2074!'

'Bettina. Volume.'

'Sorry, Roo. I'm just so excited. As soon as I found out I put my joggers on and jumped in the Monaro to tell—oh, this was weird. I stopped by the servo to get my morning Fanta and a breakfast donut—they were out of hundreds and thousands, which was a bit of a bummer— and bumped into the Education Minister and that staffer woman and I was like, "Have you guys seen Twitter?" and they were all weird. Maybe they were stocking up on Depends. My mum gets a bit embarrassed when she shops for incontinence supplies.'

'Connie Fife wears Depends? Poor woman.'

'Could be the other chick.'

'Which other chick?'

'You know, the one who never puts her face on.'

'It couldn't have been.'

'It was.' She sat at the kitchen bench.

'They loathe each other.'

'Maybe they're reconciling. How sweet is that? After years of anger and hatred, two bosom buddies rekindle their friendship. And their therapist told them to go for a morning rendezvous to watch the sunrise. It's their morning ritual. They get up, fill up the car, park some-where near the lake and shoot the breeze. Do you think they're dating?'

'You're not hearing me. They hate each other.'

'I think they're just shy. Like the other day when I saw them at the lake they were chatting away like BFFs, but this morning, when they knew I was there, they went to opposite ends of the store. Society puts so much pressure on people to fit a certain paradigm and now they're coming to terms with their sexuality. Okay, future. Where were we?'

I texted Chief.

What happened between Jack and Connie?

She rang.

'That's an odd question to ask at five o'clock in the morning,' she said.

'Hope I didn't wake you.'

'No, I've been basking in the glory of the sound guy's indiscretion.'

'Me too.'

'I don't know what happened, Roo. They were inseparable in the nineties, went to uni together. Jack is godmother to Connie's kids and was her Chief of Staff until about five years ago when Jack left and went to work in state government before coming back to run Cecil's office.'

'But Bettina saw them together this morning.'

'Where?'

'At the petrol station. I don't get it. One minute they hate each other so much that I have to be the go-between and the next minute—'

'It's politics, Roo. It's dysfunctional.'

'I guess.' I paused. 'How did you sleep?'

'I had a nightmare that you left your evening purse at the ball and everyone read the emails. Make sure you lock them up somewhere, won't you.'

I popped the clasp of my purse and pulled them out. 'They're all here.' I put a cup of tea in front of Bettina and went in search of something to put on my freezing feet.

'Phew.'

'Let's chat about it later,' I said, pulling on Luke's footy socks.

'Better go,' Chief said. 'I'm about to meet Max at the office. Can't wait to tell him about the sound man.'

'Enjoy that. You both deserve some good news.'

I opened the curtains in the lounge room to the frosty dark outside. Nothing to see but a hazy streetlight. I closed them again and went back to the kitchen, half-listening to Bettina's capsuling. 'Anyway, Roo's giving me that look, so I'd better—OMFG. Future, you guys probably don't even use paper anymore, but if you go through a retro phase for funsies (some people in my day are trying to resurrect the typewriter—LOL) get your hands on some of this snow-white beauty.'

She waved a sheet of paper to her invisible audience.

'It is, without a doubt, the best printing paper ever made. Leave it to the Germans to combine functionality, aesthetic and environmental friendliness. Do you even have Germans now? Hopefully you just have global citizens and extraterrestrials. The whole nation thing is a bit passé. Peace out.' She pressed stop.

'What were you banging on about?'

'This!' She thrust it in my face. 'Feel its quality. You'd never know this was recycled.'

'Bettina!' I snatched back the emails.

'Sor-ree, it was on the bench, and you know how I get about superior stationery.'

'Looks like run of the mill A4 to me.'

'Run of the mill? This stuff's extraordinary: 120 GSM with the sheen of high-thread-count cotton. It retains its smell for weeks. No, this is the real deal. It's no fair that the Treasurer's office gets it.'

No.

'The Treasurer's office?'

'Yes, sirree. They're the only ones. Not even PMO uses it. I was thinking about bringing up the inequality of the stationery distribution at the next Girls' Club.'

'Bettina, are you sure this is what you say it is?'

She felt it again and sniffed it like a wine snob. 'Totally.'

'Come with me.'

The Monaro sped to Parliament House, shocking roadside cockatoos.

We burst into Chief's office to find her shaking. 'I can't take this anymore. It was at my house, wrapped around the newspapers with a rubber band. I found it when I left. My house, Roo.' She held out a sheet of paper.

'Give it to Bettina,' I said.

She raised her eyebrows.

'She knows.'

'Bloody hell, Roo.'

'Just give it to her, Chief.'

She obliged.

'Is it the same stuff?'

She held it up to the fluoro light, flicked it with her fingers and sniffed it. 'Exactly.'

We read it.

Resign or this goes public. You and your boss have until noon.

'I have to step down,' said Chief. 'It's the only responsible course of action.'

'Did all this happen when you were working for Connie Fife?'

'Yes.'

'And Jack was too?'

'She was my boss.'

'So she would have had access to your emails.'

'I guess, but—' She paused. 'That fucking cunt.'

'I think you mean "those fucking cunts". Come on. Let's have some fun.'

Gotcha

'Thanks for agreeing to meet me, Jack. Especially at such short notice.'

'No worries, chook,' she said, her eyes alight and her gunmetal grey hair at its glossiest. 'Must say, I was a bit baffled by your message. Something about Di and the PM making an announcement with Connie Fife?' She leaned forward in her office chair. 'I appreciate the offer of a heads-up.'

'It's more for the Treasurer,' I said. 'But sure.'

'Of course.'

I leaned back on the couch in her office. 'It's been a really tough couple of weeks, as you know. The government's been on the rocks, we're polling terribly and the party's agitating for change. What you don't know is that the PM and Chief have been the victims of a vicious blackmail campaign designed to distract and burn them.'

'Sounds bloody awful. No wonder you've all been a

bit all over the place. What's it all about?'

'It's personal, culminating today in a threat that if they don't resign by noon their reputations will be decimated. So, after consulting their families, the PM and Chief are on their way to Melbourne with Shelly and Connie to make an announcement.'

'Shit a brick. Sounds serious.'

'Anyway, given our close relationship, I wanted to keep you in the loop. Your role, as I understand it, will probably change dramatically as a result of the announcement.' I unzipped a folder. 'Here. This is what they're saying.'

Five, four, three, two—

'Um, pumpkin, what the fuck is this?'

'What?'

'I think you've given me the wrong document.'

'Oops. Sorry.' I gave it a perfunctory glance. 'Nope, that's the one.'

Her panicked eyes darted between paragraphs and back again.

The Treasurer's Chief of Staff, Jacqueline Sloane, has been blackmailing me and my Chief of Staff, Diana Freya, for some time, threatening Ms Freya with her career and me with mine in the form of persistent and systematic anonymous correspondence.

In addition, she has been found to have leaked government information—often false—to journalists in order to embarrass the government.

The personal threats have been based on her knowledge that ten years ago, when I was a backbencher and Ms Freya a staffer, we had a fleeting relationship the year before I was married. I told my wife before we married; she counts Ms Freya as a close friend.

This morning I referred this matter to the Australian

Federal Police who are taking the matter very seriously. They have launched an investigation and, I am informed, intend to press charges.

The Treasurer asked for, received and accepted Ms Sloane's resignation.

The rest of us in this government remain focused on nothing else but governing.

She wrapped her dog tags around her finger until her skin throbbed violet. 'That's bullshit.'

'It isn't.'

'Where's your proof?' Her vocal chords betrayed her.

'Each threat is printed on paper unique to your office.'

'What are you on about?'

'You used envelopes with old stamps postmarked well before the date of receipt, so they weren't posted; they were hand-delivered.'

She scoffed and bit at the cuticle on her right thumb. It bled.

'The IT boffins confirm that, as the senior staff member, you alone had access to Di's emails when you worked together all those years ago. You had the foresight to keep them, as I'm sure you have with others over the years, preserving dirt to use as future collateral. Impressive, really. Evil, but impressive.'

'Hey, Nancy Drew, I don't want to interrupt your flow, but what on earth are you prattling on about?'

'And then there's the pillow talk with Oscar Franklin—I should've seen that earlier. You stroke my ego, I'll stroke yours. I'll give you stories, you run them until we both reach simultaneous career orgasm.'

She flicked her lighter on and off. 'Are you done yet?'

'No, but you are. Connie Fife is willing to testify. She said she caught you in the act and confronted you about it, pleading with you to stop.'

The muscle in her cheek spasmed. 'No, she didn't.'

'Yes, she did.'

She drew her lips together, draining them of blood. 'And what did she suggest my motive might be?'

'She said you always thought PMO was yours to run and with Cecil at the top you'd get there. She said you're consumed by hatred and the pursuit of power.'

'I don't believe you.' She picked up her BlackBerry and dialled.

'She won't answer. She's on a plane, on the way to Melbourne as we speak. They're meeting with investigators when they get there. It's over, Jack.'

'That filthy, lying whore.' Spit flew out of her mouth, hitting the desk in front of her. 'The first day I met her, at uni, she told me she was born to be PM, like it's her divine fucking right and it's my duty to get her there. It was her plan. Take the PM down a notch, crush his spirit, force his hand and, hey presto, she's got the numbers in the party room and I'm her Chief of Staff.'

'You have one option, Jack: resign.'

'I'll call your bluff. Masters is not going to go out there and admit he cheated on his wife. Not now when his stock's so low.'

'Try us.'

'All I have to do is hand over the emails and, boom, he's gone.'

'And all we have to do is hand over the evidence and, boom, you're in jail. Resign. Pack. Leave.'

'You can't make me, sweetheart.'

'I just did, sweetheart.' I pulled my phone out of my pocket. 'Did you get that, Bettina?'

She unmuted me. 'Yep. LOL. Total blackmail fail.'

Yes

'Shhhh, turn it up.'

'Bor-ring.'

'Debs!'

'All right, all right.'

We squinted at the tiny wall-mounted hospital television.

'It's been an eventful day in Canberra with the shock resignation of a senior cabinet minister. Education Minister Connie Fife made the announcement in Melbourne, following a meeting with the Prime Minister, citing her wish to spend more time with her family.

'Ms Fife said she was grateful for the support of her constituents and proud to serve in the parliament for thirteen years and as a minister in the Masters government for two.

'Prime Minister Max Masters wished her well and thanked her for her service to the government, saying there would be a notable absence on his front bench.

'Government sources say the vacancy in Ms Fife's South Melbourne seat is likely to be filled by the former Chief of Staff to Mr Masters, Luke Harley.'

'What the fuck?'

'Fifty dollars, Ruby.' Aunt Daphne's knitting needles clicked. At this rate Will was going to have different coloured booties for every day of the month.

'Can I pay you in babysitting?'

'No.'

'Did you know about this?'

'He might have mentioned something about considering it—'

'Why am I always the last pooping person to know anything?'

'...In other political news, a micro-blogging sound engineer has achieved overnight fame after he risked his job to post a private conversation with the Prime Minister.'

'Seriously, Aunt Daphne, did you think, "Hmmm, my niece might like to know that piece of information"?'

'I thought you didn't want to talk about Luke.'

'...The television apprentice, known only as Jim, inadvertently recorded the candid exchange while attaching a microphone to Mr Masters prior to an Eleven Network interview last week.

'The exchange prompted a flurry of other stories about the PM from the Australian public. A number of Australians say they have received passing visits, career advice and animal-grooming tips, and Marlene from Kirribilli claims the Prime Minister holds a spare key to her house in case she locks herself out.

'On the back of the news, bookies say the odds of the

Masters government being returned at the next election shortened substantially.'

'I'm going to hang out with my cousin,' I said. 'I'll see you lot later.'

Aside from the occasional yawn, Will was a good listener. He had to be, what with Daphne, Debs, Fran, Clem and I around to fill the quiet time.

He flexed his fingers and pointed to the Growth Stats chart above his crib. In five days, the show-off had already doubled his body weight, which made my week seem trivial in comparison.

'My friend, I have a few things for you. First, I brought you a letter from the Prime Minister.'

He yawned.

'Shall I read it to you?'

Dear Will,

Welcome to the world.

Get big soon.

Sincerely,

Max Masters PM

'And my friend Bettina got you something,' I said. 'It's just arrived.' I reached into the purple metallic gift bag. Inside were two items wrapped in blue tissue paper, one marked with my name, one with Will's.

Inside his was a brand new dictaphone with a printed label: WILL LLEWELLYN-PARTRIDGE'S TIME CAPSULE.

I smiled and opened mine, a tiny package no bigger than a coin.

It was a watch battery wrapped in a Post-it note.

It's time. B.

Will drifted into another power nap just as Debs came in to feed him.

'Come on, big fella,' she said, lifting him and settling into the nursing chair. A vial of breast milk connected to a nasal tube.

'How are you feeling?'

'Pooped,' she said, straightening his beanie. 'I'm going home in an hour. Can't bear the thought of leaving him here. Then Daph and I will be coming in here three times a day. Still, it'll be fun getting his little bachelor pad ready. Want to hear some good news?'

'Please.'

'The doctors think he'll be ready to come home next week.'

'That's wonderful, Debs.'

'I know. And scary. What if we poop it all up? Sprout's so weeny. What if I break him? Daph won't even let me touch the oven in case I break it. You should've seen me trying to change his pants for the first time yesterday. His shit's jet black and it gets everywhere.'

'Look at you, you're going to be great. Anyway, you've got support. Fran and Clem are going to hang around for a bit longer and I'll be here. I'll fly down every weekend.'

'And there's Luke,' she said. 'He comes every morning for a chinwag with Will. Luke's pretty much the only man in Will's life right now other than his sperm donor, who keeps talking to him about how *divine* the curtains in his nursery are.'

Will scowled. 'That's good that Luke comes,' I said.

'He's miserable, kiddo. You both are. Forlorn as a pair of French horns.'

There was something familiar about the woman washing her hands beneath the Anne Geddes poster. I couldn't quite place her.

'Ruby?' she said, approaching me.

'Yes?'

'Principal Martin.'

'Oh, Mrs Maaaartin! I thought you looked familiar. This is my cousin Will and my aunt Debs.'

'Nice to meet you both.'

'What are you doing here?'

'My granddaughter is just over there,' she said.

'Amy's your granddaughter? She's the one I want Will to marry.'

She laughed.

'No joke. She has pluck. I love her booties.'

'Thanks,' she said. 'I knitted them. I just thought I'd pop by in my lunch hour to see her and drop off the matching beret.'

She unwrapped a few layers of tissue paper.

'If I were a beret, I'd want to be that one.' It was hot pink. 'So how are things at Kirner Primary?'

'Not bad. My staff have been fielding a lot of questions about anarchy since your talk.'

'I'm so sorry,' I said. 'I was feeling a little disheartened about politics. Let me know if there's some way I can help.'

'Well, we have an assembly in an hour.'

Crap.

'I—I—have a thing in an hour.'

'A thing?'

'Yes, a political thing; you know, important stuff.'

'No, I don't. You said you wanted to help. Assembly's in an hour. If you want it, the floor is yours.'

'I don't have a car.'

'I'm going by train.'

'I'm allergic to public transport.'

'We'll take you,' said Debs. 'As soon as I finish feeding Will.'

'Where are we going?'

'Aunty Ruby is going to speak at a school.'

'Whose school?'

'Dan's.'

'I like Dan. Will Dan be there?'

'Probably, darling.'

We rounded a corner. Clem leaned into me. I ran my fingers through her curls.

'I think it's lovely that you're speaking to a school group,' said Daphne. 'It's important to inspire young people, don't you think, Debs?'

'That's why she's doing it,' said Debs, stuffing her face with sushi. 'This is round two. Round one saw a little girl ditch her political ambitions in favour of an acting career.'

'Ruby! What did you tell them?'

'I may have been a little bleaker than intended,' I said. 'Anyway, would you all be quiet so I can plan something a bit better to say this time?'

My phone buzzed.

Any chance you could give me Fran's number? Elliot.

'That's brazen,' I said, passing Fran my phone.

She reddened.

'Fran!'

'What does it say, Mummy?'

'Nothing at all.'

'Why would Aunty Wooby show you nothing at all?'

'Let me guess. The hot vet?' asked Debs.

'How do you know Elliot?' asked Daphne.

'You told me about him.'

'No, I didn't.'

'Yes, you did.' Debs looked pleadingly at me in the mirror.

'I think I might have,' I said.

'Oh, yeah, it was Ruby.'

'How did you know he was hot?' asked Fran.

'Who's hot, Mummy?'

'No one, darling.'

'Shoosh! I need to concentrate.'

'It's too late,' said Daphne, indicating. 'We're here.'

'Shit.'

'Aunty Wooby!'

'And another fifty.'

'See you all later,' I said.

'Ha! She thinks we're not coming in,' said Debs, unbuckling her seatbelt.

'Come on, Clementine,' said Fran, taking her by the hand. 'The answer's yes, by the way,' she whispered.

'Yes?'

'To passing on my number. If it's okay by you.'

'Of course it is,' I said, poking my tongue out at Dan as we passed him. He poked back. Clem went to sit next to him.

Twenty minutes later, we'd reached the end of *Advance Oz Tray Affair*.

'Good morning, boys and girls.'

'Gooood mooooorning, Misssssussss Maaaaaaaaartin.'

The sunlight drilled into my eyes as I sat on the same,

rickety plastic chair as I had the week before. My jeans stuck to my legs. Sweat marks formed under my arms and I needed a drink of water.

'Some of you will remember our friend Roo.'

'Boooooooooooo.'

It was a boy's voice. I couldn't see him because of the bloody light. It was like being in an interrogation room.

'Now, come on, kids. That's not how we treat our visitors, is it?'

'No, Misssssussss Maaaaaaaaaaaartin.'

'Anyway, an hour ago I bumped into Roo and mentioned that some of you were feeling a little sad about politics. She felt really bad about it and wanted to come here to clarify what she meant. Let's make her feel welcome.'

About four people clapped. I presumed they were my family members.

'A very exciting thing happened to me just after I saw you all last week. My aunts had a little baby. His name is Will and he is magnificent. Anyway, he made me think about a few of the things I said to you all.

'Can anyone remember what I said? Yes, you. Three pigtails. Fewer teeth. Front row.'

'You said you can make money go around the world in rockets.'

'Not quite, but close. Anyone else?' I shielded my eyes with my hand. 'Boy. Hat with a hole in it. Fourth row.'

'You said wine is evil because it made you come to Australia and a thimbleful of HR managers are trolls.'

Principal Martin slapped her forehead.

'You said being prime minister is even worser than being school captain. It's harder, nobody likes you and everyone makes fun of you.'

'Yes, thank you, Jemma. A neat summary. I want to tell you all, especially you, Jemma, that since then I've become a lot more upbeat about it all.

'When I look at Will, I wonder how a person so little and helpless could be so hopeful about the world. His dreams are massive. He's a tiny eating, pooping dream machine. But then people like Will hit puberty and become grown-ups and grown-ups forget to dream.

'We get grumpy and then we give up. I now realise how dumb that is. Yes, holey hat boy?'

'Dumb is when you can't hear or speak.'

'Really? Give me a five-minute demo. Good work. Anyway, as I was saying, grown-ups are dumb. We get cynical. Does anyone know what a cynic is? Yes, pigtails. Let's hear it.'

'Is it when you fake-sing with your mouth but no music is coming out?'

'Not quite. In fact, not at all. That's lip-synching, but it often takes a cynic to spot a lip-syncher. A cynic is a person who assumes the worst in people and refuses to find hope in life. Cynics often think they're smarter than everyone else. I know, because I've been one. But they're not. They're ning-nongs.'

'What's a ning-nong?'

'An idiot.'

'My teacher says idiot's not a nice word because some people are born idiots and they can't help it.'

'Numpty?'

'Like Humpty Numpty?'

'That's Humpty Dumpty.'

'Do cynics fall off walls too?'

'No! I'm just saying, the smartest, wisest, bravest people

are the ones with hope, imagination and faith in their fellow human beings, like Jemma. Let's call them hopers.'

Sunshine lit her braces.

'Why don't you call them hopics?'

'It hasn't been five minutes yet.'

'I know another hoper, someone very dear to me. He has decided, after two years as the director of a think tank, he wants to become a member of parliament, which is great, even though he does err on the ning-nong end of the hoper spectrum and has the most shocking taste in ties, including one that looks like butter chicken with bits of saffron rice stuck to it. That's my favourite. He's a chronic nag, makes the world's best lamb ragout and delivered the worst marriage proposal in human history.'

Ruby.

'Any questions? Just yell them out. I can't see you because the light's in my eyes.'

'What's puberty?'

'The messy, hairy, bloody, sticky limbo between childhood and adulthood. Next?'

'Does Max Masters have a robot butler?'

'Yes, his name is Jorje, he takes thirty-six AA batteries, enjoys hiking and specialises in brownies.'

'Blonde?'

'No, he's a Brazilian robot. Shiny, bald.'

'I meant the brownies.'

'Oh. No, they're seventy-five per cent cocoa solid. Anyone else?'

'Do think tanks have weapons?'

'Yes. Ideology. Next?'

'Will you marry me?'

'Bless. Probably not. I'm thirty and a terrible girlfriend

and I never return DVDs. Perhaps wait till you're older and then ask me. Your voice is quite deep already though. How old are you, out of interest?'

'Old enough.'

Clouds passed by long enough for me to make out a blob of butter chicken and Clem, sitting beside Dan, filming with her gnocchi.

'Marry me, Ruby. I've been a complete dick.'

Gasp.

Luke walked down the aisle towards me.

'I've been a bigger dick.'

Gasp.

'I know,' he said.

'Why did no one gasp at that? He could have said, "No, I've been the biggest dick."'

'Stop saying dick!' said Principal Martin.

Gasp.

'Two hundred and fifty dollars!'

'As I was saying'—he got down on one knee—'let's be dicks together.'

Pigtails giggled. 'I can see your bum crack!'

'I can see you picking your nose!' I said, getting down to Luke's level. 'You had me at dick.'

To the collective 'wooooooooooooooo' of the several-hundred primary schoolers assembled and the hooting of my family, Luke and I pashed.

'Is it five minutes yet?'

Acknowledgments

They say second books are tougher. They're right. It took a village to get me through this one. Chiefs to single out include:

Albert Tse, my husband, who scooped me off the floor, let me wipe my nose on him and told me I could do it. Often.

Mum and first reader Thérèse Rein, whose reassuring laughter over Skype and all-enveloping hugs spurred me on.

Dad, Kevin Rudd, who made me tea while I edited, and passed down the genetic gift of terrible dad jokes.

Brothers, Nick and Marcus Rudd, for not reading the sexy bits. Seriously, skip the first chapter. That goes for you too, Grandma.

My BFF, as Bettina might say, Nicole Brizuela, who walked me through the finer details of giving life to pre-term bubbies like hers, my delightful chap of a godson, Christian.

Friends and family Sue Cato, Catherine Chan, Renée Coffey, Fleur Foster, Mia Freedman, Frances Lockhart, Alex Mihos and her dad, Zara Shafruddin, Rita Wockner, Lou Ye and Nai Nai, all of whom imparted wisdom, encouragement and food when I needed it.

Readers, one and all, whose kind words, letters, emails and tweets keep me going.

Bookshops and libraries, for welcoming Ruby and her creator to your shelves.

Alison Arnold, my editor, for knowing Ruby as well as I do. Despite all the poop life threw at her this year, Ali edited this manuscript with the skill of a surgeon and the bedside manner of a GP. She made it pump.

Michael Heyward, for cherishing all of my characters and sharing them with the world. I write to be read. Michael, Jane Novak, Kirsty Wilson, Chong Weng Ho, and the whole crew at Text Publishing make that happen.

There are two others I'd like to thank.

First, Ruby Stanhope, who told me her story and made me write it down. It is the story of first-term blues, work-life balance (whatever that is), women, love, friendship, family and self. When I read what I had written my head told me to change it for fear of misinterpretation, but Ruby was persistent, tenacious, unrelenting.

At times, she was a pain to work with, like a dear friend going through a mid-life crisis—without the bald patch and Bugatti. But with a sharp kick up the arse from a little bug I like to call purpose, she rediscovered herself. I love her as much today as I did when first I heard her voice.

Second, my hugest thanks go to Bettina Chu. She champions hope, pities the power hungry and thinks cynicism is so last season. There ought to be more Bettinas.

Note that no crystal balls were gazed at in the making of this novel.